Halfa Moon

Joan Bannan

abbott press®
A DIVISION OF WRITER'S DIGEST

Abbott Press books may be ordered through booksellers or by contacting:

Abbott Press
1663 Liberty Drive
Bloomington, IN 47403
www.abbottpress.com
Phone: 1-866-697-5310

ISBN: 978-1-4582-1185-9 (sc)
ISBN: 978-1-4582-1184-2 (hc)
ISBN: 978-1-4582-1183-5 (e)

Library of Congress Control Number: 2013917828

Printed in the United States of America.

Abbott Press rev. date: 10/17/2013

To my daughter
Tina Marie Mangini Fikejs
with love
and gratitude

Acknowledgments

Thank you, Tina Fikejs, Jane Casebolt, Marylyn Caliendo, and Sandy Isganitis, for encouragement. You believed in me when I did not believe in myself.

Thank you, Tina Fikejs, Sandy Isganitis, Denise Davis, Jacki Sutter, Susanne Lakin, Roberta Davidson, and Susan Batty, editors and proof readers extraordinaire.

Thank you, Tony Mangini, for vetting my imagination when it comes to law enforcement details.

Thank you, Jennifer Mangini for ICU, ER, and paramedic wisdom.

Thank you, Paul Caliendo for the use of your laptop when I was in Mexico. Sorry about the shift key.

Damian Kyle, though we have never met, listening to you encouraged me to stay on my path and carry on in spite of adversity. Thank you for helping me realize that the preparation of my character as an author was more valuable than a daily quota of written words.

Thank you Mrs. Buckette, my high school English teacher. I never forgot that you told me I should be a writer.

Thank you James Scott Bell for your mentoring genius at your seminars and in your outstanding, how-to-write fiction books.

Thank you Dianne Collard for your supreme understanding of forgiveness by example and in your book, *I Choose to Forgive*.

Thank you for invaluable research information, Wes Davis, Jeff Thompson, Jo and Bruce LeBlanc, and Ben Drew, on staff at John Muir Hospital.

Thank you to my grandchildren, Julia Mangini, Christina Mangini, and Andrew Fikejs, for reminding me about the science of a waning and waxing moon.

Thank you Janelle Lim, Heather McMullen, and Sarah Goddard, my Abbott Press project managers, and thank you, Abbott Press for your production expertise that brought *Half a Moon* to market in a timely professional manner.

CHAPTER ONE

The Accident

I was only four when my sister died and my mother kidnapped my brother and me. I've tried so hard to remember more about the town we lived in and other clues that would help me find my daddy. Both that town, and the tiny house we lived in, were hot, hot, hot! I supposed it couldn't have been perpetually hot, but I don't remember autumn, winter, or spring.

I've read that a child's personality is formed by the time she is five. I wonder how different my personality would have been had I not experienced the brutal shock and grief of my sister's death before those formative years were complete. And although my mother and I were already at odds, I wonder if she may have had a kinder disposition had she not lost her firstborn child to such a heartbreaking accident. Perhaps our relationship would also have fared better if we had not both blamed me for Laura's death.

I have lived for seventeen years with my shame and my guilt, unable to talk about it with anyone. The only person near me who knows I had a sister is my mother and she doesn't talk about it either. The lingering humiliation preoccupies my consciousness and my nightmares. It should have been me, not Laura, who died that day. I didn't pull the trigger, but it was my fault.

All I can remember about where we lived is the street name, Nueva Lane. Daddy worked at a Texaco gas station and was attending a college. My mom worked at a hotel, and whatever she did there paid tips. For this, she always wore black capris and an ironed white blouse. Memories preceding our tragedies have dimmed and faded, but I clearly remember all the details of the day Vanessa shot Laura.

—◦◦◦—

"Mama, do you have to go to work?" I looked up, trying to catch my mother's emerald eyes.

"Yes, Margaret, you know I have to work." She always seemed to be mad at me. She wasn't angry at Laura or our brother, Ray. Just me. I often followed her around so closely that when she turned quickly, she would trip over me. The angrier she got, the more I tried to cling. I felt that she didn't love me as much as she loved them.

She was standing over the foldout ironing board that was housed in a cupboard in her bedroom wall. I could smell the bleach steaming from beneath the iron as she savagely pounded it down and then slid it across her white blouse. Her face was red and her nostrils flared. "Permanent press, my a—" She flicked a glance at me and didn't finish her sentence. "If your father had taken this out of the dryer last night, I wouldn't be running so late!" She whipped the blouse from the ironing board, slipped it around her shoulders, and flipped the pearly buttons through the buttonholes as she simultaneously slipped her tiny feet into black flats.

"Excuse me!" She barked furiously. I backed up so she could bend over to unplug the iron.

"You look pretty, Mama," I volunteered sheepishly.

"Thank you, Margaret." I think she agreed. She caught her reflection in the mirror, tapped the bottom of her bobbed brunette hair, puckered her red lips slightly, and lifted one eyebrow. She tucked the blouse into her slim black capris, and then, resting her hands just below her tiny waist, she turned sideways, then far enough to look over her shoulder to appraise her butt. As she turned her face toward me at last, she grimaced, but she was not looking into my longing eyes. She was frowning at my bandaged arm.

"Now remember. Stay in your grampa's yard. Don't go to Vanessa's, OK?"

I felt the blood beating in my face as I looked down at the bandage. Grampa's yard had turned into a place of torment and misery since Vanessa, a much older girl, had taken to bullying me. At first she'd just used words. She mocked both Laura and me for wearing the cool, colorful sundresses that Grama Estelle was always sewing for us. "Oh look. Little prim and proper misses."

Vanessa always wore dirty, raggedy jeans that were too long on her. The bottoms had worn off into uneven fringe. I had seen her wear only two T-shirts. Both were several sizes larger than her thin frame. One was faded red and had the remnant of a picture on the front that looked like a brown whirlpool. The other was faded navy blue with crinkly yellow letters on the back that probably spelled the name of a restaurant or something. Whatever the word was, I didn't know the meaning. Both shirts looked like the kind that men wore when they worked in the garden or on cars—not the kind they wore to work or to church. Her curly dark-blond hair was matted. After all the strands of hair had woven into one knotted mass, someone had pulled it all back behind her head and cut the matters straight across at about chin level.

Vanessa had singled me out as her favorite victim. The teasing progressed to poking and pushing as she rudely taunted me. She usually waited until she thought I was alone, as she had yesterday. She said, "Is that a new dress?" She grabbed the front of my dress, wiped her dirty hands on it, then pushed me hard enough to rock me out of balance. I fell against a tree. As I tried to break my fall, my arm got chewed up by the rough bark. As soon as she saw that I was crying and bleeding, she turned and ran home.

3

Our house was the first house on Nueva Lane closest to the main road. Grama and Grampa's house, and their huge apple orchard, were at the end. Halfway between our house and Grama's house was a tiny building where Vanessa lived with her mother, who never seemed to be home. Daddy called it a shack.

My chest felt like someone was squeezing me too tightly. "Oh, Mama, I don't want to go to Grama and Grampa Taylor's today. I want to stay home." I knew I was whining.

"You can't stay home. You and Laura need to be Grama's helpers with Ray. That's what big sisters do." She grabbed my hand and pulled me at adult speed through the bedroom door, then into the hallway. "Come on now, let's go get see what They're up to. They're awfully quiet!"

As we rounded the corner into the kitchen, we saw Laura hoisting Ray down from his high chair. I think my mother knew Laura's determination would give her strength not to drop the toddler; nevertheless, Mama hurried across the room to help. She heaved the twenty-pound, fifteen-month-old Ray from Laura's arms and smiled at her six-year-old-going-on-twenty-one-year-old daughter. "I think he weighs more than you do."

Laura returned our mother's smile and dutifully picked up our brother's diaper bag. The strap reached below her bottom. The bag barely cleared the floor. Laura opened the car door, tossed the diaper bag in ahead of her, then climbed into the backseat of our Ford minivan. She spread her arms wide for Ray.

Mama placed the squirming boy in her lap. "Hold on tight." It was only a mile down the lane. We all knew Laura would win the wiggle match. I scrambled into the front. Mama raced around to get behind the steering wheel.

Our dingy gray-and-white minivan disrupted the dusty road and left a trailing cloud as we passed Vanessa's house. I slid down beneath the dashboard and curled into a small "invisible" ball until I felt the car stop. I watched Mama jump out of the driver's seat, run around to our side, open both doors, and reach in the back for Ray.

When she opened my door, I felt dust settling on my face. As I stepped out into the silent heat, I could smell rotting windfall apples beneath the trees that surrounded Grama Estelle and Grampa Red's gravel circle at the end of their driveway. My mother snapped at me to hurry as she grabbed the diaper bag and jerked it onto her left shoulder. Her face showed strain as she heaved Ray out of Laura's arms to settle him onto her right hip.

"Hello, Estelle."

My father's mother stood waiting behind the screen door, pushing it open at the last possible minute. Three of the swarming flies opted to rush in. "Aren't you late, Norma?"

"Yes." Mama squinted her eyes, and her neck muscles lined up like little poles.

I was not the only one familiar with my mother's biting tone. Grama Estelle blushingly countered, "I know Frank appreciates you working so he can finish getting his degree. College is where he belongs. He always did so well in school."

"Yeah, well, just try it sometime. It's hard to get three kids out the door, get dressed for work, and be on time" Mama bit back. "Frank will be home before I will. He'll pick them up around three thirty." She kissed Ray on the cheek. "Here ya go, big boy."

Ray started screaming as she transferred him to Grama. He reached back for Mama with both arms, causing our petite grandmother to toddle.

I stayed inside as long as I could that day until Grama pretty much kicked us out of the house. Laura and I went out to the field beyond Grampa's farm-equipment shed. We always used the shed as home base for games of hide-and-seek behind the bigger apple trees. It was my turn to seek first, but before I closed my eyes and leaned against the powdery shed to dutifully start my countdown, I turned and looked longingly toward Grama's house. It seemed very far away. I opened my eyes and brushed off my sundress, hoping the gesture would simultaneously brush away a rising sense of fear. "Ready or not, here I come!"

A shadow detached itself from the shade of the shed and morphed into Vanessa. "I'm ready."

I looked down at my arm rather than into Vanessa's bullying stare.

"Does that hurt?"

"No," I lied meekly.

"Leave her alone, Vanessa." This from my protective big sister, who had apparently returned when she spotted Vanessa.

I bolted around the nearest corner of the shed. I could hear my pulse swishing in my ears. My sweaty palms against the wall of the shed turned the dust into a light film of mud. I peeked back around to see that Laura was alone again. I ran to her. "Where is she, Laura?"

"She went the other way to head you off. She's on the other side of the shed. Come on. Let's go back to the house."

Laura took my hand, and we headed toward the kitchen screen door, but Vanessa stepped out from behind the shed and commanded, "Stop!" She stalked forward with Grampa's rifle cupped beneath her right arm, the barrel resting on her left hand, her trigger finger at the ready. Then she added brazenly, "Or I'll shoot!"

I had seen Grampa's "varmint gun" in the shed before. Grampa told us to never, ever, touch it, and he promised us he would never shoot anything in front of us, like squirrels, gophers, or the feral cats that roamed the fields and howled so loudly at night. We could hear those screaming cats at both our house and Grampa's. The shed was always locked. The door must not have been latched completely.

I screamed. Laura stepped in front of me with her shoulders back; her chin set bravely high; her arms stiff, like a toy soldier.

Vanessa fired the gun. Laura fell back, pinning me beneath her in the dirt. I saw Vanessa's jaw drop and her skin turn white except for instant dark circles under her eyes. She looked down at the gun, then dropped it as if it were burning her hands. She turned and ran. This time, though, she ran into the orchard, away from the houses, toward the other road on the far side of the trees.

I wriggled out enough to see Laura's thick lashes flickering up and down like the wings of a dark moth trying to fly away. "Maggie. I'm thirsty. I want some water." Her eyes rolled back and she closed them. "Waa-ter."

"Graaammaa!" I wailed. I could barely catch my breath because I was bawling hysterically. Both my head and my stomach felt like they were water balloons that someone instantly filled up until they were too full. I peed in my underpants and felt humiliated.

Grama Estelle was already running across the field toward us. Laura squirmed and jerked a few times, then she lifted her long lashes one last time. She tried to speak, but pink foam was oozing from her nose and mouth so all that came out was a gurgly sounding cough. Her brown eyes were open, but they didn't look like they were seeing anything.

I squirmed out from under her. I was still crying uncontrollably. I pulled Laura up to my height, then draped her arms around my shoulders. I don't know if Laura was helping or if I had some kind of superhuman strength, but we began to move toward the house. Grama intercepted our clumsy journey.

"Stop, Maggie. I'll carry her." She pried the lifeless arms from around my neck. Holding her with one arm, she gently stroked Laura's hair back from her face and wiped her mouth and nose with her apron. Grama seemed to know it wouldn't help my sister to reach the house. They both collapsed into the sandy soil. Laura was lying across her lap. Grama was trying to catch her breath between each wrenching sob. I nestled down into my "invisible ball" alongside them and put the thumb of my left hand into my mouth. I was still crying violently. My chest heaved in and out, causing sharp sucks on my thumb. I used my right hand to lift one of Grama Estelle's arms at the elbow so I could scrunch myself under it. I wanted to feel comfort, like the little chicks that cuddled beneath the wings of Grama's hens.

From where I lay, I could see the gun gleaming in the dust.

Grampa Red came running in from the orchard. I felt him pry me away from the pile of dirty dresses, entwined arms, blood, and tears. He brushed his wife's face gently with the back of his hand and uttered, "I'll be right back."

He carried me into the house. I was so embarrassed because I knew he could feel my wet pants. His shoulders were slumped. He was muttering something to himself, and I could feel his body shaking. He was blinking liquid from his eyes. We passed through the living room, where Ray was crying in the playpen, then down the short hallway, then into their bedroom. He gently lowered my wet, stinky, dirty body onto their huge bed. He pulled a tissue from the box on the nightstand and blew his nose. In spite of near-hundred-degree heat outside and eighty-five-degree stuffiness in the house, he covered me with a thick, fluffy comforter and kissed my filthy forehead. I heard his long, shuddering breaths as he turned to leave.

I yanked my thumb out of my mouth and tried to beg him not to leave me, but no sound came out. My chest was still heaving and trembling each time it pulled in air. I drew the quilt up to my nose and stared at the ruffly curtains. I heard Grampa's voice in the kitchen. It shook as he told someone that there had been an accident and gave them the address. I heard the receiver clunk into the telephone base, then the kitchen screen door slam shut with a bang. Ray, who had quieted when he saw Grampa come out of the bedroom, apparently considered the bang his cue to resume screaming.

I listened beyond the wailing, hoping to hear Grampa or Grama return—or even better, Daddy—but no. Ray's screaming calmed to whimpers, then hiccups, and after a while he was quiet. I tried my voice again meekly. "Grampa? Grama?"

Ray called out, "Deedee!" This was his best attempt at "sister." Laura had been Deedee too.

I didn't want to talk to Ray. I returned to the security of the mound of covers and my thumb, to wait and hope that someone would come to comfort us. My chest, tummy and head ached. *No! No! No! No!* crashed around inside my head.

I whispered, "Daddy, I'm thirsty." This reminded me of the last thing Laura said, and then I cried myself to sleep.

Through a groggy wakefulness, I heard Grama's soft voice, then another voice that was deep, with a quality of kindness and confidence. I understood the words he said, but he pronounced them in a way that was different from how I was used to hearing them. I clung to the comforter that slid to lower me until my feet touched the floor. I padded to the bedroom door and peeked through the hall into the living room. Grama was opening the screen door to let in a man.

He had a dark face, black hair, and balding forehead. His clothes—even his shoes and belt—were entirely white. They matched his bright white teeth, which he briefly revealed in a gentle smile when he greeted my grandmother. Grama started talking, and then sobbing. The man put his hand on her shoulder and helped her settle into her rocking chair. I knew that he could see me through the crack between the hallway door and the doorjamb, but I wasn't afraid of him. In fact, I wanted him to see me and felt drawn to him, but I stayed at my post. I decided he was an angel.

The man moved out of my sight, most likely to sit on the sofa. I listened to the muffled voices on the other side of the door for a while, once in a while picking up a word or two. I heard Grampa's work boots scrape the kitchen floor. He had come in through the side door and was talking to someone who also had heavy footfalls. I caught a glimpse of a man with a tan uniform. He had a badge pinned to his shirt. In spite of a desperate desire to eavesdrop, to hear every word, I was hearing less and less. My eyes blinked heavily several times, each time closing for longer, until I felt my body slump down onto the hardwood floor in exhaustion.

I woke up lying on the couch. My head was on Grama's lap. She was stroking my hair. The man in the uniform was sitting across from me on a chair. Grampa was standing behind him.

"Hello. My name is Officer Morgan—what's yours?"

I bolted up and started blubbering to him. "She—she stepped in front of me." I was sobbing and hiccupping. "Laura—" I coughed and began to barf. I threw up on the policeman's shoes and the front of one of his pant legs. Grampa picked me up and carried me to the bathroom and held my head over the toilet, where I wretched again and again.

Between my gross noises, I heard the front door close. Grama came into the bathroom and said, "I'll take care of her, Red." I heard her whisper, "He'll come back in a few days after she's calmed down." Grama wiped my sweaty forehead with a damp cloth and rubbed my back and arms. The vomiting finally subsided. I fell asleep with my head resting on the toilet seat.

CHAPTER TWO

A Gift

I woke up in my own bed. I looked across the room to see Laura's bed neatly made and undisturbed. I felt of wave of sorrow and fear. I could not imagine life without her. I felt achy all over, especially around my eyes and in my stomach. I wasn't sure if it was dusk or dawn. I could see that someone must have removed my dirty dress while I was sleeping; I was wearing comfy jammies. The sound of my parents arguing and the inevitable sound of Ray crying had woken me. I wanted to stay in bed. In fact, I had an overwhelming desire to stay there forever, but I needed to get up and use the bathroom. Besides, I was still thirsty.

Our house was almost the same as Grampa and Grama Taylor's, though theirs had nicer furniture, and was far less cluttered and a great deal cleaner. It was a small box with a living room, dining room, and kitchen on one half of the box and three bedrooms and a bathroom on the other. The living room and dining room were all one room. There was a double-door-sized archway from the dining room into the kitchen. I slipped out of my bedroom hoping no one would see or hear me, but as I crossed the hall and headed for the bathroom door, Ray spotted me from his playpen in the living room. He raised his chubby arm to point at me and exclaimed, "Deedee!" My mom and dad went suddenly silent. Silence that sounded like it would explode. Daddy walked over, knelt down to my level, and said, "Hi, pumpkin. How are you?"

He looked awful. His face was flushed. His eyes were rimmed with red. I looked over at my mother, who was still wearing her white blouse and black capris. I knew then that it was still that same horrible day.

I reached up to my daddy with both arms. "Oh, Daddy!" I started to bawl as he lifted me into his arms. I could feel his chest shaking too.

My mom snapped at us. "OK. That's enough. Margaret, you need to get to bed. Frank, we are not through here. You put Margaret to bed. I'll put Ray down."

After the much-needed bathroom stop, declining anything to eat but guzzling down a glass of water, Daddy tucked me back into my bed. I remember looking into his eyes thinking that we were seeing deeply inside each other to a place past our faces, into each other's hearts. "Daddy, I didn't mean to—"

"I know, honey. It was an accident. Maggie, try to stay awake for just a few more minutes. I want to give you something tonight." He turned on the night light, then clicked the light switch to turn off the bright overhead light. A strange dread tugged at me as I watched him disappear from my bedroom, gently closing the door. I stared out my window into the darkness. I could see the pinpricks of light from the stars and a slice of light from half a moon. One star near to it was much brighter than all the others. In my head I sang Jiminy Cricket's song "When You Wish upon a Star," and then I wished I could start my life over.

As he was reopening my door, I heard my mother's sharp voice. He replied, "Just a minute, Norma. Yes, she can. It's amazing. I read to her every night while you are working. She started reading to me a few months ago. Besides, this will comfort her even when she isn't reading it." I noticed how kind his voice was and how softly he closed the door to shut out whatever she sharply retorted.

"This is for you, Maggie. I wrote your name and today's date in it." He handed me a soft leather-bound book. It was warm where his large hand had been.

"Thank you. What is it?"

"A Bible. I'll read it to you for a while. It's different than the little books we've been reading together. You won't be able to understand a lot of the words yet, but as fast as you're learning, it won't be long before you'll be reading it to me." He nodded and smiled knowingly.

I didn't open it. I tucked it under one arm and held it tightly to my chest as if keeping it near me would keep him near me too. I knew he wouldn't stay and read tonight because I could feel Mama's resentment seeping through my bedroom door. She would be insisting he return any minute.

He smiled at me. "You probably shouldn't sleep with it, honey. You might accidentally curl the pages."

I handed it back to him. For some reason, I noticed how beautiful his long fingers were that wrapped around the soft leather. He then placed the book on the shelf beneath my nightstand. "I need to go talk to your mother."

I wrinkled my nose and twisted my mouth to one side, which made him chuckle. "Good night, Daddy. Will you be here tomorrow morning when I wake up?"

He bent down and kissed me on the forehead. "I don't think so, pumpkin." I heard his breath go in and out erratically. "I need to go early to take care of stuff." I knew it was Laura stuff.

As I was falling back to sleep, the tension returned to the other room. Daddy's words were too quiet to understand, but once in a while I could hear Mama's angry tone and pick out some of her words. It seemed to me that the argument was not about Laura. I remember thinking that she didn't like Daddy either. I knew for sure that even if she liked me a little bit before, now she didn't like me at all. In my exhausted drowsiness, I put one hand on my forehead and the other on top of my aching heart. I did not like me either. *It should have been me. I should have been me. Oh Laura. No. No. It should have been me.* My last thought was, *I wonder where Vanessa is.*

CHAPTER THREE

Exodus

The days following Laura's death were just craziness. The hot, hot sun beat down on our backyard cement patio and the roof of our small house. There was a constant parade of sweaty people wiping their foreheads or trying to find a breeze. They moved throughout the house, onto the back patio, and outside to the front yard. We didn't have air conditioning. We borrowed fans from everyone we knew. Depending on what time of day they came, they congregated as much as possible in the shade. If they chose the front, they heard a constant hum of bees in floribunda roses. If they were in the back, they heard birdsong from the families of birds that Daddy enticed with well-supplied bird feeders to live in the bushes in our backyard. The visitors gratefully accepted cold lemonade and iced tea from the people who came from Daddy's church.

The man in white was there a lot. I was fascinated by him and covertly watched him. He never talked directly to me, but he smiled at me often and sometimes curled his hand in a little wave. I returned the curly gesture. The phone rang and rang and rang.

The day of Laura's funeral was the hottest day of all. The church was wonderfully cool, and I was tired. I wanted to lie down on the padded pew and go to sleep, but I knew it would not be allowed. I sat up obediently with my hands folded in my lap as the pastor droned on and my parents sat weeping. People behind me were gasping and taking deep breaths. I saw the man in white, but he was not wearing all white that day. He wore a light-colored suit and a white shirt.

The graveyard was on a hill with very few trees. A canopy was set up near the grave, but the shade was not enough to protect Grama Estelle, who fainted in Grampa's arms a few minutes into the graveside service. I had a gnawing ache that felt larger than the gaping hole in the ground. Through my tears, I hysterically cried out, "No!" when they lowered my sister's body into the darkness.

When we got home, many of the comforters who had come before, came again—plus at least as many more. Except for the man in white, all the strangers seemed to be avoiding me. I didn't care. Laura was gone and that was all that mattered to me that day.

The quiet servants from the church had been busy while we were away. There were trays of hot food, bowls of cold salads, platters of fried chicken, and plates and plates and plates of cakes and cookies. I had never seen so much food at one time, but I could scarcely eat. This seemed to irritate Mama, but worried Grama Estelle and Daddy, who were my champions. No matter how many others vied for their attention, one of them was always by my side holding my hand or seated on a low chair, or sometimes even on the floor at my level. Sometimes Daddy would pick me up and hold me while he talked with the sorry, sad people. Once he picked me up while he was talking to the man in white. His voice, and the way he moved his hands as he talked, fascinated me. His voice was soft, low, and kind. I wanted to know him better, but I would not get that chance.

I felt a stinging hollow inside, like fire inside of me, hotter than the scorching sun outside. I felt ashamed when I saw people steal glances at me and whisper to each other.

Ray, who liked very much to be the center of the world, loved this larger, busier universe. People picked him up and talked to him, then put him back down so he could play near me. I was comforted by his innocence and apparent cluelessness. Though Mama was undeniably sorrowful, she, like Ray, seemed to like the attention. She greeted people and moved around a lot. She talked about Laura, but it always sort of sounded like it was about her, which of course it was. No mother should have to bury a child. She did not reach out to comfort Ray or me, and she avoided Daddy. It was as if she were angry and frustrated, not just sad. She seemed distracted by something besides our horrible tragedy. When everyone had gone and the house was quiet, she became detached as if going through the motions of living in our house, but her mind was far away.

Laura had been my constant companion, friend, and protector. Of course, I was no angel, but before she went to heaven, I believed that Laura was. It made perfect sense that an angel should be in heaven, but I selfishly pined for her to come back to earth to us.

The morning after the funeral, a grating metal-to-metal screech jarred me awake as Mama viciously scraped the silver curtain hooks across the cheap curtain rod to blast sunshine across my bed. Something in her tone kept me from protesting, though I couldn't remember her ever coming in to wake me. She usually preferred that we sleep in. With dramatic flair and urgency, she tossed a clean sundress at me.

"Get dressed. Wear this." She pointed to a raggedy suitcase on the floor with its jaws open wide. "Put your jammies in that bag." It was already stuffed with most of my clothes. The closet door and my side of the dresser drawers were gaping open. I was groggy, trying to remember what day it was. Daddy would already be gone either to his class at college or to his job at the gas station. Not surprisingly, I could hear Ray crying in the living room.

Sorrow flooded in to wake me fully. I rubbed the sides of my still aching head. Each breath hurt coming in and going out past my heart. If Laura were here, Ray wouldn't be crying. *Oh please no. I wish Laura was here.* She would have heaved him into the high chair and given him some cereal and milk. We often woke before Mama and, with Laura's help, began most days without her.

As soon as Mama rushed out of my room, I hurriedly dressed and threw my nightclothes onto the floor next to the mouth of the suitcase. I rolled over onto my tummy and slid my legs toward the floor. As my feet settled and I let go of my covers, the floor felt like it was dropping, as it did the first time I rode down in an elevator. I felt a bit dizzy, and my stomach was sore. I spotted my Bible on the nightstand. I hurriedly sandwiched it between some of my clothes at the bottom of the suitcase. I folded my jammies and placed them on top. I frantically looked around my room to see if there was anything else I wanted to pack—yes, my Madame Alexander Wendy doll that Grama Estelle gave me for my birthday was on top of the dresser.

Wendy kinda looked like me. Her long hair was a dark brown, neatly woven into two braids tied with pink bows. I picked her up and leaned her back to watch the lashes of her little brown eyes close. I straightened her up again so her eyes would open. I ran my hand along the top of her head, pulled the pigtails to the front, then straightened the skirt of her pink gingham dress. I wondered if Mama would let me take Wendy, but decided not to chance it. I gently tucked her beneath my Bible and jammies.

I went over to Laura's nightstand and opened the drawer. I glanced at the bedroom door, then quickly snatched up Laura's golden cross. Daddy had given it to her when she turned six. It was plain gold with a tiny diamond in the center where the shafts crossed. I fought with my selfish feelings. I was grateful they didn't bury it with her. I pulled Wendy back out and slipped the cross into the back of her panties, then placed her carefully back into the suitcase out of sight. I picked up my brown bear that had fallen from my bed onto the floor. He probably rolled off my bed during the night, but I imagined him going "eeek" and jumping off the bed to hide from Mama when she barged in to disrupt our sleep, our room, and our lives. I comforted him with a few pats, as Laura would have comforted me, then clutching him tightly, stole out to the living room. My eyes filled up with tears at the thought that I would never again have Laura's comfort and so much more. She was also my best friend.

There was a strange man standing intimately close to my mother, obviously mesmerized by her long-lidded beautiful green eyes and thick black lashes. He stopped caressing her arm and took a step back when he saw me. My legs felt like they were giving out beneath me. I reached out to the arm of the easy chair for balance and choked my poor bear as my other arm constricted him. My first feeling toward George Randallman was hatred. My first impression of him was that he was rich and gray. He was shorter than my daddy, but taller than my mother. His clothes looked expensive: gray slacks, crisp white shirt worn with the collar open, and a gray suit jacket blazer that opened a bit wider at his stout middle. He had grayish-blue eyes and mostly medium-brown hair mixed with gray. His overall blend of gray and brown reminded me of a mouse I once saw scurry across Grama Estelle's kitchen floor. His wavy hair was combed back from a receding hairline and over an obviously thin soon-to-be-bald spot at the back of his head. The only exception from this impression of medium gray was the huge gold watch on his left wrist.

He tried a nervous smile. "This must be Margaret."

I gave him a defiant glare and demanded, "Who are you?" I had no intention of letting his phony smile disarm me. As young as I was, I was savvy enough to know this was all wrong, especially for Daddy.

George Randallman shot my mother the first of many pleading, sheepish looks I would see over the next seventeen years.

Mama said sweetly, "Margaret, this is George. He's giving us a ride to California." Her kind manner was surprising.

"I don't want to go to California. I want to stay here." I turned deliberately to glare at George. "With Daddy."

George avoided my stare. "I'll get the suitcase in Margaret's room."

Mama was across the room and down on one knee, eye-level with me in less than a second. She placed her hands on the outside of each of my arms and squeezed them together so hard that it felt like "my wings" on my back were touching each other. She whispered, "Don't you ruin this for me, young lady. Keep your mouth shut." Her cold green eyes made me think she was more of a robot than a person. This frightened me so much, I thought I might pee my underpants again, but I was able to hold it until I could go to the bathroom.

I wiggled free from her and ran to the playpen, where Ray was standing at the edge of his baby prison. He let go of one of the bars and stuck his meaty hand through to meet my face, and said, "Deedee."

I hugged him through the wooden bars. I saw his stuffed diaper bag on the floor and a bulging black garbage bag next to it. I was sure it contained everything we had in the house that went with a toddler.

Mama pried us apart, picked up Ray, and carried him to his high chair in the kitchen. She grabbed a plastic bowl off the side shelf, poured Cheerios into it, and dumped some onto Ray's tray. He started grabbing them. He had two fistfuls stuffed into his mouth before she finished pouring milk into the bowl for me. She put the bowl down at my usual spot at the kitchen table and told me to sit down. She poured milk into Ray's sippy cup before she turned to leave the kitchen. I expected her to insist, "Don't make a mess," but she didn't. I realized she didn't care if we made a mess in the house that Daddy would come home to alone. My achy head pounded again as *No! No! No!* once again echoed and blasted in my brain. I pushed the Cheerios away, put my forehead down onto the table, and cried.

———

I kept my mouth shut as the mean robot commanded, but I watched the reflection of a portion of George's face in the rearview mirror for opportunities to express my hatred and anger. When I could tell he was checking on me, I responded by sticking out my tongue or making other nasty faces.

We were comfortable enough: me on the soft leather seats, Ray in his car seat. We each had a small blanket. When I would get cold from the air conditioning, I would put Ray's around him before covering myself with mine. When we stopped, the cool car was a stark contrast to the hot asphalt or cement path to gas station bathrooms. I would make sure Ray was free from his blankie until the car cooled down again. I was rising to Laura's role as Ray's guardian. No one was assigned to protect me. This was the beginning of haunting loneliness that I felt for many years to come.

George was quiet for most of the trip, but I could tell that my antics upset him. He averted his eyes each time I delivered an insolent taunt. Sometimes I could see his color rise in his face. I sensed that I was wounding him, and I was thrilled with the power. My mother, whom I decided defiantly to henceforth refer to as Norma, sat very close to George in the front seat, but she was unaware of my malice.

In his defense, I confess that George was kind to Ray and me. He was quite willing to stop frequently so Norma could change Ray and I could go to the bathroom. He bought us as much food and soda pop as we wanted, but regardless of his generosity—and the fact that in his presence Norma was remarkably more patient and kind with both Ray and me—I refused to even consider liking him.

During one of our stops, I left Norma and Ray in the cramped, smelly bathroom and found George standing in front of the chips.

"Oh, hi." He smiled nervously. "Do you like these?" He held up a bag of Cheetos.

I calculated the mess they would make in the backseat of his luxurious car and said, "Ray loves them."

"Ok then, How about you?"

"I'm not hungry."

He looked distressed, then said awkwardly, "Well, er maybe you will be hungry later. How about some popcorn?"

I just glared at him.

"I'll get this, OK?" He still held the bag of popcorn.

I followed him to the counter. I looked up at the pimply faced clerk. "He's not my daddy. He's kidnapping me from my daddy."

George's eyes got wide. He pasted on a phony smile, and said nervously to the clerk, "No, it's not like that. I'm with her mother— oh good." He looked relieved as he saw Norma beside me.

She was furious. She practically threw Ray to George, yanked my left arm so hard that my shoulder would be sore for days. She pulled me out of the store, across the hot asphalt parking lot, opened the back door of George's car and tossed me in so cruelly that I rolled until my head bounced against the metal bar on Ray's car seat. "Listen, you little brat. I'm doing this for you. Trust me! You don't want you to have the same rotten childhood I had. I told you to keep your mouth shut so shut it and keep it shut. No more!—" She was yelling. A blue vein had drawn itself from above her left eyebrow to her hairline "—about where we came from or your daddy." She said "daddy" like it was a curse word. "Do you understand?" She said it more like a command than a question.

I nodded, irritating the bump on the back of my head as I moved against the rigid metal bar. I was too scared to cry. She was rarely nice to me, but I had no clue she could be so violent. Norma escorted me to and from bathrooms for the rest of the trip. I was no longer allowed to pick out snacks.

When it got close to dinnertime of the first day, I felt shade cover the dark car as George pulled under a covered archway. He pried his arm from Norma's clutches, got out of the car, and stepped through a darkly tinted glass door. I thought about Daddy, who was probably arriving about now at the empty, messy house, and I started to cry. *Poor, poor Daddy. First he lost Laura, now he has lost us too.*

Norma viciously turned in the front seat to face me. "Quit bawling! It's your fault you had to leave home. If you hadn't killed your sister—" Then she started to wail a high-pitched sound that was more rage than sorrow.

My throat closed up. Everything froze. I heard no sound as my mind clicked back through the confusing images of the last week, stopping at one conclusion: no one had seen Vanessa shoot Laura. They all—Daddy, Grampa, Grama, the man in white, and all those people who came through our house and to the funeral— must have thought that I shot her!

I began to sob uncontrollably. I found it difficult to breathe as horror and shame churned through my belly. I pulled the handle and kicked the heavy car door open with both my feet. I leaned out over the rippling heat of the driveway and vomited out the little bit of food and soda in my stomach, and then burning, acrid bile.

Returning to my place in the car, I cried out, "I-I-I-didn't shoot her!" Then I just cried.

Ray, of course, joined us in our wailing, so that by the time George returned carrying a key with a large white plastic thingy hanging on it, his luxury car sounded like the feral cats of Nueva

Lane. His anguish was so visible, had I not hated him so much, I would have felt sorry for him. He took my mother into his arms and comforted her. Ray and I were on our own. I took his chubby hand in mine and leaned my head against the upholstered rail of his car seat. He rewarded my kindness by pulling my braid with his other hand.

George settled some of our stuff into a motel room with two ginormous beds. The carpet smelled like bug spray, the bathroom like Pinesol. George stepped out of the room so Norma could scrub us as clean as she could in a five-minute washcloth torture. After tossing a clean sundress in my general direction, she shoved portions of a squirming, kicking Ray into a clean T-shirt and shorts. I pulled the clean sundress over my head and turned toward the mirrored closet door to see the cheerless girl staring back at me through large brown eyes with dark circles beneath them.

I felt so misunderstood. And yet, I knew they were right. I did kill her. It was my fault. Vanessa was aiming at me. It should have been me they placed in the coffin, and then lowered into the ground.

When George returned to the room, I saw he had changed into a beautiful gray-and-black silk Hawaiian shirt. He set down the shirt that he was carrying—the one he was wearing when he walked out the door—then he lifted Ray up from the bed where Norma had triumphed in the dressing battle. Norma said, "Wait!" She lifted his arm by the elbow and removed a tag by breaking a string that was dangling under his armpit.

Ray studied George's face as he was carried across a large heat-rippling asphalt parking lot to a restaurant that had a sign with huge painted fish hovering above the door. I felt conflicted by Ray's obvious contentment. I did not want Ray to like George, but neither did I want my brother to feel as miserable as I did.

George opened a heavy glass door that gave way to a green marble entry. "Ladies?"

We marched in ahead as Ray tugged at the tuft of longer hair at the base of George's scalp.

There were islands of tables with white linen tablecloths resting on a highly polished wooden floor. I couldn't remember ever seeing one white tablecloth; certainly I had never seen a whole room full of them. A man in a white shirt and maroon tie lifted one eyebrow when he saw Ray, but he immediately motioned to someone to bring a high chair as he showed us to our table. The high chair was made of dark wood and didn't have a tray on it. As George settled Ray into the chair and then slid him up to the table, I wondered if anyone else was wondering, as I was, if our white tablecloth would ever recover from the upcoming Ray assault on food.

The restaurant smelled like the bakery at Grama Estelle's Safeway. The thought of her reminded me of my inconsolable loss. I felt my eyes fill with tears and my nose started to run. I picked up my napkin and wiped them both. My mother shot me a disapproving look, which frightened my tears dry. Waiters and waitresses were carrying baskets of hot bread wrapped in white linen napkins around the room. When one of these was delivered to our table, Ray was in hog heaven. George patiently buttered more and more bread for Ray, but his attention was definitely sucked into the vortex of Norma's movements above— and I suspected also—beneath the table. Norma kept closing her eyelids and then opening them in slanted sideways glances. George was enthralled. She occasionally stroked the hair on his forearm as they talked. It reminded me of the way Grampa Red used to pet his dog.

When we came back to the motel room, there was a portacrib set near the wall by the bathroom door. I noticed that someone had tidied up. The dirty clothes that we left on the floor were folded neatly and placed on the dresser next to the TV. Dirty washcloths and towels were replaced with clean ones. We promptly made another mess. Norma picked up a tiny bottle from the bathroom sink and poured it into the bathtub as she ran warm water. The bath was great comfort to me emotionally as well as physically, even though I had to share it with the wild and wiggly Ray.

George and Norma slept in one bed and put me in the other. I pretended to fall sleep long before I actually could. I covered my ears to shut out the movements and noises from the other bed. I cried silently, soaking my poor brown bear with my tears.

The next morning we packed up and George loaded the car, but we didn't go very far. We stopped right away for breakfast. As usual, Ray ate more than I did, but I remember eating half of a huge pancake. George didn't say anything, but I could tell he was pleased to see me eating. Norma was still nicer than usual to Ray and me, but it was just plain weird the way she was acting toward George. The word that kept coming into my mind was *gooey*.

The second night of our ride to California, we stayed in a much nicer motel room than the first. George's key was not a key at all, but a card. He pushed it into a slot in the door, and a green light came on. The door unlocked. It had a little kitchen in the room and big glass doors through which I saw, for the first time other than on TV, the Pacific Ocean. When we opened the glass doors to a balcony, the seabirds cawed and called to one another in a noisy chorus. Some of them flew close to the open doors and mewed like Grama Estelle's house cat. I thought I heard dogs barking, but George said they were sea lions.

I was delighted to be so close to the ocean, the birds, and the sea lions, but I wasn't about to let George know anything he did or said made me feel happy, so I just said in a bored manner, "Oh." Nothing he could do would absolve him of the blame in my heart for helping Norma take us away from Daddy. What I needed more than anything was forgiveness, but I was way too self-absorbed to consider offering it to someone else first.

In our three days of travel, I believe Ray woofed down more french fries than he had in his entire previous year. I was still not hungry, but Norma seemed to be on a mission to control me. She would manipulate with, "Take just one more bite." Or, "You need to be a good eater." Or, "We can't leave until you drink all of your milk."

The time in the car on the third day didn't seem as long. When we got out to make necessary stops, the heat coming up through the bottom of our shoes no longer burned our feet. Just before dark we arrived at our final destination. George pushed a remote control button on the console above the rearview mirror. We waited for a double iron gate to swing on its hinges away from the car. We rode through a virtual tunnel of oak trees on a cement driveway that was banked with tall green bushes. The driveway and tunnel curved to the left, then rose to a platform in front of a house that was larger than the first motel we stayed in. George drove straight toward it, but then went around it. He pressed another button on his console that commanded a garage door to rise. It was the middle of three garage doors. We pulled in between a big white car and a red sports car. The big white car resembled a minivan. It had a shiny chrome circle on the hood. I would find out later that the red car was a Ferrari. We had just traveled three days in a Bentley.

CHAPTER FOUR

Wedding

The Randallman estate, gardens, and acres of surrounding hills were named Hillhollow. The property had been in George's mother's family for three generations. His father's family had property in the exclusive Black Rock area of Bridgeport, Connecticut. George's grandfather and father were already gone when we became part of his family. I'm not sure I ever heard why they had died young. All I knew is that they were all named George, and two of the George Randallmans were now gone. His Black Rock great uncle, who was thankfully not named George but William, was approaching eighty and never had children. William's wife of fifty-two years passed before him, so our George was in line to inherit another boatload of money very soon.

Norma was delighted to learn all this. She married him immediately. I'm not sure how she instigated her divorce with Daddy or how she succeeded to disassociate Ray and me from him, but all our names were changed from Taylor to Randallman about a year after we arrived at Hillhollow.

Hillhollow was aptly named. The three-story mansion was surrounded on three sides by a high circular wall of rock about a mile in circumference. It was as if God's hand had scooped half of a hill away, leaving a canyon floor of fertile soil. This flat half circle was graced by ancient oak trees that had thrived for many years, protected by the half sphere of curved wall. At the top of the gutted hill rose other hills that looked like seashells someone had lined up carefully into rows. There were no houses on the seashells. I learned later that they were part of the Randallman estate. For most of the year, the hills were light brown, but during the winter and the first part of spring they were emerald green.

I was in awe the first time I saw Hillhollow and each time I discovered more of its elegant beauty. I grew to love this beautiful home and its setting that was so carefully planned and maintained. The canyon floor that surrounded the mansion was judiciously landscaped with a pool, a rose garden, shrubbery, and abundant flower beds. At least a few of the flowers were blooming in the cold months, but in the spring, the Hillhollow gardens were nothing short of breathtaking.

Where the natural circle of wall broke away, Hillhollow was fenced and gated with tall vertical iron that revealed the plush gardens to observers on the road below, but stated clearly that entrance was by invitation only.

The small wedding was held on the Hillhollow estate in the yard immediately behind the mansion. No other children attended besides Ray and me. Apparently, George was the owner of an elite architectural firm. About twenty well-dressed men and their phenomenally dressed wives or dates came to eat well, drink well, and wish well. A very skinny, loquacious, sharp-witted great-uncle William flew in from the East Coast. He had a full head of wavy white hair. His obvious vigor and enthusiasm for life was, no doubt, a disappointment to Norma. He didn't look like he would kick the proverbial bucket any time soon. I liked him. He smiled and winked at me. I tried to wink back, but I think I closed both eyes instead of just one. I decided to learn how to wink by practicing in front of my bedroom mirror.

George's mother rode in from the rose garden on a motorized wheelchair. She was wearing a black coatdress with bright-yellow piping. Her wide-brimmed hat was also black, with a one-inch yellow taffeta band and a small tuft of black and yellow feathers. She headed directly toward me on path of angled pavers that sliced the impressive rear garden in half, the drone of her wheelchair and its travel in a straight line, reminded me of a bumblebee on a mission.

Mrs. Randallman was reserved when I first met her. As I got to know her better, I learned that she was quite talkative, opinionated, and very wise. It was obvious that she was suspicious of my mother's intentions, so I immediately liked her too. She had a wonderfully expressive face, in which I not only saw disapproval of Norma but also kindness and sympathy toward Ray and me. The estate was so vast and I was so small, it wasn't until the day of the wedding that I found out she lived in a house on the property with a round-the-clock staff that attended to all her needs.

The ceremony was brief and simple. We settled into chairs set up under the shade of huge oak trees off the back veranda. My eyes kept wandering to the ginormous swimming pool to the left. A fountain played in a rock ridge above it, and then water flowed out of the fountain to cascade into the pool dazzling in the sun. I could smell the clean mist laced with chlorine. It was lovely background music for the party. A mostly bald minister, who seemed to have a stuffy nose, wore a white, blue-trimmed robe and a long, blue scarf, droned on about what I—an avid watcher of recorded movies—had come to know as the "usual" things that are said at a wedding ceremony. Likewise, the vows were ordinary—nothing original from either Norma or George. I was only half listening, distracted by my anger—I could not believe they were getting married!—distracted also by sad thoughts for

Daddy who was alone. Then, I heard the minister ask if there was any reason these two should not be joined together.

I blurted out, bravely. "For real? How about Daddy?" Norma hadn't threatened me since that stop during our trip to Hillhollow. In fact, she had been a lot nicer to me since we moved in about a year ago and straightaway hired a nanny to take care of Ray. My heart was beating really fast. I had surprised myself. I thought, *Oops! Did I say that out loud?* I was outraged by their boldness to get married.

I felt all attention riveted on me. The minister was totally flummoxed. He stood silent, sternly looking at Norma, who burst out in fake laughter. She turned abruptly around, twirling her floaty, knee-length lime-green dress, and faced me with her bouquet of white lilies. "Oh, Margaret. Hush now, darling." She twirled back to face the minister and said, "You know how all little girls are in love with their daddies." Back to me, she said, "You cannot marry George, honey. Sorry. I saw him first."

The congregated guests broke the tension with tempered laughter. Some of them shot condescending looks in my direction. George's mother, however, who sat in the first row with me, reached her boney hand across the vacant chair between us, picked up mine for a brief moment, and gave it a gentle squeeze. For the rest of the service I tried to count the glistening jewels on that hand, her other hand, in her earrings, and in her necklace. My favorite was the rectangular red ring she wore on her right hand. The large ruby was surrounded by small sparkling round diamonds. Before I knew it, we were past the part where I wanted to mock Norma for making a vow and mock George for believing her. The service was over.

At the reception, I was hanging out sipping Pepsi out of a champagne flute in the west corner of the veranda. The sun was shooting beams through the boughs and leaves of the massive oak hovering nearby. George's mother motored up a ramp through the west archway to my side. The ramps made sense to me now. She sat erect with one hand in her lap, holding a yellow-piped black patent-leather handbag that matched her shiny black-and-yellow spectator shoes. Her other hand rested on the wheelchair control panel. Her voice was kind, even, and direct—a relief from the usual patronizing tone often directed toward me.

"Hello. I'm Mrs. Randallman. I understand your name is Margaret. Is that what you prefer to be called?" Had she been standing, she would have been tall. Perhaps it was her willowy frame, but she seemed taller than George with his middle-aged-man's belly. She had blue eyes, a beautifully shaped thin nose, and a sharp chin. I could see the hair at her temples was very light; under the back of her hat, the hair was reddish brown.

I felt like I should straighten my back, level my chin, and pull my shoulders back slightly, just to deserve to be standing in her presence. "Hi. My daddy called me Maggie, but no one has called me that since we left him." I fought back tears and thought I could read sympathy in her face. This woman was caught in the middle of my frustration and loneliness, but she was not my enemy.

She nodded once. "I see." Then she said very tenderly, "And would you like me to call you Maggie?"

"No, thank you." I took a breath to steady myself and replied, "I just read *Little Women*, and I've decided I'm Meg."

Her well-shaped darkened left eyebrow went up. "You are only five? And you just finished *reading Little Women*? Did you mean you watched the movie?"

"No. I read the book to Danielle, our nanny. She started reading to me, but I asked to switch places with her. She helped me with some of the words. How did you know how old I am? Did George tell you about me?" She nodded again. "My daddy taught me to read." I gulped, trying again to keep from crying.

"Hmmm." Her eyes flicked upward as if she were grabbing a thought from the right side of her brain, and then she directed them back to my face, "Well . . . what else do you do with most of your time in this great big house, Meg?"

At this point, my mother staggered up. Her voice seemed overly loud as it intruded into our quiet corner. "Hello, Margaret."

I was surprised that Norma would speak to or even acknowledge me at this event because beforehand she had made very clear that it was to be all about her, but then I remembered my outburst and shuddered. I prepared myself for a verbal whack. I didn't think she would actually hit me, or yank my arm, in front of others. Then I realized that she wasn't talking to me. Apparently, I was not the only Margaret in this conversation.

Margaret Randallman replied levelly, "Hello, Norma."

I had recently seen a Western movie on TV where two cowboys faced off with their hands hovering over the guns that hung in holsters on their belts. There was a whistling kind of music playing in the background. I imagined the same eerie dueling music playing here. Mrs. Margaret Randallman lifted her long eyelids, pushed a button on her chair, and spun to directly face Norma. Norma flinched and studied the champagne flute in her hand. She took a gulp from it before continuing her interruption. "I see you have met *my* Margaret."

"Yes." Mrs. Randallman seemed to enjoy saying, "I believe she prefers Meg." Margaret confidently and patiently waited for Norma to make eye contact, but the champagne flute seemed far too interesting.

Norma flinched and fidgeted with a little ring that had a green jewel attached. It was a bracelet for the stem of her champagne flute. If she set it down, it would be easily identified as her glass. I knew there was little risk of that glass leaving her hand as long as people were walking around with refills.

As usual, she talked about me as if I was not there. "Well, I named her Margaret! I will decide what she's to be called, not her." She shot a sideways glance at me. I could see red veins around the white that surrounded the green iris of her eyeballs. I always wondered where that conversation would have gone, because an interruption interrupted her interruption. Danielle joined us, carrying Ray on her hip. When he spotted me, he exclaimed, "Deedee Meg!"

Norma was appalled. She didn't spend a whole lot of time with Ray, so I doubted that she was aware that Ray was learning to talk in major run-on sentences. She probably also felt ganged up on because of the "Meg" thing. Her mother-in-law gave her a satisfied smile.

I felt powerful standing beside her. It was reinforced when she reached out a thin hand and placed it comfortably on my shoulder. It gave me courage to stand up for myself. I mustered up an expression that I hoped delivered self-confidence and said simply, "I prefer Meg." I felt a twinge of guilt and regret. I still wanted my mother's love and attention, but no one would suspect that I did. I had mastered subtle impertinence. In my head, I was still following her around too closely, clinging to the hope that she loved me, yet feeling very strongly that she didn't want me near. In a twisted tactic, I gave her reasons not to like me, hoping she would prove me wrong. She didn't try. I rationalized that she loved me, but that I had driven her away.

For the past year I had practiced a lot of self-pity and self-condemnation. I felt rejected by Norma. I missed Daddy, Grama Estelle, and Grampa Red—and more than all, Laura. I felt misunderstood, but also guilty for surviving Vanessa's gunfire.

As usual, Danielle was dressed casually and plain. Her dominate feature was her impossible eyebrows. Eyebrow might be a better description. Though the dark hair was sparser between her eyes, it definitely continued as one line above her deep-set blackish-brown eyes. No one could blame her for choosing a grubby T-shirt and jeans to care for my little brother. He had a propensity for grime and slime. You'd think, though, that she would have chosen something a bit nicer for the wedding. As I look back on our time with Danielle, I had a feeling that Norma chose her because Norma thought Danielle was homely. On the other hand, I found Danielle pretty. To a child starved for kindness and love, someone who offered it had unique beauty. Norma let her go after a few years. I think she was jealous of the bond Ray and I had with Danielle.

Danielle only needed to take a break. It was normal for a twenty-year-old girl to want to use the bathroom without the aid of a rambunctious two-year-old, but Norma's plan for the day had not included Danielle's needs. The playpen that was usually on the veranda had been hidden away. The kitchen was rowdy with caterers. She could hardly turn him loose in the rose garden, and she was wise to know that if she had taken Ray to his upstairs room, he would howl outside the bathroom door and the dog would probably join in as he did when he heard a siren in the distance.

Norma guzzled down the remaining champagne in her glass while Danielle was explaining that she needed a little break. I felt sorry for Danielle, not just because of Norma's momentary rudeness, but for Norma's ongoing attitude that seemed to imply that Danielle was inferior.

I sat down in a nearby chair and stretched out my arms for Ray and said, "Maybe after you go to the bathroom, you could get something to eat too."

Danielle nodded and smiled at me as she settled Ray onto my lap, then hurried off.

"Eat?" This, with gusto, from Ray. "Eat!"

I could see that Norma's greatest concern was that her glass was empty. She slurred, "Wull you scuse me?" She turned to search for the woman dressed in black and white carrying a champagne bottle wrapped in a white cloth napkin. I wondered if she noticed that the entire catering staff was dressed the way she used to when she worked at the hotel.

Margaret Randallman cringed as she watched Norma stagger off, but then turned her chair toward us. I'm sure she would have preferred not to be in a wheelchair, but to a five-year-old, it looked like fun to be able to push buttons to roll and spin so easily.

"So this is Ray." She smiled at him. "Would you like me to fix a plate of food for you?"

My brother's pudgy cheeks dimpled when she said his name. "Food!" He sat contentedly on my lap holding a deep handful of my hair. Danielle had painstakingly curled my long locks into semi ringlets. Ray probably missed the usual thick braids that served him well as handles, "Food! Deedee Meg!" He bounced a couple of times.

When Mrs. Randallman returned with the food, I deposited Ray and the paper plate on the bench that ran beneath the railing. She had managed to find kid-friendly food among the gourmet oysters, shrimp, and crab. You couldn't blame her for not knowing that he would have eaten anything. Seriously, anything! I had to keep him from eating yucky bugs when we played together outside. He dug into tiny sandwiches and petite cakes with delight. He soon had macaroni salad in him, on him, and all around him.

"Meg, I hear you have been pulled out of school."

"Yes. The kindergarten teacher put me in the first grade. After about a week and half, the first grade teacher sent me to the second grade. The second grade teacher sent me to the principal, who decided I should have some private tutoring."

"How many tutors do you have?"

"Three. They come on different days. Mrs. Glydon comes for math and science. Señora Escalerra is teaching me Spanish. Miss Palmerton is my history, language, and reading teacher. She is teaching me about the California missions."

"That's what they teach California children in the fourth grade." She paused and smiled, watching Ray obliterate any sense of order to the food she had brought him. He looked up and grinned at us through a delighted, messy face. Then she turned back to me. "Do you have any music lessons?"

"No, but sometimes I play George's grand piano."

She tilted her chin up slightly. "Do you read music?

"No, I just play stuff I hear on my CD player or the radio." I couldn't remember anyone except Daddy ever taking this much interest in me.

"I see." The same beautiful eyebrow went up, and she smiled at me mostly with her eyes. "Would you like me to teach you how to read music?"

"Sure! That would be awesome!"

She gave me a full smile in response, then turned the chair slightly and used her whole hand to point. "You see that path down the middle of the rose garden? If you go to the end of the third row and turn right, you will see another path that leads between two oak trees and then to the back door of my house. There are two French doors." Turning back to me, she said, "The ones with little window panes." She stated it like a question and sketched a little rectangular box in the air with both hands. "They're often standing open. Just call hello through the screen. If they're not open, tap on one of the windows. I also have a grand piano that you can practice on."

"Cool! Every day? I'll have to ask Danielle though."

She asked rhetorically, "Not your mother?"

"No. Not Norma."

She smiled knowingly. "Let's start with one weekday—any day except Wednesday would work for me. Would like to go to church with me on Sundays?"

"Yes! Please! My daddy used to take us to church." I blinked back tears.

"Let's talk about that when you come too."

CHAPTER FIVE

Friends

We decided on two days a week for the music lessons. I was excited to start reading music, but I was even more excited to visit with Mrs. Randallman. As I was getting ready to go to my first lesson, I headed through the kitchen toward the sliding glass door. Our chef had arrived to start preparing the evening meal. "Hi, Barbara! I'm so excited!"

She was bending down, reaching into the cupboard beneath the stovetop island. She came up with a sauté pan, set it on the front burner closest to me, and smiled. "Oh yeah? Why is that?"

"I'm going to Mrs. Randallman's cottage for a music lesson."

"What?" This from Norma, who was descending the anterior staircase. "Where did you say you are going?" She appeared at the arch between the kitchen and dining room, glaring at me with disapproval.

My excitement turned to fear. "To George's mother's house." I saw Barbara steal discreetly into the walk-in pantry.

Norma had the knack of making one word sound like an accusation. "Why?"

"She said she would teach me music." My hand was gripping the handle of the sliding door so tightly, my fingers hurt.

"No." Her emerald eyes seemed to glow like lasers. "You don't need to bother Mrs. Randallman for music lessons. I will hire a music tutor." She stood smugly, lifting one brow. "Sit down!"

I felt heat rise from my neck into my face. I released the handle, walked to the nearest kitchen chair, and sat. I was still, however, deeply frustrated and disappointed. I was sitting on the outside, but I was standing up on the inside. "Now what? Do you want me to sit here the rest of the day so you can control me?" I sat upright staring her down. I won.

She flinched and looked toward the decanters on the bar across the dining room. They were distracting her so I kept up my barrage of questions. "Are you going to call Mrs. Randallman? Will you tell her the truth—that *you're* the one who doesn't want me to visit with her and that *you* don't trust her to teach me music?" She was headed for the bar, still unable to look at me. "Or are you planning to lie and say I didn't want to come to her house?"

I could tell she was flustered. She looked nervously at Barbara, who had reappeared in the kitchen but then spun on her heel and disappeared back into the pantry. Norma switched to a more approving tone. "Well, er, I suppose that *would* be good for you." Then, nervously she pulled a tumbler forward and picked up a decanter. "Tell Mrs. Randallman I said, 'thank you.'" Her hands shook as she poured two inches of amber liquid into the glass.

I steadied my tone to match hers. "I will."

She lifted her glass and drained it with her head tilted back. When her chin was level again she said to her empty glass, "Thank you."

I rose from the chair and went back through the kitchen. Norma had her back to me. All her attention was focused on refilling her glass as I slipped through the sliding door.

I scurried down the center of the rose garden. My heart was beating fast. My brain was sorting out the disturbing scene. I was disgusted with myself for being so rude, and yet a small part of me felt justified for finally standing up to Norma's unreasonable control. Self-abasement was winning the battle though. What a horrible, ugly person lived inside of me!

I saw the French doors. They were indeed open. As I got close, the air came alive with birds flying every which way. One of them bumped into a window, but after he bounced off, he resumed flight and seemed to be fine. I saw several bird feeders in the bushes near the back patio. I pushed away the memory of Daddy's bird feeders and leaned into the screen to shade the glare with my head. I could see a large immaculate room decorated beautifully with muted coral, deep navy blue, and seafoam-colored fabrics. Ivory lace peeked out from behind the floral fabric of the draped windows. The floor was medium-toned wood covered with large, flowery, area rugs. These contained sculptured off-pink flowers resting against a navy background. To the right of the room was the grand piano. Straight ahead, I could see an archway that led to a wide green marble entryway. At the far end of the hallway was another set of double doors with crystal-cut glass inserted into polished wood. The afternoon sunshine sparkled though the crystal. Slivers of light threw illustrations onto the brilliantly polished floor.

"Hello? This is Meg. I'm here for a music lesson?" I was breathless from my fury and my scurry. I took a deep breath. "Hello?"

A woman entered from the left into the hallway. The first thing I noticed about her was her dimples. "Hi, Meg! I'm Karen, Mrs. Randallman's . . . well, er . . . I'm not sure what my title is." She laughed a throaty, contagious laugh. She spoke with an accent I had heard on TV. I guessed she was Scottish or Irish. "I live here with her. I'm sort of her secretary, companion, and house manager. In the old country I would be called the head housekeeper, but here in America everything is so much more relaxed."

She certainly seemed relaxed. As she slid open the magnetic screen door, I could smell roses. I realized, since there were no real roses in the room, that it was her fragrance. She was full-figured and freckled. She wore very little, if any, makeup—just shiny lip gloss. Her eyes were a light brown, almost golden. Her shimmering strawberry hair was very stylish in a sweeping bob, longer in front than in the back. She wore black mid-length knit pants and a tangerine three-quarter-sleeve T-shirt with "Right Arm" printed down the right arm. It had a V-neck that ruffled a bit at the base of the V. It hung long over her pants, but stopped in time to show off her bottom. "Mrs. Randallman will be here in a min—Oh! Here she is." She dimpled again.

Margaret Randallman came quietly motoring in from the right into the hallway. "Hello, Meg. I see you have met my friend Karen."

"Friend. Now there ya go. I like *that* title. I answered an ad to be a nanny in America, and instead of changing nappies and waiting on sniffling wee ones, I ended up being a friend to a regal lady." This to me. Then to Mrs. Randallman she said, "Would you like me to serve tea or lemonade?"

"In a little while would be wonderful, unless Meg is thirsty? No? Not yet, Karen, but thank you."

Karen dimpled yet again, winked at me, and then sketched a little Z of a wave before disappearing off to the left, from where I had seen her enter the beautiful room. I had a feeling she wasn't far away.

Margaret Randallman was less intimidating when dressed more casually, but she still exuded dignity and poise. She was in a soft pants outfit made of lightweight fabric with tiny ribs in it. The ribs resembled the waves in the seafoam blue-green fabric that matched many of the colors in the big room. Her eyes looked a bit blue-green too, rather than just blue, as I remembered them. Her hair was indeed a shade of red, but the sides and top were light because the dark red was mixed with a gray that wasn't really gray. It was more off-white, kind of blond, but with a hint of light red. She wore it very short in the back and on the sides, but the top was kind of long for such a short haircut. Her makeup was perfect. Her smile was wonderful.

"So, Meg, welcome to my home. Please come and sit here on the couch." She motioned to a spot at the left end. "We have some things to talk about besides music." She motored up next to the end of the couch so that we were sitting next to each other.

We did not talk about everything that first day. But for the next few years, at future visits we often took time to talk about my past. In all the conversations, I could have answered what I suspected were her underlying questions if I had told her about Laura and the accident.

That first day, however, she asked me what I could remember about my trip to California, and then she asked a lot of questions about my life before I left my former home. I told her about dusty Nueva Lane, with our house and Grampa's. I left out Vanessa. I told her my father's name was Franklin Taylor, and gave her my grama and grampa's first names. She went, "Hmmm," when I told her my grampa's name was Red. She asked me when I had first met George, so I told her about the dreadful day he showed up in his big silver car that took us away from Daddy. I felt the blood rush into my neck, then my face.

"You don't like him much, do you?"

Still blushing, I thought it over for a minute and said, "I guess I don't not like him. I just don't like it that he likes Norma."

She said flatly, "Neither do I."

"You don't like her much, do you?

She laughed at my echoing question. "Well, I certainly like you and Ray. I think George does too. He's very lucky that you and Ray came along and I think he knows it."

"So we agree? We both think George was under some blinding spell when he picked Norma?"

She accepted my precociousness with laughter, and I joined her. Then she was quiet for a moment, seemingly digesting what I had said. "My darling girl, is it confusing to you? Your relationship with your mother?"

I nodded, feeling a sting behind my eyes and my throat tightening. I was still remembering my ugly behavior in the kitchen.

"I'm sure she loves you."

I didn't want to argue with my new friend, but I didn't believe she was right. "The worst part of it is, she took us away from Daddy."

"Yes. I can certainly understand that. You miss him, don't you?"

"Yes." I let the tears flow.

She patted the top of my hand. "There, there. It's OK. Go ahead and cry. Maybe somehow we can find out more than you remember."

We did finally get to the music that day. She showed me how to properly place my small fingers on the keys and taught me how to practice scales. She called to Karen, who arrived shortly with some music theory books for me to write in, and a couple of simple books with notes in them for me to practice at home. Mrs. Randallman patiently sat near me as I went over the piano keys, calling them by their alphabet names. We had tea in delicate cups with etched flowers and golden rims. I didn't tell her it was the first time I had ever had hot tea. Nor did I tell her it was the first time since I left Grama Estelle and Daddy that someone had visited with me just because I was me—not because they were paid to feed me or teach me or clean up after me.

I remember the most important part of that first day, though, was when she asked me, "So. I think we need to decide what you

43

should call me. Mrs. Randallman is a bit formal for someone who is your step-grandmother." She looked down at the soft fabric of her pants and unnecessarily smoothed it with her hands. Then, she looked up. "What would you like to call me?"

I nodded my head in the direction where I had seen Karen exit the beautiful room. "Karen said you are a regal lady." I grinned. "May I call you My Lady?"

I could tell she was pleased, and I think I surprised her a little. "Why yes. That is such a nice name for you to call me." I saw a hint of color rise in her cheeks.

In all the visits to follow, My Lady took time to ask about my feelings and often asked me about my mother. A few years later, we settled as usual side by side, she in her chair and I at the end of the couch. She was wearing lemon-yellow linen slacks with a pale-yellow silk blouse. I noticed a small book on her lap. Pictures of stunning roses wallpapered the cloth cover. She saw my curious look toward the book, but she didn't respond.

I had just left an encounter with my mother and was feeling confused and rejected. It must have shown on my face.

"Meg, my dear, is something wrong?" she asked compassionately.

"Oh, My Lady, you know me so well! As I was headed out the kitchen door to come here, Norma asked me how I was and how my music lessons were going." I stopped to take a breath. "You know what? I was so surprised and delighted that she was interested, I started telling her how great you are and how we talk, not just do music. I closed the sliding door and came back into the room to tell her about your home, about Karen, and you." I stopped. I felt my throat tightening up and the back of my eyes hurt.

"And?" she asked softly.

I took a long, slow breath. "And it was as if she was a robot, like C-3P0, and she powered down. She totally lost interest in what I was saying. She turned her back to me and walked away. I just stood there with my mouth open in the middle of a sentence telling her how I felt about my time here with you and Karen. I thought she asked because she actually cared! I don't get it. She asked me, but she really didn't want to know. You know what?" I said angrily, "I don't care either."

"Yes, you do," she said wisely.

I turned my head to look at her and surrendered. "Yes. I suppose I do. I don't want to, but I do."

"I know you love her." She reached across to pat my hand. A sunbeam crossed her beautiful ruby ring and caused it to sparkle. "And I believe in her own way she loves you too." We sat thoughtfully for a moment with her hand resting on mine. "Can you think of times when you feel like she loves you?"

"I think so." I flipped my hand beneath hers, turning my palm up and gave her a hand hug. "Yes, I can. Sometimes she comes into my room to say goodnight. I love those times. You know what I really like about them?"

"What is that?"

"She usually comes in after a shower. She isn't wearing makeup and her hair is all wet and messy. She seems more like a real person. She asks me how I'm doing in my studies and I think she listens to my answers. Then, the best part is she kisses me on the forehead and says she is going to say goodnight to Ray." My eyes filled up. I sniffed and I sat back hard against the couch. "She doesn't say that she loves me, but you may be right. She probably does."

A satisfied smile lit her eyes. Her unparted lips curled up at the corners. "When you have hurtful, confusing moments, try to remember those evenings when she comes to say goodnight. Whatever is pure, whatever is lovely, if there is anything good for you to remember, think on these things."

"Wow. That's like poetry!"

She smiled fully. "It's a small part of a Bible verse." She picked up the book from her lap, opened it, then gently dragged her thumb to cause the pages to fan, then fall. They were all blank. "This book is for you. I will not always be available to you, so if you find yourself wishing you could talk to me about your thoughts and questions, record what happened that caused those thoughts and questions. Then bring this with you the next time you come to see me." She handed it to me. She reached into a side slit pocket in her lovely lemon-yellow slacks. "And here is a pen." She handed it to me. "I like these pens. They write so smoothly, you don't stop to think about the process of writing. You just glide onto the paper what is going on in your mind."

"Thank you." I studied the book in my hand—the second book someone had given me as a gift. I handed the precious book and pen back to her. I needed to take a breath to tame my emotions before I asked, "Would you write your name and the date inside it for me, please?"

She took them from me, but did not look down at them. Her eyes met mine. Our moment was similar to the one Daddy and I shared the night he gave me the first book. "Yes, of course, my dear Meg." She opened the book and wrote what I asked, but she added, 'I love you.' She handed it back to me with the page open.

The page blurred after I read it. "I love you too." I whispered and grabbed a tissue from the box on the table to wipe my nose.

After my piano lesson that day, we visited a while longer. My Lady asked me how things were going with Danielle and about my relationship with Ray. She wanted to know how my school lessons were going and which ones I liked the best. Then, as usual, she asked a question about my past. After a moment of silence, she asked, "What about your other grandparents?"

"Other?"

"Yes. You told me a long time ago, during your first visit, I believe, about your father's parents." She paused patiently, knowing I would eventually get to where she was going without her actually saying it. She unnecessarily clarified. "Your mother's parents," she said. "Didn't you know them?"

I sat there a little dumbfounded wondering why I had never asked myself the same question. By the time we had this conversation I was eight, but at such a young age, more often than not, stuff is still coming at you, and you sort it out as it comes in, rather than reach out for it. "I don't remember anyone ever talking about them," I said honestly.

"Does she have any brothers or sisters? Did you call anyone 'aunt' or 'uncle'?"

"Only a friend of Daddy's. We called him 'Uncle Tom.'"

"We? Ray too?"

I felt a flush of blood coming to my neck and face. I was afraid if I told My Lady about Laura, she wouldn't love me anymore, "Um, er . . . Daddy and me—we called him Uncle Tom, but he was not Grampa Red and Grama Estelle's son. He was a good friend of Daddy's. Grama and Grampa knew him really well though. I don't know why we called him uncle, but he was not very friendly with Norma. I remember that he always called Daddy, Franklin. They both thought it was really funny. I don't know why. Nobody else called him that. Everyone else called him Frank."

She looked at me suspiciously. I knew she knew I was not telling her something, "Your mother must have had parents." The two vertical wrinkles between her brows got deeper.

I said mischievously, "Or she was hatched."

She laughed, "Like a bird?"

"Or a reptile," I said cheerfully.

47

CHAPTER SIX

Spoiled and a Little Rotten

Margaret's offer of piano lessons and church turned out to be so much more. The first time we went to church, I pulled Laura's gold cross out of my Madame Alexander doll's panties and put it on my neck. I never took it off until I was thirteen, which was when Margaret took me to a jeweler to buy a longer chain for it. The jeweler also cleaned and polished the cross to a beautiful luster. My heart ached at the thought that it should have been around Laura's neck, not mine. My shame was ever with me. Thereafter, I always wore the cross, except for stopping at the jeweler's each time I visited the mall so he could clean both chain and cross while I waited.

"Where did you get that?" Norma noticed the cross when I got the new chain.

"Um, Mrs. Randallman gave it to me," I answered semi-truthfully. I confess that I often tucked it under my clothing if I knew she might see it, but unfortunately—or maybe it was fortunately—the real reason she had not noticed it sooner was she was spending less and less time with me.

"Oh. I seem to remember seeing one like it before." She looked like she was trying to remember, but at that moment most of her senses were slightly impaired. She was well into that evening's happy hour.

Ray wasn't just invited to join us for church. We both started spending more time with My Lady, and then we were both offered swimming lessons. I was nine and Ray was six. I knew Karen was "waiting in the wings," as usual, when the topic of swimming came up. My Lady, Ray and I were sitting on her bird-surrounded patio after church, finishing sandwiches.

"I saw you both splashing in the shallow end of the pool yesterday." She motioned her arm toward the pool and said, "This is the proper way to point, with your whole hand or perhaps two fingers, but not with just one."

I practiced an exaggerated gracious swing of my arm and open palm to point toward the pool area and said cheerfully, "Thank you, My Lady."

"You are welcome." She smiled with her eyes. "Actually, I heard you before I went over to see what was going on. Your laughter and squeals echoed clear over here. I have a friend from church that runs a swim school. Would you like me to invite her here to teach you how to swim?"

Before Ray and I could answer, Karen briskly came out the patio door, talking. She was wearing a red T-shirt that reminded me of one the comic book character "The Flash" would wear. "M—Did you say someone was coming here to teach people how to swim?"

"Y-yes, Karen." My Lady seemed a little surprised at the question and Karen's sudden interruption.

"Well, I say that is the perfect thing to do. Those two wee ones should know how to swim with a big swimmin' pool here like that."

Smiling, My Lady replied, "Why, thank you, Karen. I thought it was a good decision." She looked sideways at me to see that I was also smiling.

Karen took a deep breath and then began enthusiastically, "Why, yes. It's so warm here in California, people need to learn how to swim, even if they didn't learn when they were bairns because they lived in an area that was too cold and pretty much no one learned how to swim unless they were lucky enough to live near a lake for the one month out of the year when it got warm. Yes. That's a very good idea. Those wee ones should have lessons. Though both of them aren't really so wee, are they?" She finally took another breath. She was right about our not being "wee." Ray was almost as tall as I was, and we both had grown almost as tall as Karen. We would be tall like Daddy and Grampa Red, not tiny like Norma and Grama Estelle.

I could tell that Margaret was controlling her laughter when she politely inquired, "Karen, do you know how to swim?"

"Well, I can't say that what I do would be called swimmin'. It's not that I'm afraid of the water, but all I've ever done in deep water is hang onto something else and float a bit." She blushed then with embarrassment. I wasn't sure if she was embarrassed because she didn't know how to swim or if she realized that she butted into our private conversation.

My Lady, poised as always, considerately replied, "Would you like to take lessons when Meg and Ray take theirs?"

Karen eyes welled up, and her voice cracked a little. "See how you are, M? You are 'bout the nicest person I've ever met in my life. Where I was born, people like you didn't bother to take any interest at all in people like me." She pulled a Kleenex from her right pants pocket and dabbed at her watery eyes, then blotted under her nose.

I got up from the patio chair, went to Karen, wrapped my arms around her and said, "Isn't it nice to be a friend of My Lady Margaret, or as you and Ray call her, M?"

She warmly returned my hug, then began crying full on before she broke free from our embrace to go get a whole box of Kleenex to mop up.

So, My Lady, wearing a beautiful yellow sun hat, watched each week from her wheelchair as Karen, Ray, and I took our swim lessons from Wilma Rightmire, who owned Rightmire Swim School. Karen was so amusing that our lessons were doubly fun and entertaining.

Little by little Margaret and Karen took over where Norma fell short. Ray and I were so loved and welcome at the cottage. From their reaction, you'd have thought that the events of our day were the most interesting news on the planet. Though I still harbored the shame and secret of my past, I found peace during those six years between the ages of nine and fifteen. I also found myself very much in love with my new life at Hillhollow. I knew I should be searching for Daddy, but the disgrace of my former life, and the comfort of my new life, immobilized me. I felt loved by My Lady, Karen, and especially Ray. He was my new best friend.

Ray went to school, but I didn't. When he got home each day, I would listen to his stories of how he interacted with teachers and friends. He was smart, but he often asked me to help him with his homework. We often teased each other lovingly while we prepared our meals together when Chef Barbara wasn't around to prepare them for us.

When Karen and Margaret found out we often ate by ourselves, they invited us to meals that included complete etiquette lessons. By the time I was twelve and Ray was nine, we knew which fork or spoon to use and to always wait for the hostess to take her first bite before we started eating. We also learned to pause to say something grateful to God as we considered the food before us. We learned how to properly set a table so everything was exactly one inch from the edge of the table: forks on the left, knife blades turned toward the plate on the right, spoons to the right of the knife, water glasses placed above the point of the knife. If possible each person had eighteen inches of space. This, of course, was no problem at Margaret's huge beautifully polished dining room table. We learned if someone asked for the salt, you always passed the pepper too. Ray got in the habit of rising when a lady came into the room, and again if she rose from her chair. He stood beside his chair until I was seated or sometimes assisted with my chair to seat me. Margaret taught him to be aware of wheelchair movements, so he would stand when she rolled back from the table, as if she stood.

Karen was truly treated as a friend, not a servant. She was always invited to Margaret's dinner table. And dinner was, to some extent, formal. My Lady didn't "dress" for dinner like my PBS heroines, but when we joined her, we stepped it up a bit. We didn't just come in the clothes we wore that day, me around the house for home schooling, or Ray at school. My Lady wore her everyday clothes, but her "everyday" was dressy casual. Unless she had plans away from home, My Lady had a cook and servers for that last meal of the day. Karen prepared and served Margaret's less formal meals and tea.

Some of the etiquette, or what I know now were "finishing school" lessons, were just for me, not Ray. My handbag was what I had previously called a purse. A purse was technically a little bag that held coins within the handbag. My neck, if I needed to refer to it, was called my throat. A lady "tweezed," not "plucked," any unwanted hair. Both Ray and I learned that if we needed to use the bathroom, there was no need to describe why. A simple "excuse me" would do.

One day, close to my thirteenth birthday, on our way home from church as we chatted in the backseat of her luxurious Mercedes Benz SUV, My Lady, astute as always, must have sensed my loneliness. She suggested that I get a pet.

"What about a small bird?" I don't remember why, but Ray was not with us that Sunday. He was already beginning to have a separate life from me. He went to a private school every weekday. Norma paid a car service to drive him. He had probably spent the night at a friend's.

Ben, My Lady's driver, looked at me in the rearview mirror. "I love birds!"

Margaret chuckled. "Yes, you certainly do." Then to me she said, "I gave Ben a budget to feed the birds and to buy that fountain that he keeps clean for them on the north side of my patio and garden."

"I know. You have a lot of birds! They go crazy whenever I come to your back door. Their little bodies scatter, and sometimes they buzz me before they flutter their way up into the trees." I felt a pang in my heart.

"What's wrong, Meg?"

"Just a memory." I swallowed hard, took a deep breath, and then exhaled slowly. "Daddy fed birds in our backyard on Nueva Lane." I could see the sympathy in My Lady's eyes and could tell from the welled-up eyes in rearview mirror that Ben also felt my pain.

I gulped and took another breath. "I'll do some research on pet birds."

I decided on a budgerigar. I followed every link on the Internet to help me decide, and then I read everything about bird training as well. It never occurred to me that a parakeet might not be as smart as some of the other varieties of parrots, so I had unrealistic, grandiose plans for training my little feathered friend. I adopted a very young green-and-yellow parakeet and named him Einstein. Ben took us to the pet store. Besides the budgie, Margaret bought a large cage, a small travel cage, several toys, a playpen, and of course vitamin-enriched parakeet seed. I welcomed Einstein's noisy combination chirp-and-squawk chatter into my lonely rooms at Hillhollow. It turned out, because I was ignorant of limitations, I taught him things no one would have suspected a budgerigar could learn. I potty-trained him to fly to the top of his big cage in my bedroom or to his playpen in my sitting room when he needed to poop. He loved me dearly and spent a lot of time on my shoulder or on my desk trying to chew my schoolbooks and papers. Sometimes while I was studying, I would put my finger under his belly, then hold him over the garbage can, commanding, "Poop!" and he did. I often found myself laughing out loud at his antics, like trying to use my pencil as a slide.

After about eight months, he started mimicking phrases, such as "sucha pretty bird," "you're *so* cute," "silly bird," and of course, "I love you." At first, after a busy morning of flying back and forth from cage to shoulder, to playpen, to laptop keyboard, then books and papers, he would get sleepy and tuck his head behind his wing and take a bird nap. As time passed, this nap was often on my shoulder. But as he got older and totally attached to me, he would lie down on my lap, stretch out his neck and belly, and fall asleep enjoying the warmth of my body. I could not believe how much I loved him.

However, in the case of a parakeet, there is the real danger that your pet will actually eat your homework. Fortunately, I could print out a second copy of most papers that needed to be formally turned in. My tutors were forgiving of notebooks where I recorded my work. Many of the papers were merely "tasted," not destroyed.

Einstein was an excellent judge of character. He loved Ray and Evelyn, Hillhollow's long-time head housekeeper, but he didn't like Norma at all. I actually started to warm up to George a bit when I realized that Einstein liked him, but my heart was not open to love George. Every time I looked at him, I felt a deep, deep ache for Daddy. I had very little patience toward George and Norma. In fact, I was often unkind. I often mocked Norma under my breath and sometimes even to her face. Truthfully, I was a brat.

It was during this time that I started reading the Bible that Daddy had given me. I brought it out from a safe cupboard after Einstein, the chew monster, was in his cage and covered for the night. I was not getting its intended messages. It would be some time before I changed my attitude toward God. I saw Him as wise and all-powerful, but only to an end that I could increase my wisdom and attempt to manipulate His power for my selfish designs. I memorized "judgment" verses that I saved up to apply to Norma.

Norma had changed from her gooey tone toward George, often berating him openly in front of Ray and me or anyone that was working in the house. It seemed to me that her wrath came out of nowhere and that the "punishment" did not fit the "crime." For instance, when she had asked George to clear off a kitchen countertop, and he accidentally spilled a little water that got a couple of pictures wet. From her tirade, you would have thought that they were Picasso sketches. They were merely simple snapshots of Ray and me in the pool. Her tone implied that he was clumsy and stupid. Her hand went up to eye level, her finger pointed directly at his face and then down at the wet countertop. "Did you do this on purpose? Look at the mess you made now! These are ruined. Can't you be careful with anything that is important to me?"

While she ranted on and on, I stood quietly behind him and whispered one of my memorized Bible verses: "Better to live in a desert than with a quarrelsome and ill-tempered wife." He smiled—when she wasn't looking, of course.

Shortly after George's old chocolate Lab died, we adopted a black Labrador puppy, who Ray ingeniously named Midnight. We had all arrived home after going out to dinner. Midnight was enclosed in the kitchen with newspapers. Norma whined at George to put the puppy outside right away. Midnight was so happy to see us and to be released from his makeshift kitchen prison, he was wagging all over. George waited patiently as both Ray and I hugged him and received out obligatory doggie kisses and whacks from his vigorous tail. Before our welcome home greeting was complete, Midnight squatted and started peeing on the hardwood floor.

Norma went ballistic, throwing a temper tantrum and screaming, "I can't have anything nice around here. Get that dog out of here. Clean up that mess. I told you to let him out. Don't you listen to me? Clean up those newspapers too. We didn't need another dog. I told you this would happen. This is a *real* hardwood, you know." As if George didn't know the amenities of his own estate.

I mumbled to myself, "These are grumblers and faultfinders; they follow their own evil desires; they boast about themselves and flatter others for their own advantage."

I kept reading the Bible searching for verses that cut her down, but it was easier to find verses about forgiveness and love. I longed for both. I prayed to God that He would help me find Daddy, and that Daddy would forgive me for my part in Laura's death.

Nothing could heal the ache I felt in my heart at losing my daddy and grandparents, but having Margaret, Karen, Ben, Midnight, and an iddy biddy birdie buddy helped a lot. Midnight, incidentally, spent a lot of time in my rooms and basically hogged my bed. Most nights, I had to push him with my legs to make some room for myself. He was very well-behaved around Einstein, who took the dog in stride but didn't taunt him with close maneuvers. I never left them alone, however, unless Einstein was safely locked away in his cage.

One day I had an "aha" moment like a slap in the face. It was a day that I had not been invited to My Lady's and I was terribly lonely. I decided to go visit unannounced. I grabbed my journal and walked down the path with Midnight at my heels. As I came across the patio, the birds flew away in crazy panic. Midnight looked at them with interest, but sort of a "duh" expression. I was thinking that I was glad the birds were afraid of me so that no one else, or any predator, would be able to catch them or hurt them, but if they only knew how safe they would be in my hands and also in the presence of the gentle mannered Midnight . . . I smiled to myself, then turned to the closed door. I leaned into one of the French door windowpanes to shield the light's reflection. No one stirred within—not even Karen. I stood there for a moment disappointed and unreasonably feeling dejected. It dawned on me what a huge part of my life they had become over the last ten years; I was a very small part of theirs.

The upside of those rather isolated years from ages five to fifteen was what I was able to accomplish while filling the lonely hours. When Ray and I were not soaking in the attention and love we got a couple of times each week at the cottage, I immersed myself in music and my studies. I started to apply to colleges and quite a few accepted me. I chose Stanford so I could commute from Hillhollow. It was about an hour and half away, depending on Bay Area traffic. Hillhollow had become to me like Tara was to Scarlet O'Hara. I loved its beauty and the people and pets that enriched my life, especially, My Lady. I drew strength from it. Hillhollow's stability replaced the insecurity I brought with me from my shameful past. Besides, I was too young to live in a dorm since I had graduated from high school soon after I turned fifteen.

CHAPTER SEVEN

College

It was hard to make friends at Stanford. I felt like a mutant in the eyes of most of the students and probably my teachers. One of the Bay Area news channels did a segment about me graduating early from high school and my full academic scholarship. Before the interview, I wondered how on earth they had heard about me, but that mystery was easily solved. Many of their prepared questions were directed to Norma as they praised her amazing parenting skills. The film crew was directed to Hillhollow's back terrace and gardens. Norma looked smashing. She wore a sexy, deep-V-neck black rayon dress, four-inch platform heels, and plenty of diamonds and emeralds. Her makeup, of course, was impeccable.

The cameraman found it easy to stay focused on her. The interviewer, a woman named Shari, was also obviously impressed with Norma's accomplishment to homeschool a daughter that aced the SATs and was ready for college at fifteen. I pretty much stayed in the background, but of course the camera and interviewer eventually needed to include me.

Shari brought the microphone to me and motioned to the cameraman. Norma tailed the front of the camera lens, came alongside me, and tenderly put her arm around my shoulder. With her four-inch heels and my flats, we stood eye to eye. I could smell alcohol, which was usual, but it was foreign to feel tenderness and kindness. In response, I put my arm around her waist. I held my palm up to the camera and said to Shari, "May we have a moment?"

"Of course." She motioned to the cameraman to cut.

Norma spoke first. In a low tone that was meant for me alone, "I really am proud of you—you know that, don't you?" she cooed.

"Thank you." I felt a little shaky. Tears were stinging behind my eyes as I searched her face in hope that this moment was genuine. It wasn't hard to convince myself that she really did love me. I had never felt it, but of course, she loved me. Maybe she was just incapable of showing it. I wondered if something had happened to her when I was born so soon after Laura, or if Ray had come along too soon for her to sort out being the mother of three small children. I wondered in horror if perhaps Daddy had done something that had crushed her into a self-protective mode. I stubbornly pushed that thought away, but knew—as I saw her in this vulnerable moment with her guard down—that for some reason Norma Randallman shielded her heart with an outer façade of confidence in her flawless beauty and with a defense that disguised itself as an obnoxious offence. I hugged her with the arm that I had around her and used some of her words. "I love you Mama. You know that, don't you?"

She started to tremble, but gained control when she sideways hugged me back. She didn't need to say it. I was assured and she knew it. Neither of us wanted to degrade her immaculate makeup.

"OK," I called to Shari, "we're ready." Norma stayed admiringly by my side during the rest of the interview.

Alas, our relationship did not change. We immediately went back to our roles: Norma, an angry control freak, and me, still a spoiled brat. I'm sure any future Stanford students who saw that news segment, looked at me with curiosity or possibly resentment.

I was too young to stay in the dorm, so each day that I had classes, Ben drove me in Margaret's car from Pleasant Valley to Palo Alto. I worked my school schedule around Margaret's schedule and, whenever possible, around the impossible Bay Area traffic.

Einstein rode with us. He loved riding in his travel cage, listening to the road noises. He chirped happily or jabbered all his mindless mimicked phrases for Ben's and my amusement.

After Ben helped me load the backpack full of books onto my shoulders, he would move Einstein to the front seat for their ride home. One day as soon as he was moved up, I heard Einstein say, "Hi! You're *so* cute." Ben laughed, of course, and politely exchanged pleasantries with the silly bird. He was a quiet, respectful man, but I sensed from the playfulness in his eyes that he was restraining a gregarious personality. It took even more restraint to drive a precocious young woman who asked personal questions.

He was dark-skinned with no wrinkles at all. His curly hair used to be entirely black, but was starting to get streaks of beautiful silver on each side of his face. He was thin and always clean-shaven regardless of the latest facial hair trend for men. His eyes were light brown, with specks of green and amber. I suppose my curiosity about him sprang out of my lonely existence, but daily as I began my inquisition, he patiently answered my impertinent questions. He lived in Pleasant Valley in an apartment only a few miles from Hillhollow. He was not married but had a longtime girlfriend, Betty, who worked in downtown Pleasant Valley at a bakery. "She makes great pie," he said enthusiastically. "I love pie." He liked driving for a living, especially for "Ms. Randallman," who treated him well. She was not demanding, except that she expected the car to always be in prime mechanical condition and immaculate inside and out. These demands were enjoyable because, as he said, "Detailing cars is relaxing for me." I exceeded my cheekiness the day I asked him if he was going to ask Betty to marry him. He blushed and said meekly, "I guess I've never had the confidence to think she would want to marry me."

"Of course she does! You are so wise, kind, and *so* handsome!" It was my turn to blush. My entire experience with romance was, of course, from the unrealistic world of novels and both British and Hollywood movies.

About three weeks after that conversation, when we pulled up in front of Hillhollow, he asked me to wait a moment because he wanted to show me something. It was an engagement ring. "Do you think she will like it?"

"Oh, Ben! It's beautiful. She'll love it." I felt like cupid. Ben and Betty. It sounded so perfect. I wondered if the love cherub would ever shoot an arrow of romance in my direction. I realized I had added a new friend to the life that started over when I wished upon a star. Since I refused to count George, Ben was the first man I learned to adore since we abandoned Daddy. They invited me to their small wedding held at the Pleasant Valley courthouse about three months after he gave her the engagement ring.

After a few years, I finished my undergraduate degree in computer science, and planned on getting my master's in the same. At eighteen, I was old enough to stay in the dorm and Ben patiently taught me to drive, but the chauffeured commute time had developed into a well-established study time. Besides, I didn't want to leave Hillhollow, my baby Einstein, or Midnight. So, rather than brave the new world of a Stanford dormitory, I continued to commute with Ben. He beamed when I told him of my decision. His wide smile showed his perfect, beautiful white teeth.

There was another memorable man in my college years. I smelled him before I saw him, and he smelled wonderful. I was reminded of a clear rushing river surrounded by spicy pines and evergreens. In my head, I called this fragrance "forest river breeze."

It was my first day at the Stanford campus. I stood stupidly planted in the middle of a walkway simultaneously studying my class schedule and the campus map. The forest river breeze caught my attention. I looked up from the papers.

He was patiently standing in front of me, apparently waiting for me to emerge from my direction confusion. "Hello, can I help you?" he asked.

"Oh! That would be wonderful!" I was stunned when I looked into his blue eyes surrounded by thick, straight lashes. I thought to myself, *Short, fair, and handsome.* His hair was dark blond, with light-blond streaks that showed off its waviness. His build was sturdy and "cut." It spoke of athleticism.

We both seemed to have pushed the "Pause button" momentarily, but then he came alongside me. I felt his warmth, so comfortable and right. He looked down at my map, and my schedule spread out in my hands.

"This way." He pointed properly, using his whole hand. They were large hands for his short stature. I found out later that he used the long fingers on his beautiful hands to play piano, guitar, bass, and cello. "Can you believe it? We both share the same first class." He smiled confidently. I saw him glance at Laura's cross. He walked confidently also. Neither of us said another word as we walked together for five minutes. I was delighting in the forest river breeze.

When the professor called my rescuer's name, I found myself even more captivated. Stratton Davis was really cute. After class he walked up and said simply, "Uh, hi again. I'm Stratton."

"I know. Hi, I'm Meg." I was hoping my cheeks weren't radiating enough heat for him to feel it in his general direction.

"I know." He smiled, and I felt a twinge somewhere between my breast and navel that I had never felt before. "Some of us are putting together a study group, and we wanted to know if you would like to join us."

"Sure. When and where?" I wasn't sure if I was breathing.

We met right away with several other students and worked out a weekly plan that was good for everyone's schedule, including, for my part, Ben's and Margaret's. Our meeting place was a table in the dining commons. Each time we met, we sat at the same table, and each of us chose the same seats we did at our strategic planning session. Each semester, for the next four of six years that I was at Stanford, when Stratton formed a new study group, I was always asked to join. He graduated before I finished my last two years. I sat next to him exactly ninety-six times. We rarely faced each other and made little eye contact. I had cut my long hair into an angled bob and wore it that way all though college. If I leaned forward even slightly, it covered the side of my face. He probably couldn't see me when I was leaning. I doubted that he even noticed me, but those study groups were the highlight of my college experience. Hiding behind my hair did not keep me from taking in every essence of Stratton Davis. I loved listening to his low, gentle voice and breathing in his clean, fresh scent. I often wondered if he showered right before each meeting. I was taller, but height was not an issue for him. He carried himself with contented confidence.

Stratton was not "Hollywood" handsome, but to me he was remarkably attractive. His eyes were perhaps a bit large for his face. His lips were full and looked—to silly me—so kissable. He was on the Stanford men's soccer team, and he mentioned a time or two that the best therapy to clear his head before major tests was to swim laps in his parents' pool. He seemed to be a little less nerdy than the rest of us majoring in computer science and physics. Maybe it was that amazing smile, or perhaps it was his incredible sense of humor that added levity to our little "Table of Nerds." What attracted me to him the most were his wit and his brain. In fact, he was so smart, I couldn't figure out why he bothered to hang out with us. He was the natural leader of each of the groups. He simply coached the rest of us.

I didn't talk to Norma about my attraction to Stratton. In fact, during my last few years at Stanford, we hardly spoke. In our rare interactions it seemed that no matter what I did, or how I did it, she did not think I was doing it well enough. I was totally fed up with her and rarely initiated a conversation.

In spite of our detached relationship, Norma apparently felt that romance was an area of my life that she needed to control. She made a big deal of introducing me to an aspiring architect, Matt Moore. His father was a famous architect in Walnut Creek one of George's colleagues. I probably would have resisted Norma's plotting, but I had to admit that Matt was kinda cute and very sensual. He had a charming way of making every woman in the room feel desirable. He was tall, with a slight build. He wore his thin light-red hair long on the top and slicked back, but immaculately trimmed around his ears and at the nape of his neck. I would have said his eyes were turquoise rather than blue. He came from a family that had never struggled financially. Even his casual clothes looked expensive. He drove a sporty black Mercedes Benz convertible. When the top was down, his hair stayed plastered to his head. When we were out together, we turned heads.

George was not as excited about me dating Matt as Norma was. He kept Matt accountable to him and often made sure we were headed out to meet up with other people or that Ben chauffeured us when we went out in the evenings. Matt was twenty-one and inclined to have at least one cocktail in addition to whatever he drank with dinner. I recognized George's plan to keep Matt from finding a way to be alone with me at the end of an evening and mitigate any chance that he might drive with me in his car after drinking. The only time we were really alone was when we were in my sitting room at Hillhollow, but we kept the door open. He was only allowed to come up to my rooms when someone was home.

I should have taken warning that Matt was not the guy for me when one day we were on my couch in my sitting room watching the movie *While You Were Sleeping*. Matt was so close to me, I could feel the heat of his body along my left thigh. He moved in closer and put his arm around my shoulder. I reached forward for my Pepsi on the coffee table, using it as an excuse to slip out from under his arm and inch away from him a bit. He reached forward for his Mountain Dew and copied my strategy. When he leaned back on the couch, he was very close and started to slowly lean in. All of a sudden, Einstein flew in, landed on my chest, and bit Matt on the chin. Matt's reflex was to bat Einstein across the room. He landed with a thud against the wall and lay still.

I jumped up, ran to him, and gathered him in my hands. I found myself crying helplessly and praying intently for Einstein to recover. Matt came up behind me and apologized. He tried to comfort me by putting his hands on my shoulders. I violently twisted away. "Please wake up, Sucha Pretty Bird."

Einstein was so still, I was sure he was dead, but after a minute or so, which seemed like eternity, he blinked his eye and jerked a little, then rocked to his feet in my palm. He sat there stupidly all puffed up for several minutes as I cuddled him and sent warm breath into his feathers. I didn't realize that it was the very worst medical treatment I could give him. I looked it up on the Internet later and found out that most likely he was suffering from a concussion. The best possible treatment was no stimulation plus cool darkness. Deliberately ignoring my manners and not even turning to face him, I said, "Please leave, Matt. You can show yourself out."

"OK. I'm going. I'm really sorry. I'll call you later to see how your *bird* is doing." I didn't like the way he emphasized the word *bird* and wondered if he even knew that Einstein had a name.

I heard him talking downstairs to Norma at the front door. I couldn't imagine what they would have to talk about for such a long time. They talked softly, but I thought I heard Matt use an expletive and "stupid bird" in the same sentence. I disregarded their conversation and continued to pray that Einstein would recover. He did. He twitched a few times as if throwing off the stun and scrambled up my arm to my shoulder and nestled against my face. He stretched his feathery neck up to give me kisses on my cheek. I returned to the couch and sat down. Sandra Bullock's character was conflicted by being in love with one man and engaged to his brother. I couldn't help but think, *who would have thought that the love of my life would have feathers?*

I forgave Matt, but I never invited him into my sitting room again. As I think back, I don't think Midnight liked Matt much either. He didn't growl or try to bite him, but neither did he wag that ridiculous tail when he saw Matt, as he did for most everyone else. Then one day, it became crystal clear why Norma liked him so much and our clever pets did not. I had gotten out of school early after finals. As my great luck would have it—and I had begun to realize how very lucky I was—Ben was available. He didn't have Einstein, but he was close enough to the university to pick me up early. I was grateful for Ben, not just for the ride. I was feeling sad.

"What's up, little lady? Is everything OK? Since you don't have any homework, or your little buddy, do ya wanna come sit up front with old Ben?" He patted the shotgun seat invitingly.

"Yeah. I'd like that." We had not reached the freeway, so he pulled over, got out, opened the SUV's back door, and extended his hand to assist me. "And by the way, you are not old!"

He smiled at me as he resituated himself into the driver's seat. "So tell me, my little lady, what's troubling you? Are you regretting your movie-date tonight with that foul-mouthed boyfriend that almost killed Einstein, or is it something else?"

"You know, even if he hadn't batted Einstein against the wall, I don't think I could have serious feelings for him."

"He's a smooth operator, that one. I believe *charming* is the word. He slithers his way around, pretending to be one way when he's near you, but he's another when you're not."

"That's right! You've driven him home quite a few times. Does he swear a lot around you?"

"Swearing? Yeah, not that he talks much to me, but he's always yapping on his cell. He has some pretty disrespectful things to say about just about everyone, including his own folks. Especially his mother." His eyebrows went up, and he turned to face me momentarily. He nodded and said emphatically, "I know, right?"

"Really?" I thought about it. "He really is a chameleon then. I guess I just don't have much of a frame of reference to judge character. Einstein figured him out though. I would prefer not to see him anymore, but that's not why I'm sad."

He said tenderly, "You can tell Ben. You know I won't say anything to anyone."

"I know. You're the best. Thank you for being my friend."

I thought I saw his eyes moisten, and he sniffed a bit, "Hey, little lady, you rocked my world into place. After you get your burden, or worry, or whatever it is that's draggin' you down off your chest, I have some great news to share with you."

He didn't need to tell me what the news was; I already knew. "You and Betty are going to have a baby, right?"

"You little rascal. Nothing surprises you. Betty and I have been together for a long time. She's younger than I am, but we decided if we were going to have kids, we better start having them." He chuckled. "I guess it's because you have so much time alone to think, you think of things before they happen."

"Well, yeah, I do think a lot, but I'm trying out a new thing in my prayers." I felt my cheeks flush with embarrassment. "Truthfully, I realized recently that I've been mad at God for a long time. I've been blaming Him for some things that happened before we came here to Hillhollow. When God answered my prayer to keep Einstein alive, something changed. I felt like I was really talking to Him, not just trying to manipulate His power." I took a breath before continuing. "I've decided that I need to be less selfish. I'm going to try to quit blaming God, my mother, or anyone else for my past. I've spent most of my life pleading, and well, more like whining, to God my selfish requests. But even before my Einstein epiphany"—I know Ben saw my grin out of the corner of his eye—"I'd been praying for you and Betty to have a baby."

Once again, I saw his eyes get shiny. "You are a sweet little lady, Meg. I consider it a privilege to be your friend. I'm glad you decided to keep riding back and forth to school with me, rather than start driving that cute little BMW George gave you for your birthday. Now, what's troubling you?"

"It's the end of the semester, and therefore the end of the Table of Nerds study group." I sighed.

"And the guy with two last names didn't ask you for your phone number?"

I blinked in surprise. "You know what just struck me as funny? You said, 'two last names.' I think my father had two last names, and I've heard it said that daughters are attracted to men who remind them of their fathers."

"What were your father's two last names?" He grinned.

"Franklin Taylor. It's been a long time since I've seen him, so actually, I don't know him. I have no idea if he and Stratton have anything else in common, but yeah, that's it. I mean, no, Stratton didn't ask. How did you know?"

"Because every time I pick you up on a day that you've been sitting next to him, you are all flustered and happy. Looks a lot to me like you fancy him way more than you admit to yourself."

"I'm admitting it now. I realized today that I may never see him again."

"How 'bout next semester?"

"No. He's graduating."

"Oh. Sorry to hear that. Anyway, I think you should stick to your instincts about avoiding 'Slimy Red, the would-be Einstein slayer.' He doesn't have the same values, or, how can I say it?" He paused in the conversation to motion to a driver entering the freeway, allowing her to safely merge in front of our vehicle. "He doesn't have the character you do, or the heart." He shook his head. "It's not a good match."

By getting out early and missing the late Bay Area traffic, I arrived home a good three hours earlier than usual. Ben said simply, "Leave that heavy backpack for me. You don't need it right away. I'll carry it up to your rooms later."

Since I was sitting in the front seat, I leaned over and gave him a kiss on the cheek. "You are going to be a great daddy."

When Ben came around to open my door, I thanked him, then set my hand comfortably on his arm. "You know, for most of my life, I've prayed every day here at Hillhollow for a chance to see my father again. I realized today that God has given me you to fill part of that void." His eyes were visibly moist this time. Mine were too. He patted my hand that was resting on his forearm.

I bounded up the stairs to the front entrance, and then stepped onto the cool marble of the entry. "Hullo? Anybody home?" I continued up the second flight of stairs leading to the upper landing and the second-floor bedroom suites. I headed left toward my rooms, but I heard a mysterious thud in the opposite direction toward the master bedroom, so I turned around. Just before I knocked on the door of the master suite, I froze. I heard urgent whispers. Lately it seemed that Norma and George didn't like each other all that much, but what did I know about sexual attraction?

I blushed and quietly bolted for my rooms. After I set down my handbag, something compelled me to sneak back into the hallway and peek around the corner. I saw Matt, carrying his shoes and socks in one hand. He was leaning into the slightly open door to Norma's bedroom. He kissed her passionately, placing his free hand low at the back of her waist. He pulled her body intimately close to his.

I jerked back and pressed myself flush against the wall hoping desperately that he would not see me. My sweaty palms slid against the wallpaper. I was horrified and confused. I thought I was going to barf, but I summoned the strength to calm my system and stay where I could hear him descend the stairs. He took the posterior staircase. The hiss of the kitchen sliding glass door echoed to my hiding place. He had slipped out onto the veranda. I peeked around the corner again. Norma's bedroom door was closed. I dashed down the front staircase, pulled open the heavy front door, and sprinted to the edge of the house on the front veranda so I could see the side parking area. Matt was sitting sideways in the driver's seat of his car, putting on his shoes. Funny, that at a moment like that, I found myself wondering what on earth he used on his hair. In spite of his afternoon bedroom frolic with Norma, the top was still perfectly slicked back.

Ben, who had just pulled My Lady's Benz into the garage, was apparently challenging Matt for the reason he had come from the back of the house.

"Really? The floor looked shiny and wet? No housekeepers here today." Then tauntingly he added, "Meg is home now; you sure you can't stick around a little longer to see her?" Ben was apparently wise to Matt's deceitfulness. After our conversation, I knew Ben did not want Matt to stay to see me. He stood there smugly grinning because he had caught the sleazeball being sleazy.

Matt managed to get his shoes on. His face was flushed. He twisted into a driving position, ran his hand unnecessarily over the top of his glossy head, and blurted, "Leave me alone, you . . . ," adding a derogatory name for Ben's mixed heritage.

He rammed his key into the ignition, shifted into gear, and took off with enough force to squeal his tires. As he reached the corner of the mansion, he saw me standing next to one of the columns on the front veranda. He took both hands off the steering wheel and opened his palms in a universal sign of incredulity, then shrugged his shoulders. He may have meant the gestures to say, "Why me?" or "It's not my fault." Or some such innocence that would relieve him of all responsibility.

I defiantly waved my hand, just once, definitively from left to right, and held it there until he was gone. It was, for me, good-bye forever. Choosing to never see him again was the easy decision. Deciding what to say and how to act around Norma and George was going to take more effort and a lot of consideration. One of my strategically memorized Bible verses ran though my head: *"The wise woman builds her house, but with her own hands the foolish one tears hers down."*

CHAPTER EIGHT

Coffee and Daily Bread

I love bread and coffee. The latter would lead me to the former, as it is known as "daily bread." In other words, my love for coffee put me on the path to my career. It also brought me close to intrigue, murder, and answers to my deepest unanswered prayers.

When I started reading through the Bible in earnest, I started at the beginning. I searched for the first instances of bread and coffee. I never did find coffee, but when I found the first mention of bread, it was already prepared and baked. There was no mention of how people came up with such a complicated recipe. God must have told them about grinding grains and balancing grain with salt and sugar because, as I learned from Chef Barbara, bread will not rise without sugar, and too much salt will make it not rise at all. So I imagined that when God brought the animals to Adam to name, he also gave Adam and Eve the recipes for various breads—both leavened and unleavened. I also imagined He then said, "Come with me. See this bean? Wait until it is ripe, roast it in the sun until it turns dark brown, grind it until it is almost powder, and then pour hot water through the powder. This is coffee, the nectar of God."

As soon as I learned to drive, I found Peet's coffee. I took Midnight with me to the closest Peet's store almost every Saturday. I hadn't been in a while though. I had been overwhelmed with studying for finals and finishing my master's thesis. The patio was full of people. As I looped Midnight's leash under the foot of my favorite iron chair, I overheard two young women talking.

"Yeah! I know, right? That's one of the main reasons I came to work here."

"It's so rare to work at a company with so many women in high places. It gives honor to the rest of us, even if we don't want to be executives."

"Yeah. I might—"

I didn't hear the rest as I followed my nose into the store.

When I returned to the patio, I set down my cuppa, removed the safety lid, settled into the chair, and slipped off one of my fancy flip flops to give Midnight his Saturday morning massage.

"Hullo," said a lovely dark skinned woman.

"Hi."

"I'm Kirin. I've seen you here other Saturday mornings with your dog." She had a delightful British accent.

"My name is Meg. This is Midnight."

She stretched her sandaled foot to Midnight's backside. He accommodated by leaning into her foot and pounding the concrete with his absurd tail.

"Hullo, Meg and Midnight."

"No coffee?" I said as I inhaled a deep whiff from the top of my cup before sipping gently.

"My friend, Chip, is getting me some."

A deep voice over my shoulder said, "Hi. I'm Chip Swain." His face was very square with a wide, masculine jaw. His dark eyes were a bit small for his face. He had short dark hair; a low, wide forehead; and very prominent eyebrows. The sides of his hair were almost shaved. He was medium height and physically fit. "Here's your latte, sweetie."

I noticed Kirin wince and blush. "Thank you." I sensed they were nowhere near where she would be comfortable with "sweetie."

"Are you in school around here?" This from Chip. He moved the chair from the opposite side of the table close to the corner that was nearest Kirin. It was directly facing me. His intensity was disturbing.

It was my turn to blush. "I'm done with school. I am about to graduate from Stanford. I've actually completed all that I need to do, but it's not official yet."

He lifted an eyebrow and said a bit loudly, "Stanford? You look so young to have a bachelor's already."

I answered defensively, "I'm twenty-one and I'm graduating with a master's. I want to move on from school at least for a while." I sipped the coffee and partially hid my face.

He whistled. "A brain. Oh wait! I bet you're Meg Randallman."

"Yes." *Enough already with the embarrassment. Get a grip, Meg. This is not new to you.*

Kirin said, "Meg Randallman? Are you famous?"

"Not really—"

Chip said, "Yes. She is famous! She was in the news when she graduated from high school at fifteen."

"I can't believe you remember that or even saw that news segment. That was six years ago for goodness sake!"

He grinned. "Oh I remember. You live in a beautiful mansion near here and your mom is really hot!"

His memory of Hillhollow, Norma, and me, felt invasive. Hoping to change the subject I said, "Where do you work?"

Answers came over the top of each other, from Kirin, "the Lab."

Chip, "the Lab."

The two women who were still chatting about the advantages of having women promoted to high places, "the Lab."

Plus a few staggered responses from people at surrounding tables. "The Lab, the Lab, the Lab."

We all laughed. "So everyone here works for the Lab? What's the Lab?"

Kirin said, "We call it the Lab, but its official name is DPMC Research and Development. There are two others: one in Boston; one in New Mexico. Our founder is from New Mexico. After he made a boatload of money, he strategically established two others close to graduates from MIT and Stanford. This is Raj." She extended an open palm to politely point to the table to my right. "And Will."

I turned to notice for the first time two rather nerdy-looking young men, who nodded and sheepishly said hi. They were apparently unaccustomed to talking to strangers, or perhaps just to women.

"And this," said Chip, pointing his finger less gracefully to the two aspiring women at the table next to his and Kirin's, "is Heather and Christine." They smiled and nodded as did I. The way Chip said their names, it sounded as if they were very close friends, "And technically, I don't work for the Lab. I work for Ready Business Machines. I keep the printers, copiers, and other leased peripherals at the Lab filled up and ready for service, under close scrutiny of Lab security, of course," he said, releasing a nervous laugh. "I come in at least once a week." The way he looked at me made me uncomfortable as if he planned to intrude into my home once a week.

I set aside my discomfort and said laughingly, "So is this 'the Lab' coffee shop?" I reached down to respond to a doggie nuzzle. I rubbed the sides of Midnight's head. "Yes, I know." Then to the people around us I said, "And this is my dog, Midnight. Also obviously a Lab." Everyone chuckled.

Christine came over to pet him, which caused a total disruption of everything within range of the crazy tail. She wore a lot of dark makeup and looked tired, but as she looked up at me I saw very kind eyes. She had a sweet face that reminded me of my Madame Alexander Ginny doll.

"Hi." She reached out her hand to me and I shook it. "I love dogs, and this one"—she rubbed his ears the way she saw me do so a few minutes before—"is my favorite color." She was wearing all black. Her hair was also died black.

Kirin said, "Yes. A lot of people from the Lab drink coffee here at Peet's." She again reached a sandaled foot out to again caress Midnight's backside. She apparently thought he wasn't getting enough attention now that Christine had returned to her table. "You would fit in really well. You should apply for a job at the Lab. Is everything OK?"

"I'm sorry. I think I was staring at you. You look so familiar, but I can't think of where we could have met. Are you from around here?"

"Actually, most of my immediate family is in New Mexico." I'm sure I looked surprised.

"I know, right? You probably guessed India or England?"

I blushed. "Yes. I would have certainly guessed one of those over New Mexico."

She laughed graciously. "My extended family *is* from India. Once a year, all of the family here in the US go together to visit the rest of our family there. My father's family chose English as their first language in the home where he grew up." Midnight moved closer to make it very easy for her to keep scratching his back, and she obliged. "You probably just saw me here at Peet's?"

"It wasn't just your accent. You remind me of someone—your mannerisms; the way you move your hands when you talk. But I suppose that must be it. I must have seen you here." I was not convinced, but it didn't seem to matter. "What a serendipitous meeting. I am ready to start a career, using the technology I've been learning. I have been searching for a company that I feel is really right for me." I turned to Christine and Heather. "Pardon my eavesdropping, but I overheard part of your conversation as I was going into get my coffee. Does the Lab really freely promote women?"

"Yeah." Christine took a sip of her coffee. "There are a lot of women at the Lab in general compared to many tech companies and a lot are in managerial positions."

I nodded. It intrigued me to consider working for a company without a female glass ceiling. "I might send a resume to the Lab. I wrote my master's thesis on a synchronized secure protocol for an interactive knowledge-based system. As a matter of fact, I think I've been solicited by DPMC." I pulled out my iPhone to look at my e-mail and spun through my "work" folder. "DPMC. Yep. Right here. I thought about sending a resume."

"Send it to me. I work for Jack Robertson, the hiring manager in our department. He's interviewing next week for a computer science engineer. He's not our boss though. Our boss, Francis Taylor, is in New Mexico at another of our labs." She pulled a business card out of her purse and handed it to me. "Jack is great. Francis trusts him with everything. We have an unexpected opening, coincidentally in our cyber-security department." Everyone seemed to press Pause. No one lifted a coffee cup or spoke for about a half a minute, which is a long time if you have ever waited thirty seconds for a microwave.

As I studied the card in the strange silence, I shuddered, and then movement resumed. "I'll send my resume to you as soon as I get home."

The curved drive climbed steadily as it circled a small mountain. As my car wove up the hill, I caught glimpses of the fortress on a plateau about three quarters of the way toward the top. The mountain had either been excavated to create the plateau, or the property had been chosen because of a natural, level shelf. It was as I had always pictured King Arthur's legendary Camelot. I was met at the gate by a uniformed officer who had been instructed to orientate the newbie. I pushed the button to lower the window and felt a gust of cool breeze.

"Miss Randallman? I'm Jorge Garcia. Welcome to the Lab." He smiled a welcome, and then turned to the other guard in the booth. They each waved. "May I ride with you? That way I can easily direct you, first to parking, then to the cell phone lockers and entrance."

"Sure. Get in." I left the window open.

"Nice ride!"

I smiled at him. "Yes. She's my baby, third only to baby numero uno, my parakeet, Einstein, and numero dos, mi perro, also a Lab." In my nervousness, I unforgivably chuckled as I tested for the second time the same lame joke. The first day of work brought its own brand of anxiety, and it didn't help that he was dashingly handsome. *Muy caliente.*

"Habla Espanol?"

"I speak un poco. I studied it, but didn't practice much, so *very* little."

Jorge directed me through a second gate that stood open, and then to the left. I saw a parking garage protruding from the lower level of the imposing five-story fortress ahead. I knew the edifice that seemingly was giving birth to the low garage was the Lab. The parking garage entrance was a square archway. An ominous sign on its gate read "Restricted Access." At this point, since I knew that restriction excluded me, I could not go straight into the garage. I needed to go up an incline to the right or down a descent to the left to the uncovered parking areas. Jorge pointed downward. "If you go a little higher, you can park closer to the entrance side of the building, but the sun blasts that side in the late afternoons."

"Thanks for the recommendation. I prefer the shady side and don't mind the exercise."

This established the pattern that would determine my involvement in the events unfolding at the Lab. I wove through the rows of trees and pulled up under one of the liquidambars to a low stone wall at the far edge of the parking lot. The edge beyond looked like a deep canyon and a sheer drop. I shut off the car, and immediately the sound of running water filled the air. Before the asphalt was laid, the landscape architects placed rows of young liquidambar trees in squares of dirt, surrounded by concrete curbs. They started at the edge of the canyon and continued in rank so that each set of parking places was arranged to face a row of threes.

When I got out of the car, I followed the sound of water to the wall and stood beneath the tree where I had parked. I peered down into the lush green canyon to see the glint of a stream wandering beneath a tangle of trees, shrubbery, wild flowers, and brambles. Strong wind pushed against my back and briskly tossed the branches and leaves above me. I wasn't wrong about the sheer drop. There was certainly no need for security gates on the south side. Less than one foot from the outer side of the low wall, the side of the little mountain dropped steeply away. About four feet beneath me was a six-foot-wide ledge that was apparently angled toward the wall to keep the cascade of water flowing down the curve of the mountain in a ditch, rather than waterfall over the outer edge into the valley. This then was the source of the sound I heard when I turned off my car. Unlike the parking lot that was level, the water ledge climbed the natural incline of the hill. I lost sight of it as it curved around the building above. I looked the opposite direction and saw that about twenty feet down the hill the ledge ran into the opening of what looked like a five-foot-wide tunnel. I looked at this more carefully and realized the gaping hole was made of corrugated steel.

"Why do you need a drainage ditch? Wouldn't the water just cascade down that cliff?"

I held back a sigh when Jorge smiled at me with a sudden attractive smile. "Very observant." He lifted both eyebrows and nodded once. "There is a natural spring that used to run this way right down the middle of where the Lab is. The engineers created that ledge and routed it to rejoin the natural flow of water, and then down to the farmers below, not just because the farmers have always used the water but because the engineers thought if they routed it that way"—he pointed over the edge—"it might eventually cause erosion on the cliff and jeopardize the stability of the foundation of the Lab. The wall beneath us is reinforced to prevent erosion. There is a lot of water when it rains." He pointed to a substantial mountain peak above the Lab. "The spring starts up there. I think there is a considerably large lake up there too."

We walked toward the architecturally ordinary stone-and-concrete building.

"No windows?" I queried.

"Sure, there are windows, but not on this side. This side houses the super computer and all of the most sensitive areas within the Lab."

We entered through a large archway into a breezeway corridor between the Lab and the parking structure. When we reached the end of the corridor, we had a choice between a wide, concrete staircase straight ahead and an elevator on the left. Jorge turned to me and opened his palms as if to ask which one. I pointed straight and we began to climb.

The top of the staircase opened to a plaza surrounded by surprisingly large oak trees. I asked about these. "Has the Lab been here a long time?"

"No. Not that long," he said, nodding to the trees. "When they bought the property, they originally planned to use this naturally leveled table for the building, but when they got here, they decided instead to build on two levels and keep these old trees." He turned toward the upper parking lot and turned me with him by gently directing my shoulder. "And then they planted all the rest of those in the parking lots," he said, pointing to another battalion of liquidambars.

"Nice."

As we emerged from the lower level, I saw that the plaza was surrounded by a low stone wall, similar to the one circling the lower parking lot. A wide path led to an opening in the wall to the west parking area. It too had a cliff on the south and another on the north. Along the wall that separated the plaza from the parking area, sturdy privet bushes flourished in the border of dirt between the pavers and the wall. Stone pavers were in an obvious path design, kind of like the "yellow brick road." Only, instead of yellow surrounded by red and gray bricks in a swirl, they were arranged with light beige on brown so the path to and from the parking lot to the heavy glass doors of the building was clearly marked. Off-center in the plaza, toward the cliff side, was a shallow, round walled pool with a small geyser-like fountain gushing in the center. Standing sentinel on each side of the double glass doors to the building were banks of small lockers. We stopped at one of these. It looked like a wall of post office boxes.

Jorge pulled out a ring of keys, drove one of them into a lock, pulled open the little door, and slid out a key from within. "Cell phone, please." He handed me the little key with one hand and put out his other palm to receive my iPhone.

"Oh, OK." It wasn't like I got that many calls or even text messages, but I felt awkward parting with my phone. It seemed like I had carried one most of my life and had recently synced it up securely with my laptop.

"He nodded to my Coach bag. "No cameras in there, right?"

"Right. Only the one on my phone."

"Perfecto. Very careful around here. Lots of secrets to keep." Again I was dazzled by the smile that contrasted his brilliantly white teeth with his tan skin. I looked past him to see a security camera, so I decided not to grab his handsome face and plant a huge kiss on his well-shaped mouth. OK. The security camera was not the only deterrent, but the thought did cross my mind.

"No thumb drives? Good. The only laptops around are specially designed without hard drives. Under rare circumstances, some employees are allowed to take laptops home to work or on trips, but they can only access proprietary information in a secure corporate document management system behind a firewall."

"No. So if I can get a cell phone that doesn't have a camera, I can carry it with me?"

He laughed. "Yeah. Good luck with that though. There are still a few out there without cameras, but most people are so used to all the functionality and apps, they just choose to put the phone in a locker while they're here."

I switched the phone off and handed it to him. "Too bad you don't have a plug in there so I could charge it while it is stored."

"Oh there is. Do you have your charger with you?"

"No, but I'll bring one tomorrow."

The building looked less ominous from this side. It had some interesting stonework to break up the cinderblock facade and some western facing windows gleaming brilliantly. The windows reflected as if art, the fountain, the lovely old trees, the liquidambars in the west parking lot, the mountain peak, and the other side of the canyon. As we approached what I realized was the first set of two heavy glass doors, Jorge opened one side for me. We were then in a small glass room that reminded me of a vapor lock within a space ship, in a science fiction movie. In the middle of the vapor lock, there stood a waist-high round granite cylinder. He took off his badge and waved it over the pillar. I heard a click, and then he opened a door on the interior side of the vapor lock.

It reminded me of another movie, *Get Smart*, which struck up the theme song in my head. We were now in the lobby approaching a circular counter. Another uniformed man sat behind it. He was surrounded by small video screens.

I smelled the coffee. I peeked around the bank of escalators and, to my delight, spotted a Peet's coffee cart.

"Steve, this is Meg Randallman."

"Hi. Steve Cameron." He extended his hand. "First day or just visiting?"

"Hi. First day." I accepted his firm handshake. "Do you actually allow visitors?"

"On occasion. Didn't you visit for your interview?"

"Actually, no. Mr. Robertson interviewed several of us in downtown Pleasant Valley in a conference room at the Doubletree."

Jorge gently touched the top of my forearm, "I'll leave you in Steve's care. Your locker number is on the key. That is your personal locker now. I opened it with a master." He flashed me one more dazzling smile. "Bye now."

"Bye. Thank you so much." *I need to get out more.*

Steve, though cute, was not nearly as gorgeous as Jorge. However, he was like Jorge in his manner—very kind and efficient. He had an interesting face. It was square with a prominent nose. His eyes were somewhere between brown and amber. He had freckles and his brown hair was cut very short. He took my picture, morphed it into a badge, slipped the badge into a plastic holder, and slid a white plastic card into the backside of the holder.

"This will unlock most of the doors in the building and allow you to call the elevator downstairs in the breezeway. Make sure anyone who gets on with you has a badge with this bright-blue strip on it. If you suspect someone is on the elevator without the proper clearance, there is a security button right next to the bank of numbers that you can press discreetly. It will automatically alert whoever is at this desk and highlight this monitor." He pointed to a screen that showed a woman in an elevator. In my brief glance, I wasn't sure, but I thought it was Kirin.

"A card like this one," he said, still pointing to the back of my badge, "is how Jorge unlocked the doors you just walked through. You will see a white rectangle to the right side of solid doors, or a pillar like that one outside of the glass doors. This little card keeps information that lets security know who you are. It will record each you time use it to open a door. When you go into a room, you will need to use the card to get out as well. If you are escorted into one of the rooms that your card doesn't have access to, your card will get you out."

"What if there is a power failure?"

"Generators will take over. It takes less than a minute, not long. OK. I think you're all set. Shall I call Mr. Robertson now?"

"Sure."

CHAPTER NINE

The Lab

I settled into the routine at the Lab easily. I knew there were a lot of secrets and pending patents. Apparently, there were several paths of research and testing in the works. Each of these could make amazing changes to technology, and subsequently generate millions of dollars. I heard that the Lab might change history if we came up with an economical, sophisticated substitute for silicon, and that we were studying the capabilities of Gallium Nitride. But these grandiose schemes and classified research studies did not intrude into my server and security responsibilities or into my little cubicle.

My job was fun, but it was slow at first. I got to "talk" mostly to machines in their UNIX language, but there was a balance of talking with people too. Christine Channing, who had been at Peet's the day I met the "Lab Rats," as they called themselves, sat right across from me. She did not look like the usual often-haphazardly-put-together geek. She had a definite goth style. Her eyeliner and eye shadow that accented her beautiful brown eyes were always applied thickly and dramatically. Her nail polish was black. Her straight chin–length hair was black with streaks of hot pink. The dark makeup and black hair contrasted boldly with her very pale, almost blue-tinted skin. Black was her solo wardrobe color of choice, but she chose simple, professional styles. She wore long-sleeved high quality T-shirts or lightweight sweaters and probably had several pairs of identical black slacks. Christine was only a few years older than I, and may have been the youngest Lab Rat I had met. Since our responsibilities did not overlap, we would often take breaks together to go to the coffee cart, and then bring our coffee back to our cubicles.

We usually ate lunch at our desk, but one day she looked across the aisle and said, "You done? Wanna go for a walk?"

"Sure. Is it still cloudy out there? Do I need my sweater?"

"Maybe. The sun came out and it's gorgeous, but as usual, it's windy."

It was certainly both gorgeous and windy. For the first time, I followed the paver brick road out through the break in the wall that led to the upper parking lot. We walked in silence for a while. The wind surrounded us with the warmth of the asphalt that it whipped up from around the parked cars and familiar rows of liquidambar trees like the ones in the lower parking area that I walked through morning and evening.

Just before we reached the edge of the woods that flanked the west edge of the parking lot, the asphalt was covered with a blanket of leaves. Christine stumbled, reached out for my arm to catch her balance, and swore. "I'm sorry. It was one of those nasty little balls!"

"Nasty little balls?"

"Yeah! Those trees." She pointed to the closest liquidambar. "The seedpods are like a flail without the chain." She reached down and picked up the culprit that had nearly caused her to fall. "These nasty little balls have spikes, but worse, if you don't notice them you can seriously twist an ankle." She threw the nasty little ball off into the woods away from the well-worn path on which we had begun to walk.

The wind subsided a bit as we entered the forest in earnest. The path rose and curved as it circumvented tree trunks, saplings sprouting on the verge of the path, and thorny bushes that were pushing shoots to the sunlight between the trees. It was quiet and noisy at the same time. Quiet as the lovely trees absorbed us; noisy with the sound of communicating birds. I took a deep breath enjoying the freshness of the clear air and the beauty around me.

I was about to thank Christine on my exhale, when she said, "I think someone is following me."

I turned abruptly and looked behind us. She said, "No, not right now. I mean like kind of stalking me. I keep seeing this black car with dark-tinted windows outside or down the street from my house, and outside and down the street from my club."

Her voice was a bit shaky; she kept looking back over the canyon drop and the glinting stream that threaded along the ledge beneath the parking lot and wrapped itself around the Lab building. It was her turn to take a deep breath and then exhale. Her voice steadied. "But worse than that, I just feel it. You know what I mean? I feel like someone is watching me."

"How awful! Can you think of any reason someone would be?"

"Well, I've thought it for a long time, but after that girl from the Lab was murdered last month, I—"

"What?" I interrupted. "I didn't hear anything about that. Tell me."

"Yeah. I'm surprised you didn't hear about it. It's been all over the news. You filled her position. I filled in between her and you." She kicked a pile of leaves that fluttered into the air. Most likely she was making sure there were no nasty little balls hiding within.

My heart jumped and felt like it fluttered with the leaves, "Oh my! I suppose I was so absorbed with my thesis and studying for finals, I didn't watch or hear the newscasts. That was stressful craziness. How was she murdered?"

Christine took another breath to steady an obvious welling of emotion. "She was found strangled in her home."

I put my hand instinctively to my throat. "Strangled," I repeated stupidly. "Are you OK? Come, sit here." I motioned to a fallen log that had been worn shiny by weather and probably many Lab Rat bottoms. I sat mine down, leaving room for Christine's.

"They don't know if the attack was connected to the Lab. They took her laptop, but they stole everything else of value in her apartment as well."

"If they had gotten it, though, they wouldn't have been able to get any sensitive information because, as you know, our laptops don't have hard drives."

"I know that and you know that, but maybe the murderer didn't know that. Or maybe they've figured it out now that they have a laptop and they know they need more, like our SecurID tokens. If they were trying to get something from her, maybe now they are looking for another way . . ." She studied her black manicure for a moment. ". . . and another girl." She folded her hands under her arms and shivered as if a chill ran through her shoulders. "I think it's me. In fact I think he has, or they have, been watching me for a long time—probably at the same time he or they were watching her."

"Oh, Christine!" I reached out to rub the outside of her arm. "That is so scary. Have you talked to the police?"

"Yeah," she said evenly. "I called the Walnut Creek Police Department—her apartment is, er, was in Walnut Creek—and asked for the detective that handled Brenda's case. Brenda Arthur was her name. You took her place."

"You said that." It was my turn to shiver. I felt a chill run from my shoulder blades up my neck to the base of my skull. "What do you mean? Was she in cyber-security?" A huge brown spider lowered its shiny body down from a branch on a tree behind Christine. It was far enough away from her not to mention it. The spider's creepy presence triggered a second shudder.

"Yeah." She looked really sorry that she had told me. She searched my face to see if I looked upset. If she read correctly, she would know that I was greatly distressed, but was at that moment more concerned for her safety rather than my own.

She continued. "But she didn't sit where you do. She was on the floor above us over toward the windowless wall that has murals on it. All the floors are like that, like ours—with murals on the backside of the building—except the basement, which doesn't have any windows at all." The spider reached the ground and thankfully did a tiptoe dance in the opposite direction from us. I lost sight of it when it went around the trunk of the tree.

"I guess the guys who designed the building wanted the people without a window to still have a view." We both laughed. I heard the nervousness in mine.

"Anyway" She pulled out a hand to study it again. "I heard they had only questioned a few people at the Lab who knew her well. I wasn't one of them. I think the detective thought he was going to get a break in the case when I called, but I don't think he believed me. I don't know if it was because he was disappointed that I didn't have any new leads or he didn't like the way I looked." I gave her a questioning look. She pushed up the sleeve of her black T-shirt on the arm of the hand she was studying. It had a considerable amount of tattoo ink. She made a hand gesture and head nod that seemed to indicate *so there!* "Or maybe he just thought I was paranoid. He was nice enough to me, though, and gave me his card." She pushed the sleeve back down and used the same hand to reach into the V-neck of her T-shirt, pulling a business card out from her bra. "He said I could call him anytime if I thought I was in immediate danger." She turned to studying the card in her hand. "Gorsky. Detective Allen Gorsky. I don't think he was convinced Brenda's murder has anything to do with the Lab."

"But you are?" I smiled. "You're keeping his card close to your heart."

"Yeah." She chuckled and looked down at her business card pocket. "There's so much stuff going on here right now that could change the future of technology. If spies got a hold of it, they could make a lot of money—ya know what I mean?" Then apologetically she added, "Do you think I'm making too much of it?"

"No. Of course not, but I have to confess . . ." I raised my right hand. "Hi. I'm Meg, and I'm a TV addict. Crime dramas are my meat. Sitcoms are my dessert." We laughed again, this time at me. "I'm also addicted to books and movies. I reread and rewatch my favorites over and over." I patted her forearm. "Thank you for taking me into your confidence."

"I like you. You've never treated me like I'm different."

I smiled at her. "I've always been the one that's different. I like you too."

She smiled back, but then she got very serious. Putting her hands on the outside of both my arms she said solemnly, "I want you to be careful too. Keep your eyes open in case you see someone outside your house."

"Thank you." Her concern for me stirred behind an emotional door, normally locked by my resolution to accept loneliness. I found tears stinging slightly behind my eyes. I didn't think it was necessary to tell her that if someone was outside my house, they would either have had to have come over the mountain that surrounded the estate or approach the security fences and gates. And, if someone did get close to the house, they should remember to smile for Hillhollow's "candid" cameras.

Christine held the door for me. I swiped my badge across the stone pillar. She quickly stepped through the vapor lock to open the second door. When it clicked, she questioned, "What? Are you OK?" This in response to obvious recognition on my face.

"Do you smell that?" It was the scent of forest river breeze! I searched the foyer and then studied two men on the escalator. Neither was Stratton. I would have recognized him even from the back.

"Smell what?"

"He's here."

"Um, yeah? Who's here?"

"There was this guy at college. He smelled wonderful. I think he just came through this vapor lock."

"Vapor lock? You smelled a guy?" She giggled as we headed on our usual path to the escalator. "You crack me up, Meg Randallman." We held up our badges for the lobby security guard. "That wasn't just *any* guy from college, right? An old flame?"

I blushed. "Yes, but only on my part. He was very kind to me. I don't think he noticed me though, you know, in *that* way."

"Yeah. I know. Been there, done that, and bought the T-shirt. You could be wrong, ya know. He may have been intimidated by you. You are, shall I say"—she paused, apparently looking for the right word—"remarkable?"

I looked at her with a dumfounded expression, "Hardly." We reached the top of the escalator and headed for the stairwell for the final climb to our cubes.

"Have you looked in the mirror lately, or are you always in a book or watching a movie? You're striking. Not just tall and gorgeous, but a super brain on the inside—and look at those legs!" I was wearing black leggings under a knee-length shirt. "Those are enough to intimidate any guy!"

"Why? Because they're so long I can make a hasty departure? I actually can run pretty fast. When I'm not a couch potato, I run."

I thought about the possibility someone finding me intimidating and rejected it. "I was pretty young when we met. I think he saw me as a kid that needed a mentor and a friend. He was," I sighed, "great as both."

She smiled. "Dontcha think if he sees you here, he'll realize you're not a kid anymore? That is one lovesick expression on your face." She grinned. "Come on. We need to get back, but when we get a minute, I'll help you find him if he is here." She put her foot onto the first step, but stopped and turned back to look at me as soon as her footing was sure. "Seems like you might need to find *you* too."

As I settled into my cubicle, I was anything but settled. I was troubled that Christine might truly be in danger, even though she did have a detective's phone number handy in her bra. I had no idea if her fears were justified and real or imagined; the fear had a hold on her and now on me as well. And Stratton . . . if he was somewhere at the Lab—I quivered with excitement. I hoped it was not just a brief visit but rather because he worked here. But then, if he wanted to be in touch with me, it seemed like he would be. And what would I say to him if I ran into him? As I tried to picture running into him, I was overwhelmed.

I dug into my work so deeply that afternoon that I hadn't realized it was evening. I remembered that Christine had said good night quite a while ago. The ring of the phone on my desk jolted me out of my concentration. I glanced over my shoulder. In the night background of the massive windows behind Christine's desk, I saw reflections of the few remaining overhead lights glowing on our floor. Automated sensors had turned the rest of them off when movement ceased. The phone rang again. I checked my watch and noticed that was it close to seven.

I said, "Good evening, Meg Randallman."

"Margaret!" My mother was sobbing hysterically. I was certain that she was quite drunk.

"What is it, Norma?"

"Don't call me Norma! I'm your mother!"

"OK," I said levelly. "Mother, what is it?"

"Your, bro-bro-brother. He's overdosed on some kind of drug. He's at John Muir Hospital. They don't know if they can wake him up."

I felt blood leave my upper body and settle uncomfortably in my bowels. "Who found him?" I began the intricate log-off process and reached for the hanger supporting my jacket as I watched the text on my monitor detail its progress.

"He was at a party with some of his friends. They hadn't seen him for a while. He had gone to lie down in one of the bedrooms with a girl. Can you believe this? How could he do this to me? The girl came out about an hour la-later and said she couldn't wake him up. They splashed him with ice water before they called the ambulance, and then me. They're pumping his stomach. Oh, my poor, poor, ba-baaby."

I grasped my handbag from the bottom drawer of my desk and stood impatiently and stupidly staring at the monitor, ready to sprint. "Where are you, Norma?" I asked calmly, trying not to reveal my anxiety. If Norma was that far gone, George, in all probability, was also, and one of them had driven, or was still driving, to the hospital. At long last, the monitor dutifully displayed "Shutting down . . ."

She started to whine. Her screeching reminded me of Gollum in the movie *The Lord of the Rings*, when Sam tied him up with elvish rope. "Ca-can't you even call me m-m-o-o-o-ther, Margaret?"

It wasn't the time for me to say, "Can't you call me Meg?" Instead I said evenly, "Where are you, Mother?" I scribbled a note on Christine's whiteboard "My brother is in John Muir Emergency. May be late tomorrow."

As I feared, Norma replied, "We're on the way to the ho-hospital. You'll come soon?"

"Yes. I'm leaving now. I should be there in about a half an hour."

I snatched my iPhone from my cell phone locker—five missed calls. I trotted to my car as quickly as my long legs would transport me. The road from the Lab dropped down to the frontage road, and within just a few minutes, I twisted onto the freeway entrance heading north. I exercised great restraint to adhere to the speed limit. My heart ached for Ray.

My emotions were laced with guilt. I had spent little time or attention on Ray the past two semesters. He was rarely home when I was. He had a circle of friends who I thought were wonderful, upstanding citizens with wealthy parents, who could afford his private school. I was so naïve. It hadn't occurred to me until now that their disposable income could mean trouble. Neither had it occurred to me until this moment how self-centered I had become. My selfishness blinded me from realizing that he still needed me. I hoped it wasn't too late to come alongside him again, as I had when Norma extracted us from our home with Daddy.

I had to blink to keep my tears from turning the oncoming headlights into stars. Daddy. He would want to know that Ray was in trouble. If I knew how to reach him . . . if he's still alive. I took a few slow, deep breaths, blinked back tears, and kept my foot steady on the gas pedal. I continued to restrain myself, maintaining the speed of my car as close to the limit Highway 680 allowed.

Before I got to the information desk in the lobby of John Muir, Cliff Johnson who was Ray's closest friend, intercepted me, "Hi, Meg."

If my appraisal was correct, he was perfectly sober. "Cliff—"

He took me into his arms and held me against his chest. I allowed myself the freedom to totally lose it. I was shaking and soaking the front of his polo shirt. He gently said, "He's awake.

He's going to be OK. He just woke up a couple of minutes ago. Everyone is a little hysterical in his room."

I knew *everyone* meant Norma.

He continued. "I heard you were on your way, so I waved to him over the commotion and came down to meet you." He pushed me away slightly and held me by my arms. "Look at me. He's going to be OK."

I started rummaging in my bag for a Kleenex to start mopping up, but while I was digging, Cliff put his arm around me and escorted me to a reception counter with a box of tissues on it. He pulled out three and handed them to me. "Here."

CHAPTER TEN

Romance

Christine arrived at work about a half an hour after I did. She stopped in her cube for one minute, then popped her head into mine looking flushed and frightened. "How is your brother?"

"He's going to be OK. Thanks for asking. You look agitated."

"Yeah. I think I saw the black car following me a few cars back—from the time I left the house this morning. I didn't see it after I turned up the hill to the Lab, though. All clear behind me when I reached the guard gate."

'Maybe it's time to pull that number out of your bra?"

She looked down at her left boob. "What would I say?" I already told him I thought I was being followed.

"I suppose you're right. How about I follow you home tonight? If you're followed by that car, you'll have a second witness. And maybe I can pick up the license plate."

"Yeah. OK. Actually, I usually see them at night. This is the first time I've seen them in the morning."

"We can coordinate our arrivals too. I can come by in the morning and wait down your street."

"OK. Cool. Just a sec . . ." She stepped back into her cube, pulled the card out of her bra, pulled a square piece of paper out of a clear plastic box on top of her desk, and copied information onto it. Twisting back to me, she said, "Here. I put my cell number and my address on there too, so you'll know where you're following me to, and you can text me if you need to—not while you are driving, of course."

"Of course." I smiled at her for paying such close attention to the AT&T "Do Not Text and Drive" campaign and for her concern for my well-being. "I could call you using my Bluetooth. Do you have a hands-free device?"

"Yeah. I'll plug it in my ear."

I took the paper from her, examined it, then folded it in half and stuck it into my bra, which I could see from the expression on her face delighted her.

I kept an eye out for Stratton every time I left my cubicle. I was sure he was not on our floor. I didn't want to bother Christine's concentration, so I didn't remind her that she had offered to help. After settling in, I locked my workstation. I decided to take a look at the murdered girl's desk on the fourth floor. When I got onto the elevator on the third floor, it was packed with passengers riding up. I mentioned before that Stratton was not all that tall, but I knew he was there behind those that were taller. I could smell the fragrance of forest river breeze. When the door opened on the fourth floor, I stepped out and found myself in the same predicament that I was in the first time I met Stratton at Stanford. I was overwhelmed and had no idea which way to go.

As ever, he made it easy for me. "Meg?" He looked at the badge in the lanyard hanging from my neck, then looked up and beamed. "How long have you worked here?"

"Hi, Stratton." I returned a welcoming smile. "A couple of months. How about you?"

"I started at the Lab right after graduation." He gently touched the base of my spine to direct me out of the path of the de-elevatoring crowd. My entire body responded in a tingle. "They'd been 'after' me for a couple of years. Why haven't I seen you before, I wonder?" Alas, he removed his hand as we reached a cubicle alley.

He looked gorgeous. His hair was darker; no doubt it was seeing less sun these days. He wore a dark-teal shirt and a gray tie with subtle teal strips in it. His blue eyes looked almost teal. My senses were on overload. "I don't work on this floor, and this is the first time I've used the elevator."

"Are you OK? Are you afraid of elevators?" The blood beating in my face was undoubtedly perceptible. I wasn't about to own up to the electrifying effect of his touch, the unspeakable joy of seeing him, and the delight of the forest river breeze.

I laughed and hoped my morbid curiosity would explain my scarlet cheeks. "No. I'm not afraid of elevators. I am a little embarrassed though. I came up to see the shrine for Brenda Arthur. Yesterday I learned that I filled her position. Sort of creepy on my part, don't you think?"

He said compassionately, "No. It's fine. We all need to process this in our own way, whether we knew her well or not. This is not just a tragedy for Brenda's family and the people here at work, but it's also murder—something most people never have to deal with closely. Come on—I'll show you her desk. It's down this aisle." He led the way through the maze of gray-walled cubicles. I had forgotten his walk—a sure-footed, masculine, confident step. Not the swaggering arrogance of so many other men.

My admiration of Stratton's backside was interrupted when we passed a cubicle that caught my attention. "Hold up a second." It was all pink and princessy, with a pink feather boa and a pink lace valance over the whiteboard. We stopped there for a moment. Stratton was chuckling. "We did this to David's cube when he was on vacation a couple of months ago."

Still studying the décor I said, "What's amazing is he's left it this way for two months." I turned to face Stratton. "Does he aspire to be a princess?"

Stratton snickered. "Wait until you meet him. He's no princess, believe me!"

A deep voice behind me said, "Sure I am." A huge Samoan man in a Hawaiian shirt put out his hand. "David Matua—or as I'm known around here now, Princess David." His deep chuckle rippled the water landscape in his Hawaiian shirt. My hand was dwarfed by his firm but kind handshake.

"You certainly are a good sport."

"Well, I sort of started 'the cubical wars.' I left a fuzzy green-haired troll on Cindy's keyboard one evening. Then people started decorating each other's offices in small ways." He waved his large arm as if to proudly point out his furnishings. "If you go on vacation, they have more time for interior decorating."

I felt Stratton looking at me the whole time I was listening to David. I liked it.

"David, this is Meg Randallman. We went to Stanford together. She graduated this year." I could see the wheels turning as David assessed my age, but his kindness extended beyond the welcoming handshake. He spared me the questions.

"Great to meet you, Princess David." I turned to Stratton. "I should probably do what I came for and get back to work." Then I turned back to David. "I work on the third floor. Do you know Christine Channing?"

"No. I don't think so. This is a pretty big place actually. We should have a company picnic or something sometime."

Stratton laughed. "Yeah, catered. I think there are a lot of non-cooking nerds working here. Bye, David. I'll be back in a minute. I'm going to walk Meg to Brenda's desk, then down to her desk, and then I need to pick your royal brain about something."

"Bye." David was smiling approvingly at us as we turned to go. We passed a cube with Stratton's name on it. I peeked in briefly and saw a large black poster on the wall with a silver globe-like circle. It had white writing that read "It's not rocket science, you know—oh wait!" I chuckled.

Brenda's desk was covered with greeting cards. The monitor had been removed from the docking station. This platform was covered with stuffed animals, mostly some kind of stuffed turtle plus some silk plants and flower arrangements. There was a framed photo of two box turtles on the wall above the middle desk. One was sitting in a rectangular water dish. The other was resting on of a large leaf of romaine lettuce. He had pieces of banana in front of him and some banana mushing out the sides of his mouth.

We stood silently for a minute or so, then Stratton said, "She loved her turtles. It's too bad they can't talk. They probably saw her murder. Oh, I'm sorry." He put his arm around me and pulled me close to his side when he saw my tears. "Come on. Show me where you sit."

By the time we reached my cubicle door, I had recovered from Brenda's orphaned turtles, but I was really sorry to have Stratton leaving me, and he seemed a little reluctant to go. I heard him take breath in as if he was going to say something, but then instead he just peeked in the cube. "Pretty conventional."

"Yeah. I should probably bring in some pictures or get into a cubicle war with someone." I saw Christine coming down the aisle toward us. Her eyes were huge. She grinned and pointed at Stratton, lowering her hand before he saw her and in time for me to say, "Hi, Christine. This is Stratton Davis. I ran into him on the fourth floor. We went to Stanford together."

"Rivals." She shot him a mischievous grin.

"Pardon me?" This from Stratton.

"Nice to meet you, Stratton. Christine Channing." She extended her hand and he took it. "I went to Cal."

"Ah. I see. Rivals. Nice to meet you." He turned back to me. "Well, uh, I better get back. I need to meet with David about something, but I can't tell you what or I would have to kill you."

"Good one." I nodded mockingly. "Thanks for walking me back." I'm sure my eyes were saying thank you for so much more. "Maybe I'll see you now that I've seen you."

He smiled. "Count on it." He waved and headed toward the stairwell.

Stratton was not quite out of earshot. Christine and I were exchanging nods and smiles. Chip Swain was abruptly between us. "Who was that?"

I was startled and my body jerked. "Why hello, Chip. Where did you come from?"

A bit defensively he said, "I work on the first floor." He had apparently rushed to get to our cubicle alley. He took a much-needed breath. "I looked you up in the Lab directory. I rode the elevator up with others."

"As an outside vendor, how did you get access to the directory?" He stood there stupidly, not answering, so I said, "You're not supposed to be on this floor." I looked for his lanyard. It was tucked inside his shirt.

He put his hand up to his chest to cover the lanyard. "I know, sweetie, but I wanted to say hello to you. I've been looking for you." His eyes scanned the three tabletops of my desk.

I followed his eyes to make sure there was nothing lying on my desktop or on my screen that he shouldn't see. The screen was dutifully flashing colorful fractal-like shapes as it should when I lock it and walk away. "Chip. This is awkward. I was instructed in situations like this to call Asset Security."

"Whoa, sweetie. I'm just being friendly." He bowed his head in a humble position that somehow entirely failed to communicate humility. Then he looked up again sheepishly like a naughty child trying to manipulate a disciplining parent, "No need to go all crime squad on me." I could see Christine behind him. She pantomimed that she would call Security for me. He probably guessed when he saw me look past him. "No need to call them. I can escort myself back downstairs." He turned to head in the same direction as Stratton had just gone.

"You won't be able to open the stairwell door with your key card."

"Oh, you're right, sweetie." Each time he said that it made my flesh crawl. "So will you open the stairwell door for me?"

"No. But I'll walk you to the elevator and put you on a car that's going down." So I did, and I didn't say a word to him as we walked. I think, in spite of his propensity to be clueless, he knew I was irritated. He kept silent for most of the walk.

I waited until an elevator car got to our floor. I stepped in with him and pushed the button for the first floor, then stepped out. I realized that I could watch the progress of the elevator but that I could not guarantee he wouldn't get off on the second floor, or even step off when it reached the first floor or the garage, so I stepped back in to ride down with him. Then it was really awkward.

He smiled at me. "So you want more of my company, sweetie?"

"Look, Chip. First of all, don't call me sweetie." He was a medium height man. I was almost eye level with him in my two-and-a-half-inch heels. "My name is Meg—or even more appropriate for our level of acquaintance, Ms. Randallman." I felt the elevator stop at the first floor. The lights confirmed we had arrived. "Secondly, no. I do not want your company, and I'm annoyed that you've put me in this situation. You do not have clearance for any floor except this one. I should have called Asset Security."

The doors swished open. I added, "If I see you upstairs again, I will." My outward composure was intact, but inwardly not so much. He accepted my rebuke the way I would expect an insecure child to behave. He was sulky. His normal military posture gone. He was slightly bent. The doors were closing, so I didn't have time to analyze it further. I pushed the button for the third floor, then I realized the elevator was continuing down to lower parking plaza. I sighed and dutifully rode unnecessarily to the garage, then, since no one was there, was able to return to the third floor without stopping.

As soon as she saw me, Christine bounded into my cube and said, "So! Shall we start with man number one? Is that the college flame? He *does* smell good. It looks to me like it's not so one-sided." She smiled admiringly.

"That was definitely fun to run into him." I felt the redness return to my cheeks as I remembered our reunion. "I went to up see the Brenda shrine. He got off the elevator on that floor."

"You're blushing."

"I just remembered that he touched me."

"Wow. He touched you? You've got it bad!" She chuckled. "Or maybe I should say you've got it good?"

"Maybe I do. Hey! What's with that creep Chip? Has he done that before?" I shivered.

"Nope. I've never seen him up here, or even around here. The only other time I've seen him was at Peet's that first time I met you. I met him that same morning. I don't usually get up that early on Saturdays. I was actually there that morning because I was still up."

I'm sure she recognized confusion on my face. I couldn't remember ever staying up all night for any reason. "Wow. Do you do that a lot? What did you do this past weekend?"

"Oh, it was benign. I went shopping with my mom and sister on Saturday. Is there something wrong?"

I studied my nails that seriously needed a manicure, then looked up. "I was just having a moment of envy. Is your sister older or younger?"

"She's younger. Almost through college. She is what's known as a 'super senior.' It's taken her about six years to graduate with a bachelor's. She was unable to get the classes she needed. Budget cuts to the state colleges and universities make this a lot of people's story. Julie is her name. She lives at home. When Mom takes Julie out to spoil her, she invites me for some spoiling too. No sisters?"

I shook my head. "No." I thought about telling her I used to have one, but wasn't sure I could talk about it still, after all these years. All the memories flooded into my brain, and I felt my face flush scarlet. Daddy, Grama and Grampa, Laura . . .

"I'm sorry. You look really sad. I'm not going to lie. I love having a sister." Christine started talking very fast as if she could talk my obvious pain away. "For a while we fought a lot, but no one could cross either of us without one coming to the other's defense. Then, when I moved out, she and I really got close. I talk to her at least once a week, and we trust each other with everything. Oh, I'm so sorry. This is really upsetting you, isn't it?"

"I'm OK. Thanks for your concern. My mom and I have never had that kind of relationship either. So did she buy you anything?"

"Mom bought us both new bras and each of us something outer. I got a new jacket."

"Black?"

"Yeah. How'd ya guess?" She laughed. "I wore both the new bra and the new jacket to my club Saturday night." She turned to the side and stuck out her chest. "Uplifting, yeah?"

"I bet you were a hit."

Then she really got laughing. When she calmed down a bit she said, "I wore other clothes too, you nitwit."

I smiled. "Well, nothing like a perky business card holder."

She laughed some more. I think it was a continuation of the first session of laughter that got her laugh motor started. "OK, let's get some work done. No coffee break today. Thank you for following me home tonight."

Later, we gathered our cell phones from our lockers. "Where's your car, and what kind am I following?" I pulled the paper she gave me out of my bra and entered her name and number into my phone's address book. "I just sent you a text. Now you have my number too."

"I'm on the upper parking lot, and it's a black Ford Focus. Where are you and what kind of car will be following me?"

"Black? What a surprise." I smiled at her. She nodded and smiled back. "I park on the lower level. Black Sapphire Metallic BMW."

"Oooh. Cool."

It was an uneventful ride as far as my super sleuth assignment went, but I really enjoyed chatting with Christine along the way. It was soothing to have a friend besides my adopted family and my pets. I had a feeling that was new to me. I wasn't sure, but I think settling into the job, finding Stratton, and becoming friends with Christine were all strengthening me. I felt comfortable. I realized the feeling was contentment.

Christine pulled onto an asphalt driveway, and then into a carport of a sprawling apartment complex. I had stayed back from her a bit, so she was out of the driver's seat and locking her car by the time I pulled behind her. I waved good-bye and went to the end of the driveway that I suspected made a circle. I was right. Around the first curve, as I passed by a fence, I could see a nice-sized community pool. No suspicious black cars with tinted windows in the tenant or guest parking slots.

I followed Christine for a full week, both ways. We connected our Bluetooth earpieces and had amusing chats. More and more deeply, I began to appreciate her friendship and the spontaneous banter with no agenda, other than just enjoying each other's company. After we settled into our cubicles on the morning of the fifth day, she poked her head into my space. "You think I'm crazy and paranoid, right?"

"No."

"Well, if you are not thinking it, I'm beginning to."

"Have you considered that your stalker may have spotted me and backed off?"

"Hmmm." She tilted her head slightly, looked up to the right, then looked back at me and shook her head. "No. I hadn't."

"I have an idea. I really enjoy our travel chats. How about I pick you up and take you home every day? I know you have to work late unexpectedly sometimes, but that's OK. I always have stuff to do and can work while I wait. If I have a date or something"—I smiled and she smiled back—"We can take separate cars."

"Yeah. A date or something." Her eyes looked up toward the section of the ceiling where I told her Stratton's cube was located on the floor above, then back to me. She nodded. "I like it. That would be great. I can pay you for gas."

"That's not necessary. It's my pleasure. You're on the way. It'll take an insignificant amount of fuel." I didn't add that I hadn't even cashed any of my paychecks. I kept meaning to set them up with direct deposit. I wasn't working for the money.

CHAPTER ELEVEN

Ray Renewal

Ray recovered from the overdose that nearly killed him, but shortly after, he got into trouble with drugs again. This time the trouble was with the law. He was arrested at a party. He was only being generous. He offered to share something illegal with an undercover cop. The cop was there targeting a "bigger fish," but he could hardly let Ray slide. Ray was charged with a misdemeanor, not a felony, because of the small amount of narcotics in his possession. He took a plea bargain, and his sentence was reduced to a few years of probation with the stipulation that he check in to rehab immediately and serve six months of community service after his rehabilitation.

Norma was beside herself. She drank more than usual and was viciously mean to the rest of us in the household. If I had been Evelyn, the housekeeper, or Chef Barbara, I would have quit. I even found myself sympathetic to George, who joined a gym and therefore extricated himself from a portion of her wrath. Besides watching him take the brunt of her temper tantrums and general bullying behavior, I didn't know if he suspected her infidelity. I was an incredible coward who had successfully avoided any lengthy conversation with him since Norma's tryst with Matt.

I thought about one of my movie heroines, Danielle, played by Drew Barrymore, who was "Cinderella" in the movie *Ever*

After. She was so brave. My favorite scene was when she and Prince Henry get surrounded by a raucous band of gypsies and she outsmarts them by negotiating with their leader to give his word that she will be permitted to leave and take with her anything she can carry. She hoisted Prince Henry onto her back to carry him away. I wished I could muster half as much of her bravery to talk openly to George. I convinced myself that even though I was just the messenger, I didn't want to hurt George.

I also justified my cowardice by entertaining the idea that George somewhat deserved Norma's unfaithfulness. You'd think since he married an adulteress he would expect her to continue to behave like one.

But these weren't the only conflicts thrashing my courage. I wasn't ready to accept Norma's fury. My well-practiced defenses of denial and apathy were emotional Band-Aids that I applied to each instance that came up. Sometimes it was the patronizing or angry tone of her voice. Other times it was her silence when we passed each other in the Hillhollow kitchen or on the stairs. I would greet her, but she rarely replied with more than a nod or a grunt. I felt despised and rejected. Deep inside I was still that lonely little girl that wanted her to love me. My greatest fear of all, though, was that a disruption of Norma and George's union might also separate me from My Lady Margaret, whom I loved and honored more than either George or Norma.

I made time for Ray while he was in rehab. I took a few days off when he was first admitted, to spend time with his counselors and attend group sessions with the families of other recovering patients. After I returned to work, I went to the center at least twice a week. It was time well spent, not just for Ray's benefit but also for mine. Al Anon teachings "meddled" into my history and opened my eyes to my codependent, enabling behavior. I begged Norma to join us, but she declined saying she "would just die" if someone she knew saw her arriving or leaving the center.

Ray had lost a lot of weight and, actually, I had to admit that he looked good. What I didn't like to admit was that his "weight loss plan" nearly destroyed him. His robust appreciation for food had begun to catch up to him before he traded it for new addictions. His new, svelte self was utterly handsome. He had passed me in height a few years before. His dark-brown hair was thick and wavy. Dark lashes framed his eyes that were a color somewhere between green and brown. He probably put "hazel" as his eye color on his California driver's license. He was nineteen now. His handsome face had lost the boyish look. As one of my PBS British movie characters would say: he was dishy. I looked down at his large, beautifully shaped hands. They reminded me of Daddy's hands the last time I saw them—when he securely set my Bible on the shelf under my nightstand. I felt pressure building in my throat and behind my eyes.

We were drinking coffee, sitting on a comfortable couch in one of the many small living rooms throughout the center, decorated in soothing colors. The carpet was dark gray with textured bars of light gray. A bank of three large windows was across from the couch. Behind the couch was a wall-sized window between the sitting room and the hallway. The miniblinds were open. One of the three windows to the outside was open a couple of inches. We could hear bees enjoying the blossoms on the lime tree outside. The walls were covered with porous rose beige stone slabs.

Ray looked up from drawing dented patterns on his napkin on the tabletop with the handle of his coffee spoon. "Are you OK, Deedee?"

I took a breath to answer, but a young therapist bounced through the open door into our serene setting. She had dark short hair with blonde spikes jutting out of the top of her head. She was wearing navy scrubs and a thick layer of expertly applied makeup.

"Hi, Heather!" My brother shot her a winning smile. "What are you doing here so early?"

I had a feeling she was long past needing to be won over by a smile. Through the thick camouflage of foundation and heavy blusher, I detected a flush of crimson rising in her neck and cheeks. "Oh, I finished up all my chores at home and thought I'd just come in early. She looked hesitantly at me. "Can I get you anything?"

"I think we're set with coffee and water, but thanks." He raked the waves on the top of his head back with the four fingers on his right hand. This caused the muscle beneath his short-sleeved T-shirt to bulge a bit. I was thinking *This poor girl doesn't have a chance. She'll be hopelessly in love with him before he recovers and checks out of here.* He tilted the wavy locks in my direction. "Have you met my sister, Meg?"

She looked relieved. "Oh! Your sister! I knew you had a sister named Meg, but didn't you just call her Deedee?"

I elbowed him gently. "He still calls me by the first name he ever called me. It was his talking toddler lame attempt at *sister.*" He gave me a mature, mild smile that indicated my teasing had reached a comfortable level of endearment.

This set her off giggling, which seemed to bubble up easily. "Well, I'll see you later, Ray, when my regular shift begins. Nice to meet you, Meg." She turned on her heel but gave us a parting look over her left shoulder. She gave Ray a smile that generated adorable dimples. When she turned back to pay attention to where she was walking, I thought I heard her say softly, "Sister."

Ray resumed his spoon to napkin graphic design. Without looking up he said, "Maybe I should go to culinary school."

I looked at him admiringly. "Maybe you should. In fact, that's a great idea! You know your way around a kitchen, and you've always been a fan of great food." I emphatically tilted my head to make sure he knew I was studying his spoon/napkin artwork. "You've always been artistic too."

He chuckled, sat up from his drawing, and with one hand grabbed the miniscule remainder of spare tire around his middle that had all but disappeared. "I wouldn't know how to cook if it weren't for you, Deedee."

No one else had ever called me that. It was a bond that reminded me of our shared loss. I said softly, "Survivors. That's what we are."

As he added a circle to the top of his tabletop creation, I remembered how we used to have fun preparing our meals in the Hillhollow kitchen. Chef Barbara did all the grocery shopping and came to prepare and serve dinners most days, but Ray and I actually did quite well preparing breakfasts and lunches during the weeks or months that Ray was on school vacations. We also prepared dinners when Barbara was given the night off and we hadn't been invited to My Lady's. Norma and George went out to dinner frequently, so Ray and I had many opportunities to experiment with Barbara's techniques and recipes.

Since I was tutored at home, I spent a lot of time with Barbara and asked her a million questions. She encouraged these, gave me comprehensive answers, and often assigned me sous chef responsibilities. She taught me how to make soups and salads and homemade salad dressings. I learned to grill meats and vegetables—until they were "just there," Barbara would say. "Don't overcook." She also taught me how to make yummy sauces. The most ubiquitous of all was creamy white sauce that morphed into heavenly Alfredo or simple, delicious macaroni and cheese. Then, I found cooking shows on my most faithful life companion: my television.

Ray interrupted my meandering culinary thoughts by addressing my last statement. "Survivors? You're funny. We live in a mansion on a huge gated estate surrounded by servants and affluence. How did you come up with survivors?"

"Abuse takes many forms. Just because we've been spoiled financially, doesn't mean we haven't tasted emotional cruelty." Anger superseded my sadness. "Look where you are! This"—I gestured to take in the essence of the institutional gray, pink, and beige—"is the result of bad parenting. I was just thinking yesterday how I've let you down by not being around for you, but our mother has never been available to either of us emotionally. She isn't even available to you now here, when and where you need her the most." I felt the heat of blood in my face. "You are a wonderful person."

An errant bee blundered into the room and crossed to the window behind the couch, where it stupidly crashed into the reflection of the scenery outside. I was watching it as I said confusedly, "I overheard our real daddy say to Norma once, 'There is no such thing as a bad child.'" The sadness returned.

Ray got up and went to the open window. He slid it open completely, and used a magazine to coax the bee to its freedom. I saw the sides of his mouth slight turn slightly up to acknowledge his victorious rescue, then he closed the window and returned to the couch. "Well, it's up to me now. It won't do any good to put the blame elsewhere. That would only put the power to get well somewhere else besides right here." He put his palm on his chest. "It starts with me, and of course with God."

I should have been in that moment encouraging him to nurture this victory, but years of pent-up emotions erupted. "Don't you remember Daddy?" I blinked back the moisture in my eyes. "Or Grama Estelle? Or Grampa Red?"

He looked at me compassionately and, had he not been taking classes on how to correctly deal with life, he probably would have lied to avoid his discomfort. He didn't. He had learned that avoidance only put off the inevitable and often exacerbated his problems. "I really don't, Deedee. The only dad I know is George, even though I've never called him father, or pop, or dad," he said levelly. "He's not real chummy, but he's been more than good to me. He's actually been a lot nicer to me than Mom. I'm sorry. Are you OK?" He put his hand on my arm.

"And Laura," I added lamely. "I'm sure you don't remember Laura." I looked at his befuddled stare and realized that of course he didn't remember her and that it would have been my responsibility to keep her memory alive. "We had a sister." I felt a burning in my abdomen. I'm sure it was caused by shame. "She was two years older than I am. She was your original Deedee. We both were actually."

"What happened to her?" He gently rubbed my arm as he watched my ebbing tears. "Did we leave her behind?"

"No. She died just before George and Norma took us away from Daddy." I was uncontrollably sobbing.

Ray got up and walked across the room to get a box of tissue. He closed the door and lowered the miniblind cord to shut us privately within. He returned holding out the box of tissue and waited patiently as I pulled, snorted, and blotted, and then pulled, blew, blotted, sniffed, and blotted some more. After I had calmed a bit, he asked softly, "How did she die?"

I took a deep breath and felt my chest shudder. "She was shot with Grampa Red's varmint gun by a girl that Laura and I used to play with. Her-her n-name was Vanessa." A few more pulls and blots, then another trembling breath. "Vanessa was aiming for me."

He moved closer to me on the couch and put a comforting arm around my shoulders. He said to the coffee table, "And therefore, you decided that it was your fault, and all these years you've felt guilty, right?"

"Right. It *was* my fault because I ran to Laura when I saw Vanessa with the gun." I took another chest-shuddering breath and then said guiltily, "Laura took one step that put her between me and the gun."

He relinquished the box of tissues to my lap, then took my shoulders in each of his hands to turn me slightly toward him. "I believe in taking responsibility for our actions, and I believe that your fear had a part to play in this tragedy, but how old were you, Deedee? You couldn't have been more than five."

I brought up a picture of a little frightened girl onto the video screen in my head. It was as if she were someone else, someone whose terror and response I could understand, instead; someone who deserved compassion. "I was four."

I could hear him take a breath as if to say something, but no words came directly. Instead he took me in his arms and gave a consoling hug to the four-year-old Meg. He said with devastating simplicity, "There's no such thing as a bad child."

CHAPTER TWELVE

It Keeps Coming Up

I hadn't seen My Lady Margaret and Karen for a while, and I really, really missed them. I couldn't wait to tell My Lady about my new friendships with Stratton and Christine, and having renewed my kinship with Ray. Karen and Margaret had taken an extended European vacation that included cruises around the Mediterranean. I expected them home any day.

After I dropped Christine at her home, I drove around the circular parking area looking for an ominous dark car or anything suspicious. I whispered a prayer asking for her safety. I switched on the radio and heard Amy Winehouse sing that she didn't want to go to rehab. I was sad that she lost her life because she said, "No, no, no!" Then I whispered a second prayer for Ray.

A really, really stupid gray squirrel ran out from the shadows of a tree and stood stupidly in the middle of my lane about one hundred and fifty feet in front of my car. As I braked and my tires squealed, he raced to the center of the oncoming traffic lane, reversed directions in time for a truck coming the other way to miss him, then stopped again about three feet in front of my abruptly halted vehicle. He was stupidly staring at my bumper with his shiny black eyes. I said, "Lucky thing you are cute or I'd be very angry with you!"

I don't think he heard me. He dashed back into the shadow from which he'd appeared. Fortunately there was no one behind me to crash into me and cause my bumper to bump into his little stupid head regardless of my efforts. I shook my head, inhaled deeply, and spared one more thought about how stupid he was. Then I took my foot off of the brake and put it on the gas pedal to slowly resume my trip home. By the time I recovered from the adrenaline rush, I realized I was almost there.

I pushed the remote to open the gate, then dropped into second gear to take the climb up Hillhollow's drive. When I made the turn at the end of the mansion into the garage, Ben was there. I parked and got out quickly to catch him before he left for the day.

"Hi! How are you? How are Betty and Ben Junior?"

They were the right questions if one wanted to see pure joy on his face. "Hi! All good. Very good." Then he said playfully with a knowing grin, "Did you know that Ms. Randallman is home? She got home around two."

"No! Oh cool! I'll go see her right away."

I kissed him on the check, retrieved my handbag from my car, and headed around the back toward My Lady's. I could think of no reason I would need to go to my own home first. Midnight was out on the rear veranda. He lifted his head from his paws and put his ears at attention as soon as he spotted me.

"Hi boy! Come on. Let's go see My Lady and Karen." He bounded to his feet to join the chase. He romped joyfully beside me, and of course we terrorized the multitude of birds. As they took flight one of them bumped into a window. He flew away a little goofy, but thankfully fine. I was about to apologize to him in flight, but I heard voices around in the side garden, so I headed toward them through some of the circling birds who were confused by our change in direction.

Norma was talking to Margaret. Before she saw me, I heard her say, "But she was so little, they ruled it an accident . . . Oh, honey! There you are. Did you come to welcome Margaret home?"

I felt horror zigzag through my heart and my bowels. She lifted her well-shaped right eyebrow, then turned back to My Lady Margaret to sketch a half circle with her right hand. "Well, I'll let you catch up. Glad to see you arrived safely home from your travels."

Margaret thanked her courteously, then watched Norma pass me with a smug smile on her way to the rose garden path. No doubt she was headed for a celebratory cocktail. I supposed that she had always been jealous of my most cherished relationship and had planned to expose my shame to My Lady, thinking she could easily destroy it. She may have been correct.

My Lady sat there staring at me. She was pale as if all the blood had drained from her face. I wasn't sure how to read her. There was a silence so full of comment that it buzzed louder than the bees in the bushes. It broke when I blurted out, "I didn't kill my sister."

"Of course, you didn't mean for it to happen."

"No, I didn't shoot her. It *was* my fault though." I stood there thinking that she didn't need this shock, but hoped it would help her process it if I explained rather than leaving her toying with misconception or confusion. "The gun was aimed at me. I ran to my sister. She stepped between me and the shooter."

"Come here." She put her arms out to me, and I ran to them. It was always awkward trying to hug her in the wheelchair. As I embraced her, she seemed thinner than I remembered and very frail. Midnight nuzzled in to be part of the cuddle. We accepted his intrusion and patted his head, but then I pushed it away and told him to lie down. I could see Karen standing just inside the doorway to the side garden. She had no doubt heard Norma tell My Lady that I shot my sister. This would be the first time they had even heard I'd had a sister. Karen was blotting her sunken eyes with a Kleenex.

As I backed away from our embrace, My Lady continued to hold the outside of my arms comfortably. She said compassionately, "Are you OK? Do you want to talk about it?" Midnight settled comfortably at My Lady's feet.

"Not really. Not now," I said lamely. "Oh, I've missed you so much. I have so many other things I do want to talk about. So many things to tell you about that happened while you were gone." I stopped to breathe, then said calmly, "But first, how was your trip? Did you have a good time?"

"Yes, my dear. We did, but how about, instead, *this* first," She lifted a hand to hail Karen, "Tea, or coffee?"

I smiled and began to relax. I searched her face and found sympathy, curiosity, and unmistakably love. Nothing Norma could have said, or how she slanted it, would alter My Lady's love for me. "Coffee would be great. I love coffee." I sat down in the shade in one of the cushy chairs at her glass table. The umbrella over my head had a string of mini lights embedded into its skeleton.

"OK, Mr. Midnight." she looked down into his longing eyes. "You need to move." He did. She motored to the vacant side of the table also in the shade. Midnight lay down, managing to position his large body between the chair legs so it was convenient for both of us to pet him with our feet—just in case. He tapped the patio with his ridiculous tail. "I know that you love coffee." My hug and Midnight's intrusion had rearranged My Lady's perfection. She smoothed her left sleeve with her right hand, then started smoothing her other sleeve, and then smoothed her lovely pressed slacks.

"And I love you, even more than I love coffee." I smiled and accepted a Kleenex from a box in Karen's outstretched hand. She patted my shoulder as I pulled a few.

My Lady looked up from her grooming, pulled a few tissues for herself, and dabbed her eyes as she said, "I know that you do, my sweet Meg. I love you too." Then to Karen she said, "Could you make us a press pot of Arabian Mocha Java?" Obviously reluctant to leave, Karen nodded, grabbed a Kleenex for herself, and left the box behind.

We ignored the proverbial "elephant in the room"—or in this case, "the elephant in the garden," as we remained in that serene setting anticipating our coffee. A lovely breeze stirred the butterfly bush where bees, butterflies, and an occasional hummingbird all feasted on the conical purple florets. A few finches reluctantly flew in to the feeders. Some sparrows began to peck at the ground beneath, but they all jetted away again when Karen came out with the coffee. They returned in force after we settled peacefully into sipping from our mugs and chatting. The hummingbirds didn't frighten as easily. They kept their vigil at the bulb of sugar water, taking breaks to scold us, particularly Karen, with their tiny beeps.

Before I got started with my news, I insisted that she tell me about her trip. I hadn't realized that her brother-in-law, George's Uncle William, had met up with them in Greece. They had planned the trip years before when both their spouses were still alive. They decided to take the trip at last while they both could still travel. She laughed lightheartedly. I found myself admiring her graciousness and beauty. "Besides," My Lady said, "We had some important decisions to make, and it was the perfect opportunity to discuss them." I felt it was not my place to ask what those were, though it did seem like she led the conversation to this logical place expecting me to inquire.

When I finally got talking, aided by a hearty dose of caffeine, I was an utter motormouth. My animated gestures frequently stirred the birds, and I kept Midnight happy by vigorously massaging his side with my right foot. I told her about Ray first, how he had screwed up, but this latest screwup definitely seemed to be turning out to be for the best. I told her he looked great and had a spectacular attitude. I was so pleased and excited to report that for the past six weeks Christine rode to and from work with me and I could talk to her about anything. "I feel so close to her, she's like a sister—"

I paused. There it was again. My Lady's expression stayed level. She was not going to push me. I took a breath to say more, but decided not to mention Brenda's murder or Christine's fear that someone was following her. Instead I exhaled and realized I had been like a tightly wound, automated toy that had at last wound down. It was quiet except for the buzzing of the bees and the scolding the iridescent red-throated hummingbird beeped as he whirred from the bulb to the top of the butterfly bush, then dropped suddenly to drink from flowers at the bottom. The finches were cheep, cheep, cheeping in the Nigel seed feeders.

I had saved Stratton for last. I found my neck and temples warming as I talked about him, "He's come by my desk every day since we ran into each other at the elevator. You remember me talking about him when I was in school?"

"Yes. Your hero. He came to your rescue when you were disoriented. The brain, who consistently smelled wonderful. I remember." She smiled and waited patiently.

"We talk about absolutely anything and everything. He is so interesting and seems to be interested in what I tell him." I paused, took a sip of coffee, and then added unnecessarily, "I think he likes me." I felt I needed to put it into words so I could begin to believe it. "When the weather is nice, he and I eat lunch out at the tables on the upper grounds of the Lab. It's often way too windy though, so we eat together in the cafeteria the other days." My cheeks felt hot and crimson.

She laughed. "I'm sure he likes you. Have you seen your reflection lately?" She sipped her coffee, then set down her mug on the garden table. "You are lovely, Meg. Beautiful on the outside, but even more lovely on the inside. I don't know how you got this way, but you seem to be always thinking about others and putting them first." She paused, and then asked tranquilly, "Do you think Stratton shares your faith?"

I felt the blood leave my face. "Uh—I don't really know." Then I said defensively, "How would I know? It's not like it would come up in a lunch conversation at an office building!"

"My darling girl, has this gone too far for you to take a warning?"

"From you?"

Still with great kindness she said, "From me, yes, but also from your God." She reached across the table to put her right hand— the one with the ruby ring on it—on top of mine. "If you had to choose between him and your faith, which would you choose?"

"Why would I have to choose? You know I can't lose my faith!" I looked away and said lamely to the butterfly bush, "I know that the first day I met him he noticed my cross." I looked back into her eyes.

She smiled. "And he walked you to class anyway?"

I nodded. "Pretty dumb conclusion, huh." I released a breath and let some of my defensiveness go with it.

"If there was some wisdom that would enhance the possibility of success and minimize the chance of failure, would you consider it?

"From you?" I echoed feebly.

"Yes. From me. Do you believe that I know you well, and know more about man-woman relationships than you do?'

"Uh. Y-yes." I surrendered emotionally. The defensiveness was at last deflated. "Of course." Then rhetorically I asked, "I don't know much, do I? How could I possibly?"

"Do you believe I love you?" I nodded. "Do you believe God loves you?" I nodded again.

"I see where this is going." I smiled. "Cupid's arrow still thrums where it struck me. My whole body seems to thrill and tighten when I get an instant message or an e-mail from him, but you're right." I flipped my palm up to gently grasp her hand that she had set upon mine. The ring seemed to spin easily. "The Bible says something about not being yoked with unbelievers. Light can't coexist with darkness, right? Is that what you were trying to remind me of?"

"Yes, my dear." She squeezed my hand back, then took it back to her coffee mug. "So many relationships fail these days. I'm sure when they began, both partners thought everything was perfect and yet . . ." She paused to study my face. "Can you see that they may have been blind to flaws in the relationship, possibly from the beginning?"

"Yes. I suppose so."

"You suppose so?"

"My head agrees with you." I looked up as if I would see God, but all I saw was a fluffy white cloud drifting through the heavens. "My heart doesn't want to ask the question," I answered candidly.

"I just want you take advantage of the wisdom that is available to you. I've heard it said there are four likely causes that destroy a marriage relationship: dishonesty, disloyalty, differences in religious beliefs, and money."

"It's not like he asked me to marry him."

"That's true. So many people say, 'it's just dinner,' or 'it's just a movie,' but we all know when our intentions and attractions are more." She looked at me with compassion. "I want you to be happy, but I also want you to be wise. And so does God. I want you to think—so few people do." She tilted her coffee mug to see how much was left, took a sip, then set it down. "I think," she said intuitively, "there is a struggle going on within you. You may not believe this at the moment, but it's a good thing to wrestle with God, as long as you come to Him with a willingness to be honest with Him and know that you will surrender to His will in the end. He already knows that cupid's arrow struck you before you had time to vet the relationship. He may have been waiting for you to bring this to Him for His council."

All of sudden, she looked very tired to me. "I believe that this struggle will prove your character and turn out for your good." She took a shallow breath that seemed almost to sigh. "I would like to meet him. Both of them, actually. I would like to meet Christine too." I could hear a rattle as she took another incoming breath and waited for more, but she was silent.

"Are you OK? I bet you have jet lag." I got up to leave and picked up the coffeepot and my mug. Midnight jumped up as well and rapped My Lady across her legs with his tail. "Midnight! How rude."

"I'm OK, dear. And Midnight didn't hurt me. What he lacks in finesse, he makes up for in enthusiasm, and his enthusiasm brings me great enjoyment." She took another shallow breath and closed her eyes momentarily. "However, you are correct. I am tired even after this wonderful coffee. Thank you, Karen."

Karen, who, not surprisingly was stationed close by, said, "Oh now, you sweet thing. You don't need to help clean up. I've got those things." She took them from my hands. "M *is* tired though. It was so good of you to come and see her right away. We've missed you." As I stood close to her for the first time since I arrived. I realized that her eyes were rimmed with red—redder than a few tears shed over Norma's sabotage. I chalked it up to jet lag and turned to leave.

"Oh!" I turned back toward them. "When you're rested, do you want to go see Ray with me?"

"Yes, dear. I would like that very much. We can have Ben take us in the SUV with my travel chair. How much longer before Ray comes home?"

"They won't set a date. It's all dependent on his progress." I studied her face again with worry in my heart. She looked pale, exhausted, and a little gray. "Can you text me when you're ready to take it on?"

"I will. Thank you again for coming so soon to welcome me with your good news. Meg, it is all good news. You will see."

I decided another, less forceful hug was in order. I hugged Karen next. She stretched her arms wide because I'd caught her off guard with her hands full of coffee paraphernalia. "I missed you too. I love you too." I waved good–bye and turned to leave. With Midnight at my heels, we scared the birds that were scarfing up the seed greedily before their final flight home for the night. It was starting to get dark. The lovely breeze had turned cold.

CHAPTER THIRTEEN

Memories, Spider, and Scare

"So! Don't you look pretty today?" This from Christine as she ran from her apartment and got quickly into the passenger side of my car. "You look great all in black. You could be mistaken for me." She grinned proudly.

"Ha! I guess I could. Since you let your length grow out and the pink fade away, our hair looks almost the same too." I made the circle through the parking lot and got out onto the main road that headed to the Lab. "I just got this comfy sweater." I stuck out my right arm in her direction. "Feel the material."

She rubbed the fabric. "So soft!"

"It's been getting so chilly up there on the mountain." The mountain had just come into view, so I pointed to it. "The days are so much shorter now. Seems like it's dark when we go to work and darker when we get home. Plus, inside the Lab is never all that warm."

"Sounds like justification. Did you spend a lot of money shopping for clothes this weekend?" Her inquiry was supportive rather than accusatory.

"Yeah. I kinda did. Lunchtime has become pretty special time for me. I want to look great when I come here." I ran my card over the reader to gain access to the parking lot. As the gate lifted, we both waved a "queen's wave" to Jorge.

"Gosh, do you think Stratton is *ever* going to ask you out?"

"I think so. In fact, I think he was trying to the last few times we had lunch, but all three times someone came up and started talking to us when we were in the cafeteria, and then it was time to get back to work."

"Shall I run interference today? I could sit nearby, and then get up and bump into anyone who looks like they're heading for your table." She chuckled. "Anyone besides that creep Chip, that is. I'll leave it to Stratton to defend you from him. I don't want his cooties to touch me."

"Cooties?" I was laughing as I pulled up under the last liquidambar along the guardrail next to the wall in the lower parking lot and switched off the ignition. As always, it was within the three or four spots of where we usually parked. The sound of my car motor was replaced by loud rushing water.

"Boy!" I opened the car door. The roar increased. "That's really noisy today. It rained harder last night than it ever has since I started working here. Does it always get like this in the ditch below the wall?"

"Yeah." Christine got out, opened her umbrella, and came around for me as I slipped into my black trench coat that I yanked from the backseat. We were protected from the drizzle that was either the end of the last storm or the beginning of the next one in the meteorologists' forecasts. Rather than head directly for the Lab entrance, we moved together toward the front of the car, drawn to the edge of the wall. We stood there momentarily mesmerized by the furious fizz and spray. It roared from around the base of the Lab and broke over a large rock in the gully, about fifteen feet up the ditch from where we stood. The boulder had probably slowly made its way down from the mountain in various storms throughout the life of the manmade channel. I didn't remember seeing it my first day at the Lab when I stopped in amazement to study the ditch and its engineering. The water foamed and twisted in resistance as it found its way around the rock. The force on the back side caused water to break free above the rock to create a lacy gossamer streak that settled back into the main torrent. It gurgled and hissed its way down to the mouth of the tunnel below us. "Sometimes it comes down the hill so forcefully that it overflows the gully. I wouldn't want to be caught in that rush on a day like this. Last year, I saw a large branch headed downhill, so I stayed to watch it. That branch was traveling so fast, that when it hit that corrugated steel tunnel, it made a dent." She pulled my arm gently to turn me to align our vision and pointed. "See! See where the metal tunnel is crooked on the right side?"

Indeed, there was a large dent in the steel. "So powerful! The water seems to be pretty close to the top of the gully. If that next storm comes in as they're predicting, I bet there'll be a waterfall." I looked out at the swaying trees in the canyon. "It would be beautiful to see a wall of water spilling over into the canyon, but without a helicopter, it's unlikely anyone will ever see such a sight." A strong shiver shook my shoulders and caused me to bump into Christine as we huddled closely under her umbrella.

"Oh, I'm sorry. You're cold. Let's get inside." She hooked her arm through mine. She probably had no idea how endearing her gesture of companionship was to me. I'm sure she had often traveled in umbrella sync with her mother or sister. We picked up the pace and took the elevator to the first floor rather than try to fight the wind up the stairs to our cell phone lockers. On days like this, it would be nice to be in the lower locker bank. We got off at the first floor to venture out through the vapor lock to put our cell phones in their lockers, then stopped at the Peet's cart before heading up the escalator. I kept shivering until I wrapped my free hand around the warm cup.

Late morning, I headed to Kirin's desk to deliver SecurID cards for a couple of new employees. She was orchestrating an orientation day for them on behalf of Jack Robertson. Her cubicle was a little different than most. Because she was Jack's admin support, she only had three walls. Instead of a fourth wall with a little door to close it off, her large desk, facing the aisle, was the fourth barrier. She sat behind this desk to easily greet and filter visitors before they reached Jack's corner office across the aisle. She was a gracious and lovely gatekeeper. There was an opening to the right of her desk for entrance. She had a mirror above the smaller desk at the back wall of her cube.

"Wow! Hi, Meg. You look so sophisticated dressed in all black."

"Hi, Kirin. Thanks." I handed her the envelopes that contained the little key chain tokens with tiny LED screens. "This one is for Smith; this one for Rogan. Have them call me when they're ready to choose a PIN so I can synchronize it with each token's cycling passcode."

As my hand extended across her desk, I saw the reflection of a man who had approached behind me. He had a dark face and was bald on the top of his head. He utterly disregarded protocol and went directly through the opening at the side of Kirin's desk. She rose immediately to embrace him, saying enthusiastically, "Appa! I knew you were coming sometime soon, but I didn't know it was today. I thought you would wait and fly out with Francis!"

As soon as he spoke, I heard a buzzing in my memory, like a hummingbird fluttering, buzzing my head and calling *tick, tick, tick* to her friends to help me remember. The buzz came to life as soon as I heard his voice. I remembered him. He had visited my grama's house the day Laura died—the man in white. He said cheerfully through their hug, "My beautiful daughter."

Kirin turned politely to me. "Appa, this is Meg Randallman. She's been working here for what, Meg, two months or so?"

He extended his hand and turned to face me. "How do you do, Miss Randallman?" His accent sounded British, like Kirin's. When he looked at me, he was direct and polite. I don't think he recognized me.

I took his hand. "I'm good. It's so nice to meet you. Meg, please." I knew I was staring. Totally lacking poise, I said randomly, "Er, actually almost three months now." I took a breath in an attempt to regain my composure. "How do you do, Kirin's Father? Is your last name also Puri?"

"I'm fine, thank you for asking. And yes, it is Puri, but please call me Ajeet." When he released my hand, I thought he may have taken an extra moment to study my face.

"Thank you, Ajeet." I felt flustered and was quite sure it was evident. "I-I'll leave you to your reunion. I need to get back to my desk." I was gone before they had a chance to agree or invite me to stay.

I sat down in front of my monitor and listened to voices in my head telling me that I should go ask him if he remembered that day. He would know where I was from. I took in a huge breath and then let it out. It was possible, even after seventeen years, that he would still know Daddy. He might know if my grama and grampa were still alive, and if they remembered me. He would know about the accident. He would think I shot Laura.

I bowed my head and cradled my forehead in my hands. I felt my temples throbbing into my fingertips. *Now what, Meg Randallman? Here is your chance to find out all you want to know, but do you really want the answers to all your questions? Are you willing to pay the inevitable price? Everyone around you will find out too.* A "plink" from my laptop caused me to jump as it interrupted my muddled self-doubt and recrimination. It announced that a new inner-office chat message had arrived. I looked up to see the label: Stratton Davis.

SD: Hi, Meg. Lunch?

MR: Sure. Cafeteria?

SD: Looks like it cleared up and the wind has dried the tables and benches. I don't even think it's cold. It was a warm rain. Want to get some fresh air?

MR: Yes please. Just what I need.

SD: Hard day so far?

MR: You have no idea. See you in 15, north corner?

SD: Yep.

I got to "our" table before him and set down my lunch bag, then I was sucked to the wall to watch the water. I was kinda like the alien spaceship in *Independence Day* that pulled Will Smith and Jeff Goldblum to the alien mother ship. I couldn't help myself. The weather had indeed warmed up. The sunshine bit into the black of my new sweater. I pushed up the sleeves to welcome Vitamin D onto the skin of my forearms.

"Oh!" I was startled. My heart jumped, reacting to the shock. Someone was walking their fingers up my back.

"Chip!" I said angrily, "You startled me!" He was uncomfortably close. His presence felt highly offensive within my personal space, and I wanted to say, "Eew!" because he touched me in such a familiar way. I backed into the hedge of privets. "Ow! Ow!" I thought I saw a micron of joy in Chip's eyes as he recognized I was in pain.

"What's wrong, sweetie?"

With my right hand, I swatted a spider that had run down the left arm of my sweater after biting me twice on the neck. I got it just as it took a third bite out of my left forearm. "Ow!" The carcass fell from between my hand and arm and landed on the top of the wall with its hairy legs curled into its furry body. I ripped a leaf off of the privet and used it to turn over the remains. The pungent spicy aroma of the privet leaf whiffed by my nose in the wind. Chip was uncomfortably close; studying my tiny nemesis. I felt the larger threat was the human.

I said angrily, "Could you back up please? You are too close, and it was totally inappropriate for you to touch me in that manner!"

Putting his hands up as if in innocent defense and moving only a few inches away, he said patronizingly, "OK, are you OK? Do you know anything about spiders? Do you think it's poisonous?" Again I saw a tensing of the muscles in his jaw and a gleam in his eye that was scarier than the spider bites.

It wasn't a large spider—only about a half an inch in diameter. The legs and underside were deep black. The design on its back was a black background with three tiny yellow diamonds. I rubbed the small red mark on my arm. "Gosh, it stings." I was rubbing the back of my neck as Stratton arrived.

"What stings?"

When Chip saw Stratton, he finally stepped far enough away from me that, for the first time in this encounter, I didn't feel uncomfortable. "Hello. Who are you? Are you a doctor?"

Stratton smiled confidently and mischievously. It was a look I had seen before and was beginning to admire greatly. "Yes, actually I am a doctor, but not a medical doctor. Stratton Davis. Who are you?" I noticed that the normally perfectly mannered gentleman did not extend his hand. He was a quiet but strong force to be reckoned with.

"Chip Swain." He puffed up his chest a bit and gave a standing swagger by slightly rocking side to side in place. "I met Meg at Peet's Coffee before she came to work here." Then arrogantly with a wink to me he said, "I'd like to think I'm one of the reasons she did."

I scowled at him. "Hardly."

Stratton was not fooled. I was, in fact, sure that he had correctly assessed the situation and was quite aware that Chip was annoying and unwelcome. He turned his head slightly toward me and smiled. "Well, Chip Swain, will you excuse us please? Meg and I have something important to talk about during our lunch date, and I want to determine what kind of first aid she may need from this dastardly bug." He turned his attention to the spider, rolling it over with the privet leaf that I had left beside the body. He gently took my hand in his and lifted my arm closer for examination.

I could see Chip behind him befuddled. He took an exaggerated, and probably exasperated, breath as if he was going to say something else, but there were no words—just a semi-silent fit of temper. He stood there for a few seconds, then strutted away with his usual arrogant march that seemed to indicate he was protecting his manly parts from the inside of his own thighs.

"Two more bites on the back of my neck too." Then in a whisper I said, "He's gone. Well done. He gives me the creeps. In fact, he startled me into the bushes by walking his fingers up my back. He has no sense of propriety."

"Lemme see your neck." I sat down, leaned my head forward, and pulled up my hair. "I see where you were bitten. I can tell which one was first and second. The first is a little more swollen than the second, and the second is a little redder than the one on your arm." I think she was running out of venom as she went."

"She? Do you think it's a black widow?"

"No. I just said *she* because of the widow's reputation." He popped the top off one of two iced coffees that he had set on our table. Even in my mini crisis I wasn't so distracted that I failed to notice his thoughtfulness to bring one for me. No doubt that's why it took him longer to get out to the terrace.

He scooped out an ice cube with a napkin and handed it to me. "Here, put this on the one on your arm." He scooped again with another napkin, gently pulled my hair to the side after I had let it go, and pressed the ice against the other two bites. "Too cold?"

"No. It's OK. Thank you. It helps. They're all stinging. Do you know what kind of spider that is?"

"I think it's just a plant spider. They normally live in bushes and eat bugs—unless a beautiful, tasty brunette happens to startle them into a more massive adventurous meal." I could tell from the movement of his shadow that he looked over to the ledge where the fuzzy body lay. "That'll teach her!"

I laughed. "Hard lesson, death." I blushed and smiled to myself. *He thinks I'm beautiful.* "The laughter helps too, and thank you for the compliment." The ice was melting and beginning to run down my back. "I think that's enough for now. We should probably eat."

"Great idea. I'm starving!"

We pulled out sandwiches and unwrapped them. The sound of the waterway echoed over the wall. "So noisy. It's like having a picnic by a rushing river." I set a baggie of cut vegetables in the middle of the table to share.

"Oh thanks, don't mind if I do. I like it," Stratton said simply. "The force of water reminds me how puny I am. The weather, fire, earthquakes—we have so little control over this world that we treat so superciliously." He finished his philosophy statement with a phrase that surprised and delighted me. "We are no match for the power of God."

"It's true. We conquer others, harness technology, redesign genetics, but if God withholds rain, we will not be harvesting our genetically engineered crops." I hadn't forgotten my encounter with Kirin's father. I felt a tug to unload everything, but I didn't know where to start, so I started instead with office gossip. "Did you hear that Francis Taylor is coming to visit the Lab? It seems like there is a pall of fear. Like everyone here has a deep reverence for her."

"Her? Francis is a guy."

"Really? So it's one of those names like Pat, Carol, Kelly, or Adrian. I was so surprised to meet Carol Blankenship on the third floor and find out he was a man." I sipped my iced coffee. "Francis is Tom Selleck's character's name on the TV show *Blue Bloods*."

He laughed. "There you go again talking about a TV show."

"I can't help it. My television is my most valued companion besides my parakeet."

"Oh yeah! I remember you used to have your bird ride with you to and from Stanford." Then mischievously he added, "People used to talk about you, you know?"

"I'm sure they did. People always talk about each other, especially when someone is weird." I could feel the color rising in my cheeks. I could also feel the prickling of the spider bites.

"Not weird, but certainly out of the ordinary. In fact, I would say extraordinary." His expression was perceptibly admiration. I blushed and felt that strange twinge deep in my abdomen that I had only felt around Stratton.

"But you're right about the reverence for Director Taylor. The last time he was here was when Brenda was murdered." He thoughtfully studied the carrot stick in his hand. "He was supposed to leave and go back to New Mexico the day after the murder, but he stayed until everyone at the Lab that knew her had been interviewed. He did a little pre-investigating for the police. Set the police up with appointments in an informal interrogation area in that first floor conference room that doesn't require top-secret clearance." He bit off a piece of carrot and chewed it. "He made sure that anyone who knew Brenda told the detectives anything and everything they knew about her. Some people didn't like it, and they didn't like him for ferreting them out." He took a bite of his sandwich, then studied the people who had ventured into the plaza to catch the far-too-rare sunshine of late. "Some of us found it cathartic to talk about her."

"Like you?"

"Yeah me. And Princess David. He really took it hard. I think it comes with being such a big guy. He's really kind and tenderhearted. He's probably been trying really hard not to accidentally hurt people all his life. Hey. Are you OK? You look a little peaked. Maybe you should go home early."

"Naw. I need to give Christine a ride, and I'll be fine. I-I actually would love to talk to you about something, but there's no time, and I'm afraid I may not stay emotionally stable enough to tell you here."

He looked up to the left. I followed his gaze. There were huge puffy white clouds drifting in an easterly direction. Even above the tumultuous water noise I could hear him inhale. On the exhale he turned to face me and said quickly, "Would you have dinner with me on Friday night?"

I smiled and nodded an enthusiastic yes, successfully restraining a giggle of delight.

Christine and I both needed to stay late. The predicted storm that was crashing down on us had actually subsided since it unloaded its worst. It was the remnant of Typhoon Mellor that had hit the Philippines two and a half weeks before, causing flooding and destruction there. It killed at least two hundred people, but more were still missing and would probably never be found, buried under mud or washed out to sea. The force of the storm had diminished greatly by the time it moved inland into California from the Pacific, but it was still dumping a lot of water. The wind shook the large windows, and it felt like the building was rocking slightly on its earthquake rollers. Fistfuls of rain pelted the windows as if a crowd of people were taking turns throwing pebbles.

"Are you about done?" Christine had her coat on, her laptop case over her shoulder, her handbag strap on top of that, and umbrella in hand.

"Not quite, Mary Poppins, but close. Are you taking your laptop home?" I pointed to the straps across her body.

"No. I just have some personal stuff I want to take home, and I don't want it to get wet." She turned and peered out the window above her cube. There was a small sliver of daylight. The clouds above the break were fighting the darkness. They burst to brilliant purple streaked with crimson as they were struck from below the mountain by the now-invisible sun. The gap was closing. The darkness was winning.

My hand went instinctively to the back of my neck, but I resisted the urge to scratch. I was afraid I would tear my skin away and then would have a bloody mess to go with the unbearable itch.

"Mary Poppins?" She laughed as she held the umbrella up. "Yeah, I know. I'm just taking it home too. I own four, and I have all four of them here. I wasn't planning on flying into the canyon tonight." I had opened the bottom left drawer of my desk, where I kept my handbag. I reached down into it, then tossed her my keys. Her eyes popped wide as she caught them. "So I can drive your Beemer?" She looked down at the keys in her hand and dimpled a grin.

"You can drive all the way home if you want to. If you do, though, I promise to let you drive on a good day too. By the look on your face, I think this might be something you've wanted to do for a while." She nodded, dimpled again, and looked down at keys. "Do you mind picking me up near the front door? I'll only be a few minutes more. Just about the right amount of time for you to trek down to the lower lot, get totally soaked, and drive up to the upper level." I returned a grin. I regretted that I had never thought to ask her before if she wanted to drive.

"Sure. No problem."

I jetted out to the cell phone lockers for my phone. The wind wrapped my black trench coat around my calves and nearly tripped me. I ran back to the vapor lock with cell phone in hand and stood waiting in its shelter. After about fifteen minutes there was no sign of my car and Christine. No call. No text. The storm was so ferocious that I decided to backtrack to the elevator and save myself from a short portion of the tumultuous, whipping rain.

I could see the taillights of my car from the breezeway. There was also a long trail of taillights heading out of the parking area, but none of the people that were leaving had been parked as far south next to the rail as I had that morning. Otherwise someone would have seen Christine lying under the open door of the driver's side in a pool of bloodstained water.

CHAPTER FOURTEEN

911

I startled myself with an involuntary scream. I called 911 as I ran. I reached Christine long before there was an answer. I sat down in the puddle, leaned over Christine to shield her from the rain, and felt for breath. *Oh, thank you, God. She is still alive.* My heart was pounding so hard, I thought it was going to break my chest. I waited for no less than twenty rings, gasping for breath between sobs. I plugged my Bluetooth into my ear so I could have my hands free to lift her out of the puddle of water. When 911 finally answered, I was connected with the California Highway Patrol. I was hysterically crying, "Help! Please! My friend has fallen and hit her head. She's lying here in the rain next to my car in the DPMC parking lot. Yes. Pleasant Valley!" They patched me through to a local 911 operator, who assured me paramedics and an ambulance were on the way. They asked me to stay on the line and feel the artery in Christine's neck.

"Christine, dear sweet girl. You're alive. Can you hear me? It's Meg. Help is on the way." I was relieved to feel a pulse, but alarmed that she was so still.

I looked around to see if anyone was around to help and realized then, that Christine probably didn't just trip and fall. She may have been attacked and the attacker may still be nearby. I told the 911 operator, "Yes. I'll stay on the line. Can you call the security guards at DPMC Research and see if you can get someone here to help me before the ambulance arrives? Tell them we're in the southeast corner of the lower parking lot." They could. I tried to still my sickening heartbeats.

I didn't know if I should move her, but I thought it would be OK. The only injury seemed on the back of her head. Her beautiful black hair was spread out in the bloody water. I tenderly opened the wet fingers of her right hand to remove my car keys. I pushed the remote button to open the trunk. "Christine, I'm just going to the trunk, I'll be right back."

The rain pelted into the trunk as I retrieved two towels, a roll of paper towels, and a small blanket. I thanked God for Ben teaching me emergency preparedness, and then as long as I had audience with God, I prayed for Christine, asking that He do the real praying because I didn't know what to say or what to ask for. *Please, God. I can't lose another sister.*

I sat back down next to her, put one of the towels on my lap. I gently lifted the top half of her body, and slid myself beneath it. I wrapped the blanket around her. Then I took a wad of the paper towels, threw the rest of the roll into the open car door, and carefully placed a wad beneath her head. I took the second towel and put it over both of us like a tent. All my spider bites itched.

It was only a few more minutes before handsome Jorge was there. I brushed a lock of hair back at Christine's temple and told her, "Christine. Jorge is here to help us."

He exclaimed, "Oh my God! What happened?"

"She's fallen and hit her head. She has a huge bump on the back of her head and it's bleeding a lot."

He pushed the driver's side bucket seat forward and lifted Christine off my lap. He set her gently on the backseat of my car—blanket, towel, paper towel, and all. I stood behind him very wet, trembling with cold and fear. Isn't it strange what can go through your mind in an emergency? I missed the warmth of her body when it was removed from me, and I was thinking, *She's warm. She cannot be dead.*

Of course that was not necessarily true, but thank God, it turned out to be. Three rescue workers—two men and a woman—arrived in an ambulance shortly after Christine was settled in the backseat of my car, so once again she was temporarily out in the rain as she was safely strapped to a gurney and loaded into the van.

The driver ran to his position. The other man started working on Christine in the van. The woman came to me and said, "Are you OK?"

I was still shivering, and my teeth were chattering so that my reply came out in broken syllables, "I-I'm f-fine." With a gesture indicating the shiny stickiness dripping down the entire front of my coat, I said, "This blood is hers." Jorge was valiantly fighting an umbrella and trying to protect me, but the storm was winning.

"She's your friend?"

I nodded. Even my nod seemed to shiver.

"What's her name?"

"Christine Channing."

"Do you want to ride with her?"

"N-no." I was furious with my body for shaking and causing me to stutter and for the fact that above all the other physical discomfort the spider bites continued their torment. "I w-will f-follow you in my car. Can we check to see if her cell phone is on her? I think it will be-be in-in her b-b-bra. Maybe you should get it instead of him?" We both released some nervous laughter.

Indeed, the cell phone was next to her heart with the detective's business card. The paramedic pulled out both and was reading the business card as she walked back.

"I'll take that too, please." She handed me the phone and the card. I lifted the phone and faced it toward her. "I'll look for her ICE numbers and her parents and sister on this, a-and then-n I'll call him." I held up the business card. "This detective will want to know about this. I doubt she just slipped. I think she may have been p-pushed." I took a deep breath. "John Muir?"

"Yes. John Muir. It's not the closest, but it's the best for head trauma. You need to get warm." She nodded to Jorge as if to give him permission to take me away. "You're probably in shock."

She turned to step up into the ambulance. I said, "W-wait! What's your name?"

"Emily."

"Thank you, Emily. Th-thank you for taking care of Christine." My throat closed in a gulp, and tears filled my eyes.

"You're welcome." She touched the top of my arm. "I'm just doing my job." She tilted her head toward the gaping doors of the ambulance. "Drew and I will do everything we can for her on the way."

Jorge nodded his own gratitude to Emily, abandoned the umbrella battle, and put his arm around me to escort me to my car. He put the driver's seat back into position and held my arm to steady me as I got in. "Thank you, Jorge." The tears were full-on now.

"Hey. She is in good hands." He tucked my long soaking-wet coat into the car. "Try to calm down before you drive. Start your engine and turn on your seat warmer before you make those phone calls. I'm going to close this door now so you can get warm."

"W-wait! What about you?" I looked around to see what vehicle he had arrived in. Since there wasn't one, I supposed that someone else had given him a ride over "Get in. I'll drive you back to the gate." I pointed to the shotgun seat. "I'll warm that seat too." I smiled and tapped the seat.

He flashed that dazzling smile. I think he was considering declining to let me get on with the tasks at hand, but then he said, "Thanks."

After he closed my door, I pulled the rearview mirror down and was appalled by the mascara dripping down my face. I reached between the bucket seats into the back and tore one of the paper towels off the roll. The outer towel was damp, so it wasn't ridiculously scratchy on my face. I was able to remove most of the black streaks by the time Jorge was buckled in. I looked at the streaked paper towel in my hand and considered getting a dry one to scratch the bite on the back of my neck.

He exclaimed loudly over the rain, "You look fierce! All dressed in black and determined."

I laughed. It helped subside my tears. "Yes. Annoyed is more like it. Through all this you would expect that I wouldn't feel the burning itch of three spider bites I got earlier today, but they are so irritating. That's why I'm frowning."

"Ah. Determined not to scratch."

"Exactly." Then less fiercely I said, "Thank you for coming to our rescue."

He said simply, "We will see how much help anyone can give her. Do you mind calling me once you hear more? If you have time and remember, of course."

"Oh sure." I pulled my iPhone out of my bra and handed it to him. "Put your number in here for me."

He grinned. "Nice and warm. What is it with you and Christine and your intimate phones?"

I returned the smile, "She started it. I find it to be a very convenient pocket actually."

"You don't have this fragile instrument in a case."

"Funny you should mention it. I ordered a Lifeproof cover a couple of days ago from Amazon. It's probably waiting for me at home. After I put it on the phone, it should be safe even underwater. It probably won't be quite as comfortable in my left breast pocket though." I spun through Christine's contact list on her phone as Jorge typed his name and number into mine. I was warmer and calmed enough to drive Jorge back to the gate.

—◦◦◦—

I went directly to the John Muir Hospital emergency waiting room. Christine's mother, father, and sister had already arrived. I recognized them instantly. Christine's sister looked much like her, and they both looked a lot like their father, but there were traces of the mother's characteristics evident in both girls. Their father was pacing back and forth between the chair where his wife was seated and the window. I contemplated the completeness of their family and prayed that it would remain so. I walked up to them just as Mr. Channing returned from one of his short walks. I was unsure of what to say, but they made it easy for me.

Christine's sister had dark circles under her watery eyes. She asked, "Are you Meg?"

"Yes. You must be Julie." I put out my hand, but she shook her head and wrapped her arms around me and held me tightly. I melted into her embrace and hugged her back. We were both shaking. I pulled a Kleenex out of my coat pocket and wiped my eyes, nose, and hand before looking up to the parents, I put out my hand. "And I don't know your names."

"I'm Bert, Christine's dad." He extended his hand. "This is Carol." She reached out and placed her hand on top of our handshake and gently squeezed my wrist. They were both pale.

"Thank you for calling us right away. We got here at the same time as the ambulance." Carol's eyes were rimmed with red and she was shaking but spoke calmly. "They let us see her before they wheeled her in there." She pointed to a set of double doors. "She was awake and she recognized us. She waved to us as the doors were closing."

"Do you know what happened?" Bert asked. He was a big, rugged-looking man with strong shoulders. Creases around his eyes and mouth indicated he smiled often, but he was not smiling now.

"No. I don't. I wasn't ready to leave, so she took my keys. She was going to pick me up close to the building so only one of us would have to be out in the storm." All three were nodding, acknowledging Christine's sacrificial kindness. "When she didn't come for me, I went to the parking lot and found her unconscious. I'm so glad to hear that she was awake. She had a nasty bump to the back of her head and—"

We were interrupted by a call from the desk.

"Mr. or Mrs. Channing, please?"

Carol was slight and dark. She was not remarkable except for a pair of beautiful blue-green eyes. They were long lidded and banked by only slight traces of crow's feet, indicating meticulous attention to eye cream and skin care. She was dressed in a cream silk blouse and high quality gabardine black slacks. Her lovely pearls made me think that I'd caught them on their way out for the evening.

She said to me, "Do you know what kind of health insurance Christine has? She hasn't been on ours since she started working. Is there only one choice at the Lab?"

"There's a confusing smorgasbord of choices, but, here." I had two handbags clutched tightly under my left arm. I pulled Christine's bag from beneath mine and handed it to her. "Her insurance card is probably in here. She apparently tossed the bag in behind the backseat before she—fell. I didn't find her laptop case though and I distinctly remember that she had it. I didn't see anyone, but I think she was attacked."

"Attacked!" Bert was angry. "Why would someone attack her? What about Lab Security? Weren't there security cameras? They took her laptop?"

"Just the case, but they'd have thought it was her laptop. She had it laden with a heavy binder."

"Oh honey!" Carol put her head against Bert's chest and wrapped her free arm around him."

He put both his around her shaking body, and said, "I better go to the desk."

Carol backed up from him to use her shaking hands to pull out Christine's wallet and found the card. She handed it to Bert, then handed him the wallet and said somewhat hysterically, "Here. Take this too. They may need other information from her driver's license or something."

He took the wallet, and then reached for her empty hand to give it a squeeze. He looked her in the eye and nodded, and then turned to take both the insurance card and the wallet into a semi-enclosed desk.

I said, "I wonder what they do when people come in without their identification or they don't have a wonderful family like you."

"Or don't have a wonderful friend like you," Julie said generously.

It was a long wait. Bert and Carol were sitting in chairs against a wall. Bert's hand rested on top of Carol's, which was resting on the armrest between them. Carol's free hand was clutching her handbag so tightly, it looked like there was no blood in her fingers. Julie and I were almost directly across from them. I could hear her breathing deeply. There was a baby wailing in the far corner of the room. His mother was rocking, then walking, then bouncing him, but nothing seemed to make him happy. In the chairs that were back-to-back to Julie's and mine, I heard one conversation going on in what I think was Hindi. A few other people around us were speaking Spanish. A young man sitting next to me had his hand wrapped in a blood-soaked white washcloth. I asked him curiously, "Is everything still in one piece in there?"

"Yeah." He started to unwrap it.

"Oh no!" I lifted my right hand in protest. "Please don't disturb your bandage."

145

He stopped. "Maybe if I had chopped off my whole finger instead of just slicing it, I wouldn't have had to sit here so long." He grinned. "It's really busy. All the admission windows have been full since I arrived."

I kept thinking someone would come out to tell us how Christine was doing. I was also thinking, *once again*. *This is my fault. An attacker would have thought she was me.* I finally stepped outside to call Detective Gorsky. No answer. So I rambled haphazardly, leaving a long, no doubt, incoherent, message on his voice mail. I told him we worked at the Lab, that Christine had slipped in the parking lot and that she hit her head hard when she fell. I told him I didn't see anyone, but I'm pretty sure she didn't fall all by herself, she was attacked, and that she had contacted him after Brenda Arthur was murdered, and how it was raining so horribly and she hadn't come back to pick me up. In between repeating my name and phone number at least three times, unnecessarily, I reminded him of Christine's last name and told him she was at John Muir and so was I.

When I finally hung up on the poor guy's voice-mail box, I placed another call to Ben to see if he had left for home. The rain had stopped, but the hospital sidewalks and parking pavements were still covered with a layer of water, and all depressions in the shiny asphalt were pooled with puddles that splashed when the cars drove through them. The wind whipped my trench coat open. I wrapped it tightly around me and realized that my efforts to wipe off Christine's blood with a paper towel, were not sufficient. It would need to go to the cleaners. I was grateful to have a spare trench coat in my closet. I heard Ben answer.

As I started to tell him what happened, I suddenly felt tired and weak. My emotions were flat, as was my voice. I asked him to go up to my rooms to make sure Einstein had fresh water and plenty of birdseed, and to then cover him. I also asked him to tell

Margaret that my friend Christine was in the hospital. I doubted if George and Norma would even notice that I didn't come home.

"And, Ben? Do you mind feeding Midnight? I usually give him half a can of wet food on top of a big scoop of dry. There's a covered half can in the refrigerator. The cup I use is in the dog food in a covered plastic garbage can on the pantry floor. He'll need clean water too."

"Are you OK, little lady? Your voice. It's not like you. Do you need me to come get you?"

"Oh, Ben," I gulped in a little air and then swallowed. "I don't know what's wrong with me. This is not about me, but I'm feeling so alone, so lonely. And I love my friend, Christine, like a sister. I'm so worried about her. I see Christine's family, and wish I had a mom like hers, and a sister. And I wish I still had my daddy." There were no tears left to cry that day, but I felt the strain in my throat and sinus cavities. "No. I'll be OK. I'm feeling a bit woozy. This crisis seems to have just hit me physically in a new way. I feel like I accelerated faster and faster, and then hit a concrete wall. I'm wiped out. I'll get some water and maybe even some food before I head home. I'm not sure when that will be, but I'll make sure I'm safe to drive. In fact, I promise to call you if I am not totally confident of my driving ability, OK?"

"OK. I'll accept your promise. Remember it please. Even if it's very late and you don't think you should call me, please call me."

I gulped back the tearless emotion. "Thank you. I can always count on you. Thank you for taking care of Einstein and Midnight." I rambled on unnecessarily in gratitude, "Einstein will probably say 'ni nite' when you cover his cage, and Midnight will manage to whack you with his out-of-control tail."

I went back in to join the watchful family waiting for the doctor. A guy came up to the Channings and sat down in the empty chair next to Carol. He was the kind of guy you wouldn't probably notice unless he did something to make himself known.

He wore shades of taupe and brown. His hair was neatly cut and combed in a somewhat old-fashioned style. He reminded me of Sheldon on the *Big Bang Theory* sans the Flash T shirt. He was way shorter and more nondescript than Sheldon, but he sported the same hairstyle, and he was obviously a nerd. His toffee brown eyes were surrounded by short, thick lashes. He had full, youthful lips.

He cleared his throat and said, "Hi, Mr. and Mrs. Channing." He nodded across the aisle to Julie and then to me. "How is she?" He reached back to rub his neck as if it were stiff.

"Hi, Jake." Carol seemed surprised to see him. "We don't know a lot yet. How did you know we were here?"

"My cousin, Tim, works at the Lab at the security desk. He called me as soon as he heard it was Christine." The skin around his mouth and eyes were tight with strain. The tension that stretched between all of us expanded like a big rubber band to enclose him into our vigil of worry.

"Jake," said Bert, "This is Meg Randallman. Meg works with Christine. She found her and called emergency services."

Jake nodded to acknowledge me again and then said, "Thanks." He studied my face a bit longer than I thought would be normal. I sensed he recognized me. "Thanks for saving her life." I saw the worry in his eyes that said he wasn't sure that Christine's life had been spared, and he regretted what he had said.

"Hi," I said lamely. "Her mom said she was awake when they took her into surgery. That's a good sign, don't you think?" My voice didn't sound like it was mine. I took a deep breath in an attempt to revive a bit.

Jake nodded in agreement, then started a low conversation with Carol and Bert. Julie leaned to the left to be close to my ear and said, "He's in love with her. Always has been."

"Really?" I whispered back.

"Yeah. His family lives on our street, just a few houses down. For years, my dad called him her puppy dog, but neither Jake

148

nor Christine knew that." She lowered her voice even more. "Christine is totally clueless, and Jake has always been too shy to give her any reason to notice. Whoa! There is a really, really red bump on the back of your neck!"

"I know. Actually two." I moved the sweater in the back to show the second bite. "Spider bites." I started to pull up my sleeve, but a doctor appeared at Bert's side. Bert rose to meet him. Then we all rose.

"Mr. and Mrs. Channing?" He looked awfully young to be a doctor. He was medium height. His skin was dark, as were his kind eyes that were surrounded by very thick, straight black lashes. He looked like he was from India, but his English was perfect and without accent, unless California has one. "Christine is stable," he said.

I know I was not alone feeling relieved. "We have her sedated. There is increased cranial pressure and a strong possibility of brain bleed."

Carol gasped in a short breath. I saw a flicker of worry cross Jake's face.

Bert said gruffly, "What does that mean? Is there anything you can do?"

"We will keep her sedated and in intensive care for twenty-four hours. Then we will give her what we call a 'sedation vacation' to monitor her behavior as she awakens. If she is, well, cranky." A smile touched his lips. "Unless she is always cranky? No? Then we will sedate her again for another couple of days. She will get a neuro consult tomorrow."

"Cranky?" Carol asked incredulously. "What do you mean cranky?"

"If she has a brain bleed, she will not be herself when she wakes." He paused. "I'm sure you would like to see her even though she is not awake?"

All of us said yes, including Jake. The doctor moved his eyes to take in each face in the group and glanced at the blood stain on the front of my coat. "I'm sorry—immediate family only, and only two at a time. Fifteen minutes maximum. Then, after you see her, because she is in Intensive Care and because she will stay asleep, I suggest that you all go home, get some rest, and return tomorrow." He looked directly at Carol, and then at Bert. "You are welcome to stay in the Intensive Care waiting room, but I think tonight, if you can get some sleep, it would be good. This is going to be a long vigil."

The doctor stood there for another few seconds compassionately searching first Carol's and then Bert's face. "Do you have any immediate questions?"

Carol shook her head. Bert took her hand. Julie took mine. The doctor bowed a gracious nod to each of us and then said, "Follow me. I'll show you where the ICU waiting room is." You can all wait there, even though only immediate family can go into her room.

CHAPTER FIFTEEN

The First Randallman Death

I got tangled up in my sleep. I woke up wrapped in my nightgown, surrounded tightly by my top sheet, and my arms and wrists were twisted in awkward positions. One hand was bent extremely backward, the other uncomfortably forward and into a fist. They tingled and ached. I was aware of a disturbing dream lurking at the edge of my mind. I was thirsty, my forehead was perspiring, and, of course, the wretched spider bites burned and itched. I reached into my subconscious and summoned up terror. A reverberation of rushing water pushed the rest of the dream away. I had no desire to return.

I rolled out to disengage the sheet and stood up to straighten my gown. On "his" side of the bed, Midnight lifted his head but put it back down on his paws when I lay back on my pillow and massaged the feeling back into my hands. I resisted the urge to scratch the bites. Through the slats in my bedroom blinds I could see that it was daylight, but the sky was still gray. Thankfully, though, the wind had calmed down, and at least for now it was not raining. The storm of last night had passed. Einstein chirped an inquiry from beneath his cage cover to remind me that as long as I was moving around and it was daylight, shouldn't I uncover the bird?

I was considering taking a personal day to go sit outside the ICU near sleeping Christine, when my phone chirped at me too. "Ms. Randallman? This is Detective Gorsky."

"Oh. Hi. Please call me Meg. I apologize for such a long voice mail message. I was a bit flustered—"

He interrupted me. "No problem. I understand. Will you be going to work today or to the hospital?"

"I was just asking myself that question and hadn't yet answered it."

"You're funny. Well, Director Taylor at the Lab has offered a conference room as an interview room for anyone who can meet with me, who may have seen something last night."

"So it would be more convenient for you if I went there."

"Yes."

"Sure. OK. I have some stuff I need to check on anyway. I'm in the Cyber Security division and—"

He interrupted again. "I know. You took Brenda Arthur's place."

"Yes. Actually, Christine told me. I'll see you later though. I'm going to take my time getting there. There are other things I need to take care of." I had no idea how prophetic that was.

I showered and dressed to the morning music of my wildly chirping parakeet. Midnight had gone downstairs to see who would let him out into the yard. Einstein found the other bird in the bathroom mirror and was ecstatically making love to it. I was dressed and ready to leave and about to put Einstein into his cage, when George tapped the door frame of my open door.

"Hullo? Meg?"

"Come in." I stood there foolishly with Einstein on my finger. My first thought was that he knew about Norma's tryst with Matt and came to tell me that he and she were through and I would be moving out soon. The thought of leaving My Lady and Hillhollow was deeply distressing. I could feel my blood beat in my ears. "What's up?" He was carrying a small Amazon box. "Would you like to sit down?" I motioned to the couch.

"Sure. That would be good." He sat at the far end of the couch closest to the door. He looked slimmer and balder than he had the day he helped Norma kidnap me from my daddy. George handed me the box as I sat down at the other end and said, "This was delivered to the gate last evening."

"Oh. I'm sure that's the industrial strength cover I ordered for my iPhone." I set it down on the coffee table. Einstein jumped to the top of the couch and waddled in a silly run most of the way, then flew to land on George's shoulder. He tilted his head to stare up at George's face with one eye.

"Might it be time for you to go poop?" Einstein flew to his playpen.

George said, "Pardon me?"

"I was talking to Einstein. He'll come back after he's done his duty."

George chuckled. "Isn't that the darndest thing? I didn't know parakeets were that smart."

"Uh, excuse me? His name is Einstein." At this point Einstein returned and settled comfortably on George's shoulder. "He's obviously pleased that we noticed he was such a smart birdie."

George laughed again. "Right. You are certainly the smartest birdie I've ever seen."

Einstein fluffed and started picking his feathers contentedly, scattering a mild dust of feather casings over George's dark-blue sweater. George turned his head to watch, but then—having done that many times—I knew he turned back because his neck and eyes began to hurt. "So, how are things? You haven't had any extra expenses lately." He smiled.

"Yeah." I grinned back, slid open the drawer at the center of the coffee table, and picked up a stack of unopened envelopes. "I have yet to cash any of my paychecks from the Lab." I acknowledged the amused look on his face. "Right. I'm not working for the money. I just knew it was time for me to start a life using the skills I've learned. It's rewarding."

"I know." He smiled. "I didn't have to work either, but I wanted to become an architect. I have left my designs all over the western United States. I'm not working for the money either."

I looked at him with a new sense of admiration. I thought how my anger and blame had most likely robbed me of knowing George, and kept me from accepting his support while I was growing up. I dropped the envelopes back into the drawer and said, "I finally filled out a form to have direct deposit from now on." I pulled a box cutter out of the same drawer and sliced the tape across the Amazon box.

I looked up from studying my plan of attack on the protective plastic casings around the phone case and sensed that the normally laidback George was stressed and anxious. He looked like he lacked sleep. He looked old. I decided it was not the right time to answer his "how are things?" question with a report about the dangers at the Lab. "I bet you didn't come up here just to deliver that package or talk to me about my allowance." I made the first slice through the plastic.

"Listen, Meg, I know you only met him once, at the wedding, but I wanted to tell you in person, rather than on your cell phone, the way we usually e-talk. My Uncle William died yesterday. He had a stroke."

I looked up from my free-the-phone-cover mission. "Oh, George. I'm so sorry."

"They got him to the hospital right away, but he didn't make it through the night."

George must have loved his uncle very much. I was sure that telling me was difficult. I didn't know what else to say so I repeated myself, "I'm so very sorry, George. Will you be leaving soon to go to his funeral?"

"Yes. I was just downstairs making the flight arrangements. Your mother and I will be flying out tomorrow morning. Would you like to go to Connecticut with us?" He looked sheepishly at me. "I'll understand if you'd prefer not to go."

I felt more compassion for George than I had all the years since he took us away from Daddy and brought us to his California mansion. Since the tryst, I saw him differently, duped, emotionally abused, and manipulated like the rest of Norma's train. As I hesitated in my answer, he may have thought I didn't want to go to Connecticut because of our shallow relationship, or because I didn't know Uncle William very well. The true reason for my hesitation was I felt I should stay close to Christine. I was a bit surprised to realize that I would have been pleased, at this difficult time, to support George. However, the thought of hanging out with Norma-the-adulteress, Norma-the-drama-junky, or Norma-the-phony pretending to be sorry Uncle William was dead and leaving them a boatload of money was unbearable. I toyed with the idea of going for the sole purpose of blackmailing her into being nice to George for a few days, but just as I was weighing the possibility, a question came to mind. "Will your mother be going?"

"No, I'm afraid she isn't feeling well. Mom has had a bad cold that's traveled into her sinuses and chest. She's on antibiotics. The doctor says she needs to rest."

"She didn't look well the last time I saw her. I had no idea she was that ill. If you don't mind, I'll stay home and spend some time with her. Maybe I can read to her and play piano for her." I quoted a Bible verse to him amazingly *not* from my cynical repertoire: "A merry heart is good like medicine."

I hesitated again. "Besides, there's a big deal going on at work. You may even hear something on the news. A girl was attacked last night in the parking lot. She's my best friend and she's in the hospital." Lack of sleep left me vulnerable to my emotions. I closed my eyes momentarily and gulped back the surge of tears. "I really am sorry, though, about your uncle William. I would have gone with you if I wasn't needed here for my friend, Christine and your mother. Really," I said sympathetically as I searched his face. "I would be happy to support you." I was finding my composure.

George's eyes watered up a bit. "Thank you. He and my mom are the last in my family of the previous generation." I heard him take a breath. Einstein tilted his head to the side as if he was studying George's face. "That's nice of you to check in on Mom. She treasures your visits. I know you've never warmed up to me— no, now don't protest—I'm aware that you prefer distance from me, but I'm glad you chose to befriend my mother. She always wanted a daughter, and well, when I brought Norma home, I don't think that she was what Mom had in mind." He winced.

I snickered. "Sorry." I really was sorry. Sorry for him and sorry that Norma had been so divisive. George practically had to sneak to see his mother if he wanted to keep peace in his marriage. A lot of good that approach accomplished! I knew this was a perfect segue in the conversation to mention Norma's character flaw and most recent indiscretion, but it wasn't the perfect time to break George's already aching heart. Not that I would be doing the breaking, I justified to myself. He definitely needed to know especially now that he would have an enormous inheritance he should carefully protect and keep in his own name.

Cowardly, I decided on a topic shift. "Did you invite Ray?"

"No. I talked to the center. They don't advise it." As he rose to go, Einstein flew to his playpen and bowed to drop another poop. George's eyes followed the flight. I saw a corner of his mouth indicate a smile. "He's quite remarkable."

"Thank you." I looked over at my little feathered friend. "He's a good companion." I stood there uncomfortably knowing I should initiate a hug. I stepped closer to George and wrapped my arms around him. I felt him tremble, and he put his arms around me too. "I really am sorry. I'll be praying for you as you travel."

He stepped back from our embrace with moist eyes, "That's . . . that's really great. Thank you." I reached down to the coffee table and handed him a box of tissues. He took a couple and with both hands wiped from the outside of his eyes to his nose, and discreetly wiped that too. "Well, good-bye now. Either I or your mother will text you our plans."

I pictured Norma oozing greed out of her pores as she packed. "Before I go into work, I'll stop in to see your mother, My Lady."

He was at the door. He turned and smiled. "She told me you call her that. Thank you for that too. Please text me if you see any change in her health."

"OK, will do. I think to cheer her up, I'll try to find a few of her favorite roses. Sometimes there are still some left in the garden after the weather changes."

"That would be very thoughtful. If you can't find any in the garden, I'd be happy to pay for a florist's bouquet." He sketched a wave before he turned to leave.

I looked down at the Lifeproof iPhone cover instructions and said out loud, "Right. I'm going to test this cover weighted down in a bowl of water overnight and watch a how-to video?" Einstein flew to my shoulder and looked thoughtfully on as I snapped open the cover, settled my phone into the top half, and snapped on the back. I bent my neck to look at Einstein. "Like I'm going to take it jet skiing, right?" I could tell he completely understood and concurred with my lazy path to just trust the case to be, well, lifeproof.

As I approached My Lady's back patio from the rear garden, the birds took off in random flight as usual. The bees were busy in the star jasmine. I couldn't blame them. The sweet aroma stirred up by the rain was intoxicating. I noticed that the house, which was usually bright and open, was shuttered and dark. I carried a small bouquet of hot-pink roses. Their fragrance rivaled the star jasmine.

I tapped gently on one of the large French doors. A woman I had never met opened it for me. She wore a light-green polo shirt, beige chino pants, and sensible well-cushioned shoes. Her name tag read "Denise Davis, R. N."

"Hi. I'm Meg, Margaret's friend. Is she well enough for a visitor?

"Yes. Of course. I'm Denise." She pointed to her name tag. She told me you might stop by." I sensed a hesitation.

"She must be seriously ill for her to need you here."

'Well . . . You see, I'm not at liberty to speak about her condition, but I know she wants to talk to you. She told me to wake her if you came, but she's awake."

"I understand. Where's Karen? She'll know where to find a vase for these."

She took them from my hand. "I'll take care of them for her. She's in her room in the back."

I thought it strange that Karen was not hovering over home and mistress. I continued on to My Lady's bedroom. I was not prepared for how she looked. Her lovely skin was waxy gray. Her normally perfectly coiffed hair was fluffy without style. Her eyes were closed, but she opened them when she sensed my presence and sent me her loving smile. My throat tightened. I blinked away the tears, I sat down on the chair next to her bed and took her bony hand in mine. Her beautiful ruby ring flopped to the inside of her fingers. I straightened it back to the top and fought with all possible restraint to keep from crying. *So much for my merry heart mission.*

"My dear, My Lady, you look so . . . so tired."

"Hello, my Meg. Yes. I'm very tired." Her voice was barely above a whisper. She coughed. "I'm dying."

"Dying! No! But you can't die. George is leaving for Connecticut." As if that logic settled it.

"Yes. I know. He doesn't know how poorly I'm doing. Karen and I have successfully thwarted his attempts to check in on me. I was waiting for a better time to tell him, but then William—" She broke off coughing again.

I was in complete denial. "But you only have an infection, and you're on antibiotics, and you're going to get well."

"No, my dear sweet girl. I had a biopsy. It's more than an infection. It's a recurrence of the cancer that put me in my wheelchair. I had a tumor on my spine many years ago. I had recently completed chemo and radiation before I met you at the wedding—how long ago?" Another cough. "Has it really been seventeen years? They thought when I passed the five-year mark cancer-free that it would not return, but it's back with a vengeance. It's metastasized. It's in my lungs and my pancreas. I'll still be here when George gets back from Connecticut, but probably not around much longer after that."

I lost it. I brought her hand to my cheek and found myself crying helplessly. After recovering slightly and with my free hand taking a couple of tissues out of the box by her bed, I apologized. "I came here to cheer you up, not do this! I love you, My Lady. I will miss you more than you can possibly know." I continued to hold her hand with my other hand.

"I know, sweetheart. I love you too." More coughing. "Be a dear and hand me that glass of water."

I released her hand so she could scoot up in her pile of pillows to a nearly sitting position. I held the glass and flexed the straw for her. She coughed again, sipped, and then visibly gained a formidable strength from somewhere within. It surprised me, cheered me, and settled my emotions. It reminded me of the dignity I saw in her the first day I met her. Once again, I felt as if I needed to straighten up and be nobler in her presence. "I have several important things to talk to you about. The first is about your father."

I had set down the water glass and flipped two more tissues from the Kleenex box. I stopped mopping up for the moment to look at her directly. "You mean George?"

"No. I mean your daddy, Franklin Taylor. The man you talked about every time you came to visit me the first few years." She smiled sympathetically.

I was stunned. Daddy. I remembered taking My Lady into my confidence, spilling out my resentment toward Norma and bitterness toward her son. Complacency is a subtle and powerful enemy. Surrounded by wealth and every creature comfort, I lost sight of the determination I had when I was four to run away from Norma, George, and California and return to my daddy. It was kind of like the way people become complacent about their love for God that gets *choked with cares, riches, and pleasures of life, and bring no fruit to maturity.* Out of habit, I still prayed for my daddy and grandparents every night, but now that I was old enough to actually search for them, I had never put any effort at all into the promise I made to myself as the Bentley carried us to Hillhollow. I hadn't even taken the opportunity presented to me when I recognized Kirin's father. I was like the proverbial frog in a tepid teapot, ignoring fire increasing beneath me without making a move to leave the warmth as it rises to a boil. "You know where he is?"

"Sort of. When I got the news that made me suspect I didn't have a lot of time left, I redirected Greg, a private investigator that Emerson hired for other matters, to look into your origin. You've met my attorney, Emerson?"

"Yes," I said simply, but I was intensely curious about the other matters. My face felt flush. I felt a bit dizzy as a plethora of thoughts collided with each other passing rapidly through my brain. I was glad to be sitting down. I had so little time left with this woman whom I loved so much. And could I really find Daddy? If I did, did he hate me because he thought I'd shot Laura? I wondered if the "other matters" were Norma's adultery, but that would only be one matter. Perhaps there were *other* other matters. Maybe even George knew about the adultery. Could George be so blinded by Norma's beauty or still be such a wimp that he could overlook her insulting behavior and continue to tolerate her?

She patiently waited for me to process my thoughts, then smiled knowingly. "When you have a lot at stake, it's good to have all the facts before you make major decisions."

"What's at stake?"

"Hillhollow belongs to me."

"Really? I see." I sat listening to the busy bees buzzing loudly through the screen of her partially open window. Very busy indeed. They sounded like they were on a mission, like My Lady the first day I met her. She was so strong that day. I remembered how she didn't back down from Norma's nonverbal challenge as I witnessed the clash of their wills. Norma took the Randallman name, but My Lady Margaret held the Randallman fortune.

My Lady began patiently and deliberately. "As I said, I have several important matters that I need to discuss with you. Let's start with your mother's divorce and the adoption of you and Ray. We cannot find any trace of a divorce."

"Really?"

"Really." She nodded, and then continued. "We have all three of your social security numbers from George's income tax records. Though it cannot be true, records indicate that none of you existed before 1998. Emerson thinks, since there are only three ways to legally obtain new social security numbers, and since your mother wasn't in a witness protection program and wasn't a victim of identity theft, that she must have convinced the court that she, you, and Ray were abused by your daddy."

"No! That cannot be true," I protested.

"I know, my dear. This is difficult for you to hear." She took a sip of water to calm a guttural cough. "I believe as you do, that this was her lie. Probably the same lie she told to my son."

"Oh! Right! That makes sense." I considered mild-mannered George falling for Norma's lie laced with persuasive seduction.

"Yes. His part in your mother's crime has never settled well with me. It finally makes a bit of sense—and is a bit of a relief to me—if she told him the same lie that she told a court to get new social security numbers." She took a raddled breath. "Since her former social security number would be protected under such circumstances, Greg was unable to find where you were before. You realize what that means, right?"

"Yes. Daddy would not be able to trace us either."

"Correct." She coughed and reached for a sip of water. "We found a death certificate that recorded a Franklin Taylor in Phoenix, Arizona. No wait, please." This in response to an involuntary gasp from me. "You told me it took you three days to drive from your former home to Hillhollow. Even carrying two small children, I doubt that George would have stayed two nights in a hotel coming from Phoenix. Greg could not find any other Franklin Taylors that were likely to be him. It does not help that we don't know if he was even close to the same age as your mother. He could have been much older, or possibly a bit younger."

I took a deep breath. "So, you think he's still alive?"

"I do. And I think he is still legally married to Norma."

I ran the data through my brain several times and then back through in a different path considering Daddy, George, Norma! "Oh my! Poor Daddy!"

She laughed and then started coughing, and then stifled the cough. "We can search in several other ways. I will provide the resources, but will leave the searching up to you." She stopped to cough again and pointed to the water glass. I assisted and the coughing subsided. "Let's go out into the sunshine. Please go get Denise and have her bring my wheelchair. I want to tell you the rest in the garden." I looked out her window, and indeed there was sunshine. The clouds had parted to give us the option to enjoy the patio.

Denise assisted Margaret into a cream silk robe, and then easily lifted her frail body from the bed and settled her into the wheelchair. After a shot of cough medicine, we turned the motor off and she was ready for me to wheel her through her lovely home and out through the French doors. Denise handed me a towel. I nodded a thank you. My Lady commented on how dark it was and asked Denise to open the drapes to let the sunshine in. Denise complied, apologizing that Karen had asked for darkness. She had a migraine and had retired to her room.

My Lady winced. "I see. Well, as long as she is resting, please let in the light."

At first I thought My Lady was in physical pain, and then I realized that the wince was because she knew that Karen's migraine was probably brought on by grief. *I will never be as selfless as she is.* She was apparently more concerned about how her illness would affect others than her own suffering.

Settled at the table where we last drank that delicious coffee, My Lady began with an orderly list of things she wanted me to know. She started with my daddy. "Unfortunately, he has a very common last name, and my guess is that his father's first name, your Grampa Red, was not really Red. That was probably a nickname," she said thoughtfully as her eyes gazed across her beautiful garden to the butterfly bush. "Before you leave, I will give you a folder with a few possible Franklin Taylors that Greg found information about. He will help you when you are ready to pursue your search.

"I am not the only one who engaged the services of Emerson and Greg, the private detective. Uncle William did also." She paused and searched my face, and took a somewhat gurgled breath. "I don't think there is any kind way to say this to you, but I have

163

to tell you." She paused again. "Your mother has been unfaithful to George."

"I know."

Her right eyebrow went up. "You know?"

"Yes. I came home early one day from college and heard noise in her bedroom. I saw Matt—you remember Matt?" She nodded. "He left in a hurry." My prolonged cowardice haunted me. It seemed so easy now to tell the truth. "I should have told George," I rolled my eyes. I was annoyed with myself.

"Well, I can see how that would be hard." She took a shallow breath and signaled that she would like some water. After I handed her some she continued. "Uncle William altered his will. He left almost everything to you."

I choked and coughed before I could say, "Me? But why me? Boy, is Norma going to be, er—" I searched for a better word, but used the first one that came to mind, "Pissed! I'm sorry. That's not a nice word."

She laughed and coughed. "No. It's not a nice word." She chuckled again. "But it's probably right on." She got serious again. Uncle William has no other heirs. When you turned twenty-one this year, he changed his will to include you on my recommendation. He is leaving a substantial amount to charities that are dear to him, and he is leaving a small amount, relatively speaking, to George, but he has had no respect for George since the day he met your mother at the wedding."

"Not Ray?"

"No. Not Ray. I have made some provisions for Ray in my will. Emerson will ensure that it will be carefully controlled so that he cannot use it to destroy himself." She paused to breathe a couple of times. I could hear soft gurgling in her chest. "George has several properties in Walnut Creek. He also has a substantial trust fund that is impossible for your mother to raid. The money from William will be protected too. Emerson and William's attorney have made sure of it." As she was talking, I probably I looked more dumbfounded to her than my questions indicated. "Besides, there is a strong possibility that she is a bigamist and not entitled to anything." She closed her eyes momentarily and focused on taking a shallow, even breath, then she continued, "George lived with a woman in Walnut Creek before he made his Southwest tour to oversee that hotel chain architecture—"

"Where he met Norma."

"Yes. Where he met Norma and then brought you here." She looked at me lovingly. "When I had my battle with cancer and my surgeries, he left the woman—her name was Kiwi—and moved back to Hillhollow. He designed and had this cottage built for me." She motioned with her left hand to wave as if it were a blessing on her beautiful home. "I wanted something smaller and needed one story."

"Kiwi? Really?"

She laughed, "Yes. Third-generation hippy culture. Her grandmother, a sixties flower child, named Kiwi's mother something like Flower, or Sky, or Blossom—I can't remember. Her mother in turn decided to name her daughter after a fruit."

"What happened to Kiwi?"

"She still lives in one of his homes. He let her remain after their relationship fizzled. It's a lovely home surrounded by a large lot. It has a creek running along one side of it." She laughed a little, which caused her to cough. "You may have noticed that he lets women run over him. Kiwi oversees the property. George pays her an allowance." I lifted both eyebrows. I wondered if Norma knew about Kiwi.

"Which brings me to my wishes. I, too, am leaving almost everything to you."

"Really? Hillhollow? But why?"

"Yes, Hillhollow and this home, because I love you," she said simply.

"But George—"

"I'm leaving some money for George, but he will not be able to touch it as long as he is married to your mother." She smiled. "I think even George will not let her continue to use him forever. I've made sure that your mother cannot get to your fortune either."

"But they live here at Hillhollow," I said.

"Yes. They live here now, but it belongs to me."

"Uh, they can stay here if they want to."

"I thought you would say that." Again that loving smile.

"And Karen and Ben!"

"Yes?"

Thoughts were racing through my brain and colliding with each other. I said determinately, "I'll keep Ben on salary. I know he'll want to keep working for me."

"Does it bother you that I find you predictable? You should not find it hard to see why I'm trusting you with what I'm leaving behind."

I was in shock. I didn't really want to let myself think of My Lady dying, and yet the questions kept coming into my mind and blurting out my mouth. "Do you suppose Karen will want to stay?"

"She might. I'm leaving her a comfortable income, so she may want to move on after I'm gone, but she may want to stay right here. You see, she also loves you very much." She looked down at my right arm. "Please give me your right hand."

As I extended my hand, she easily slipped her ruby ring off her thin finger, and then slid it onto mine. "Oh, My Lady!" I cried openly. I wiped the tears with the other hand and stared down at the stunning jewels.

"You keep checking your watch. Are you supposed to be somewhere?"

I checked it again. "Yes. I asked Ben to tell you about Christine. He did, right?"

She nodded. "He told me she was in the hospital, and that you were there with her. Was there an accident?"

"No. So much worse. She was knocked down in the Lab parking lot last night. She has a serious head injury. I was finishing up work, and she went down to get my car. She was supposed to come pick me up at the top of the hill." I gulped. "When she didn't, I went down to the parking lot and found her lying in a water puddle." I wiped my eyes and finished lamely, "They took her laptop case."

"In that horrible storm! How is she?"

"She's in a drug-induced coma in the ICU at John Muir." I'm not allowed to see her—only immediate family may—but I'll go spend time with them there later as they wait."

"Please tell me everything that happened."

"Sure." I checked my watch again. "I'm supposed to meet up with a police detective at the Lab, but I want to tell you." So I told her the whole story starting with the morning Christine noticed my new black clothes and how she thought I looked like her. And I included that I tossed her my keys so she could drive my car up the hill.

She raised troubled eyes. "You realize, my darling girl, that whoever hit her thought they were hitting you?"

"I know. Once again, someone took my place. It was supposed to be me."

CHAPTER SIXTEEN

Support

Apparently it was my fortune to be surrounded by hot men. I could see Detective Gorsky through the conference room blinds. He was in a dark-gray suit, crisp white shirt, and teal silk tie. He had dark, wavy hair and a trim, athletic build. He was drop-dead gorgeous—like John F. Kennedy Jr. gorgeous. He was surrounded by three neatly stacked piles of papers in manila file folders. The conference room was on the first floor behind the guard's desk, under the escalators. The Peet's Coffee cart was directly across.

I popped my head through the door, and he rose to meet me. "No, please don't get up. I'm Meg Randallman. Want some coffee? I'm going to grab one for myself." His smile revealed beautifully straight white teeth.

"Sure. Just cream, no sugar. But I can buy—"

The scoffing sound that came out of me was something like "puh" as I waved him away. It occurred to me that I could soon afford to buy the whole Peet's Coffee company, but, like Scarlet O'Hara, I didn't want to think about that right now. There was so much to think about; I had begun to compartmentalize my thoughts. The one thing that was constantly cutting across all compartments, however, was the stinging itch of the spider bites. Stratton had been right. The first bite was the worst. It must have had the most venom. But right now I would try very hard to focus on helping this beautiful man with his investigation into Christine's attacker.

I returned with two large coffees. He saw me through the blinds and opened the conference room door for me. In that close proximity, he smelled wonderful. I stole a quick glance at his left ring finger and noticed that it was ringless. "Which one is mine?"

"Either. You take yours the same way I take mine." I pushed my right hand forward to him.

He took his cup, walked around the small table so he was facing the window toward the coffee cart, and motioned to the chair across from him. "Thank you for the coffee, Meg Randallman. I'm Detective Gorsky." He reached across the table to shake my hand as soon as it was free. He couldn't conceal his curiosity. I was unable to read him. My guess would be that he hadn't expected me to be so young. Or, I thought, letting my imagination run away with me a bit, *Maybe he thinks I'm a hottie too. Ha-ha-ha.*

I smiled instead of allowing myself to chuckle. "Yes. How do you do?" I found myself nervous but could not figure out why. I knew I was not a suspect.

He looked down at his folders and rearranged them so the one on the left became the one in front on him. He carefully lined all of them up exactly two inches from the edge of the table and perfectly aligned two inches apart. He opened the one in the center, pulled out the papers, set them on top of the folder, and made sure they were evenly stacked. He took a sip of his coffee and looked up. "I have bits and pieces of what happened, but if you don't mind going through it from the start, I would appreciate it since you are the only person who has the whole story." Someone or some action through the blinds behind me caused his eyes to flick there, but he quickly turned his attention back to me.

"Did you see anything on the Lab Security tapes?"

He smiled. "Yes. I came here last night as soon as I got your call, looked at the crime scene, and the tapes. With the darkness and the weather, they do not reveal much, except that, you were right. Christine didn't just slip and fall. She fell when someone pulled the shoulder bag she was carrying off of her shoulder." He lifted one eyebrow and tilted his head as he asked his question. "Now can you tell me what happened?"

I decided to start with the way I had been dressed in all black and how Christine always wore black and how she commented that I could be mistaken for her. He listened patiently, but I thought he was slightly annoyed that I had included my wardrobe in the story, but when I got to the part where I threw Christine my keys, I could tell he was quick to understand. "We also both have black raincoats so—"

He interrupted me. "So. It's possible that Christine could have been mistaken for you as well?"

"Yes." Then, as evenly as I could, I told the whole story to him as I had just related it to My Lady a few hours before. His cell phone rang partway through my story. It was so odd to hear a cell ring within the Lab, but because he was not an employee with access to Lab information, and he was there in official law enforcement capacity, and because he was only on the first floor, he had been allowed to bring it in.

"Yes. Thank you. Yes. I'm interviewing her now. I'll tell her." He pushed a button to hang up. I was still trying to read him. It was difficult because he was very level, professional, and intense. "That was another detective in our department. I asked him to stop by the hospital to check in on Christine. Our offices at City Hall are not far from John Muir. I appreciate you coming here to meet with me. I know you would rather be there with her family." He paused. "It's not good news—No, wait—it's not really bad news either." He searched my face compassionately. We both paused to take a sip of our coffees. I waited. "The doctors gave her what they call a sedation vacation."

"I heard that phrase for the first time at the hospital last night. And I take it she didn't do well?"

"That is correct. She was very agitated and rude, so they put her back into the resting state."

"I know it's not funny, but it seems like a good solution for agitated, rude people." It was fun to laugh, but then I said seriously, "So I suppose that means they think she does have a brain bleed?"

"Yes, but they think the sedation is all they're going to need to subdue it. I guess there are other procedures to relieve the pressure, but—" He stopped to run his hand across the top of his gorgeous head of dark wavy hair. "You know what? I don't have all the information, and I don't want to add more than what I know. What I know for sure is that she's not ready for an interview, she's going to be in the ICU for a while longer, and I knew that you would want to know what I know." Again, he looked through the window momentarily, then returned to my face. "So please continue with your story."

"That's very considerate of you." I was beginning to think he was very considerate indeed and like a magnet on the other side of the table. I finished my story as factually as I could, trying to ignore the drama of emotions I was feeling as I was reliving the incident and trying also to leave out the horrifying complications of the wet, windy darkness.

When I finished, he looked down at the paper in front of him and pulled a pen out of his left breast pocket. "Thank you. So now I have some other questions." Another a flick of attention toward the coffee cart. I could tell that Detective Gorsky missed very little of what went on around him.

"OK."

"Can you think of any reason someone would target you or Christine?"

"Well as you know, I took Brenda Arthur's job. What you may not know is that Christine was filling in that same job between the times that B–Brenda . . ." I stopped to take a breath.

Kindly, he finished the sentence for me. "And when you came to work here?"

"Yes. Thank you. This is all so ugly."

"Murder and attempted murder always are."

I thought about how he had to deal with this kind of thing as part of his job. It would always be dreadful no matter how often someone had to encounter it. "Christine told me she contacted you when she thought she was being followed. Didn't you believe her?"

I saw a smile cross his face. "It wasn't a matter of believing her but rather the lack of evidence. I couldn't dictate action in a city that wasn't in my jurisdiction."

"But you're here now."

"Yes. I'm here now because Christine called me, and then you called me. This attack certainly gives credence to the possibility that it's related to the case that *is* in my jurisdiction." I again got to see his straight white teeth. His eyes smiled too. "So what is it about this job that all of you have been doing that would draw this danger to you? What would the attacker or attackers be trying to get?"

"Passwords. We have access to everyone's accounts. These horrid people are not very smart though. They should realize that even though we administer the passwords, we don't actually have access to all the accounts."

His eyebrows went up in interest. "What do you mean?"

"I mean that we have the power to create and reset passwords, but we don't have the codes to each of the partitions of the servers. It's a multi-part security system. The partitions are kind of like the web address. Do you know the acronym URL? Universal Resource Locator?"

"Yes." He smiled again. "Like dub-dub-dub wcpd.org, right?"

"I'm sorry. I didn't mean to be patronizing. It's just that it's one of my pet peeves that people brandish acronyms around and assume that everyone knows what they mean. So what I'm saying is this: even though Brenda, Christine, and I have had the ability to cyber-morph into everyone at the Lab, we would need to have their particular training as well to know what systems to access."

"Cyber-morph?"

I laughed. "Yeah. Sorry. We can change into other people's identities using our technology in the digital world that is known as *cyberspace*." I asked another question. "So do you think that the guy that grabbed Christine's laptop case thought he was getting her laptop? There has been a change in technology since someone stole Brenda's, but it's so hard to believe someone who works here is doing this." I heard the defeated tone in my voice as I continued, "Only someone who works here would know about the change so it has to be someone at the Lab, doesn't it?"

I saw the same fractional smile. "Maybe." Then he chuckled. "You do realize that I'm supposed to be interviewing you, right? It's not that I consider you a suspect—no, really, I don't. It's just that I cannot reveal details about the investigation into Brenda's murder because there are details that only the perpetrator knows. Answering your interview questions would compromise the integrity of the case even though you're not likely to share the information with someone who's a suspect."

"Oh. OK." I felt the telltale warmth of embarrassment creep up my neck to my ears and cheeks. "I was only trying to help." I took a breath "Even if the perp—I watch a lot of TV," I explained baldly, "actually did get any of our laptops, there is yet another layer of security. If the Lab laptops are docked here"—I motioned with a large sweep of my arm to indicate all the floors above—"They're behind the firewall. But if we take our laptops off site, there is one huge mitigating limitation: they do not have hard drives. The only access to sensitive data is on the servers. In order to log in behind the firewall from an undocked laptop they would have to know our Lab username and password for our laptop, and then our SecurID PIN."

"Secure ID PIN?"

"Yes. Some people have them on a little key fob like this one," I pulled out my key-shaped SecurID token and turned it toward him so he could see the eight digits on the display. "Those eight digits change every minute. See the little lines getting smaller at the bottom? As soon as the little line disappears, the number will change, and the line will morph back into a full line across the bottom of the display, and then systematically start to diminish again. This is synced with my identity and a six-digit PIN that only I know—not even the person who set up the PIN knows, which most recently was Brenda, Christine, or me. When we set up a PIN, we open a secure channel for the person to input their PIN, and it shows up as dots on our control panel screen. After the SecurID and PIN are synchronized, the user has to input her personal PIN and then the current SecureID token number." I dropped the fob back into my handbag. "And, again this can only happen after someone is first logged in with their User ID and current Lab password."

"You implied that some people have them in a different mode?"

"Yes. That's the new technology I mentioned. People who only need access behind the firewall from their laptop have the choice to have it *on* their laptop as software. It looks like a little picture of the key fob. They start up the software and see a mock key fob picture on the screen. Those of us with key fob IDs can actually log on from computers throughout the Lab." I thought his eyes were starting to glaze over and decided I was glad I had brought him a cup of coffee before I bored him to death. "Well you asked." It was my turn to smile.

He grinned. "Yes. I did."

"Do you ever see those e-mails that detail who wins the Darwin Awards? People die doing really stupid things. Often, they are illegal stupid things."

He laughed. "Yeah, and unlike the Darwin Awards, there other reports of the stupid crooks that don't necessarily die, like the guys who tried to pull an ATM machine out of a cement sidewalk with a truck and it pulled the truck's bumper off instead, so they drove away leaving the license plate chained to the ATM."

"Really?" I found myself laughing again. "Yeah. It's kinda like that." Then I returned to sobered reality. "But this is not funny. Whoever is doing this is stupid but not funny. As you said before, murder never is. It could never be, but someone who works here *has* to be the person who is doing this because, for one thing, whoever attacked Christine got through the guard's gate at the entrance yesterday. Or someone here is working for the people who are trying to get the secrets." He gave me that *who is the detective here?* semi-smile again, and once again I felt pulled emotionally toward him. "I know. I'm sorry, but all that blah, blah, blah, blah, blah that I just bored you with makes me believe that everyone who works here would realize how futile any effort was to just get our laptops, unless . . ."

"Unless?"

"Unless the person who attacked Christine thought they were attacking me and they thought I would keep information about other people's passwords and access on my laptop."

"Can you think of anyone who would think that?"

"I suppose anyone who saw my job responsibility in the directory could think that, but he would have to assume an awful lot about how I work and how I would choose to save sensitive information." I sighed. "I only have a couple of friends and I haven't told them *anything* about how I organize and protect the sensitive information I handle."

"Well, what we know for sure is that someone is trying very hard to get to the secrets of the Lab, and they are willing to take dangerous, desperate risks to get them. They knew where Brenda lived, and they were probably following Christine until you came to work here. You've been working here for—" He looked down at his paper—"three months? Do you think anyone has been following you? I think we should have the Pleasant Valley force put a detail at your home."

"That won't be necessary. I live in a pretty secure place."

"If you live in a gated community, don't be too sure that someone cannot follow another tenant through or watchfully obtain the gate code."

"It's not like that. I live in a gated fortress. No other tenants live there except my family. We have security cameras and a full-time employee monitoring them. Whoever is on watch also opens the gate unless one of us in the family uses our remote control."

He tilted his head a fraction and studied my face. "Randallman." He nodded as if he were tapping an invisible keyboard with his chin. "Creekside Architecture. Is your property in Walnut Creek or just your father's offices?"

"No. Our home is here in Pleasant Valley, and not my fath— Oh, never mind. Yes. Creekside Architecture in Walnut Creek is the same famous architect, George Randallman, my, er, stepfather."

"Well. I suppose then that you don't need more security for now, but do something for me please." He reached again into the left breast pocket of his jacket, pulled out a business card, and handed it across the table. "When you get your cell phone out of your locker this afternoon, please put me on speed dial. As you noticed last night, 911 on mobile phones default to the Highway Patrol."

I looked at the card in my hand and started to cry.

"What's wrong?" he asked.

I sniffed and tried to wave the tears away with my hand. "I already have one of these. It's the one you gave Christine."

"Maybe I should let you go be with her and her family," he said compassionately.

"That would be good. I need to go upstairs for just a little while and take care of any urgent ad hoc that might have come in this morning, but then I'll go see her, or go be near her and see her family." I pulled a tissue out of my bag. "I'm sorry. I think I'm tired. I don't operate at full capacity when I don't get enough sleep."

"No need to apologize. You've been through a lot in the past twenty hours." He stood and reached his hand across the table, which I thought was very gallant of him since I had just washed it with my tears. I pulled out another tissue and wiped my hand completely dry before accepting his hand. "If you think of anything else, please call me."

"I will." I smiled. "And I'll make a list of my interview questions for our next meeting."

"Right." He nodded knowingly and smiled with one corner of his mouth and with his eyes.

CHAPTER SEVENTEEN

Day One of Three-and-a-Half Days

For the next three-and-a-half days of my life I felt like I was playing several roles in the movie *The Lord of the Rings, the Return of the King*. The White Wizard, Gandalf, and the kings and warriors of the West set out on an unachievable mission against the forces of evil attempting to divert the Evil Eye from Frodo. The fate of the love of King Aragorn's life, the elven princess, Arwen, was tied up with the fate of the ring, and though she was not in a coma, she was fading fast. And two poor Hobbits, Frodo and Sam, were in the heart of darkness trying to get to Mt. Doom to destroy the ring of power. Frodo both loved and hated the ring of power. My life was like that, only different. There were no wizards, elves, hobbits, royalty, or orcs, but there were certainly comas, danger, an emotional conflict of loving and hating, a need for healing, and battles with evil.

With each new challenge, all I could do was compartmentalize and continue to channel Scarlet O'Hara. Several times I determinately decided that "I just can't think about that right now." However, I did have one recourse and someone to champion my causes. I could pray.

Before daylight of the first day, that would be the first of three days filled with trouble, I had a sense of dread that drove me to my knees at the side of my bed. I hated to disturb the dog, who was snoring lightly and hogging the bed so comfortably, but I rolled out and yanked my blankie out from under him and wrapped it around me. Midnight opened one eye, tapped the comforter several times with the tip of his silly tail, and went back to sleep. I closed my eyes, bowed my head into my folded hands, and contemplated how great my Savior was. I told Him so in as many ways as I could think of, which shamefully seemed like way too short a list. Meditating on His attributes helped calm my feelings of dread and gave me a sense of trust and peace. Then I lifted my head up to look out my bedroom window while I continued to pour out my heart and my hurts. The brilliant light of the waxing moon cast Midnight's body into shadow. The bed was in darkness because of the wall beneath the window. The moon would be full in a few days. I was grateful that I was about to be a multimillionaire, or possibly a billionaire, but I could not bear the thought of My Lady dying. I was sad for George that his uncle had died. I was also apprehensive of George and Norma's reaction to the reading of Uncle William's will. Christine was still in a drug-induced coma, and the danger that put her in the hospital still lurked at the Lab. The center said Ray wasn't ready to travel. I had neglected visiting him for the past few days, and I felt guilty. And then, without really thinking it through, I talked to God about my upcoming date with Stratton and realized I didn't have any idea what to wear.

After I showered, accompanied by Einstein sitting above me on the shower door alternately chirping loudly, singing wildly to the music of the running water, and picking his misted feathers, I put on a soft, comfy purple turtleneck and a pair of black slacks. I delicately applied makeup to puffy eyes, then went downstairs to prepare a hearty breakfast. I shared a sausage with Midnight, then I called my boss, Karolina.

As usual, she was great. I asked if I could work half days for the next several days. I would start somewhere in the middle of each day and stay at work until crucial issues were handled and resolved. This gave me time to go see My Lady every morning. Mornings were better for her. My plan for these morning was to read her favorite Bible chapters to her and play her favorite pieces on the piano. If she needed to sleep, I would the play the piano anyway.

After my visit with My Lady, I drove up to Walnut Creek to see Christine. She was still in the ICU, so I couldn't technically see her, but rather I sat with whoever was there from her family. Jake was always there, quietly worrying. The doctors told us they were going to try again tomorrow, on Thursday morning, to let Christine wake up using their sedation vacation. We were all there when they told us: her whole family and, of course, Jake. While the doctor was giving us the good news in the ICU waiting room, I felt my handbag vibrate. It was the center. Ray was in crisis. He'd left during the night, and they hadn't noticed until this morning. They had no idea where he was. They had been unable to reach George and Norma.

I couldn't reach them either. I thought they may still be in flight to Connecticut. I left voice messages with the calmest voice possible, knowing that Norma would not receive the news calmly. I wasn't sure what the funeral schedule was, but it was to be a short trip. They would be traveling back on Friday, so whatever was scheduled would happen between Wednesday evening and late Friday morning. Hopefully, we would have word from—or about—Ray before then. My abdomen ached when I allowed myself to think about him.

On the way back to the Lab, I prayed that Ray would call his sponsor or return to the center. When I called with questions, they assured me that he could still make a full recovery.

"No," they said, "it was not unusual for patients to falter at least once. Yes. This is very dangerous. Some do not live through the crisis of a relapse."

My screen chirped almost as soon as I logged in. An instant message from Stratton Davis had arrived.

SD: Hi! Glad you are there. I've missed having lunch with you these past two days.

I opened up the Stratton compartment and allowed myself to consider how much I had missed him also during the craziness that began when I tossed my keys to Christine on Monday evening.

MR: Hi, Strat. I've missed you too.

SD: How is Christine?

MR: Better. They are going to try to wake her up again tomorrow.

SD: So you won't be here before lunch again, right?

MR: Right. So sorry. Coming in late each day. At least for the rest of the week.

SD: I'll be down to see you in a little while. I'm going to bring you my cell number and get yours, OK?

MR: Sure. That would be great.

How sweet, I thought. We could have just typed them to each other, but he wanted to see me. I felt a twinge of joy and knew I wanted to see him too, but was afraid to think what I looked like. I was sure the strain of the past few days was showing in my face. I got up and went into Christine's cubicle to use her mirror. Yes, I was a mess. The face that stared back at me looked tired and tense; my skin looked dull. I had puffy dark circles under my red-rimmed eyes. I had cried way too often in the past few days. Fine lines surrounded my lips that seemed to have less fullness than usual. I had come in out of the damp wind, so my hair was a bit crazy too. I could at least run a comb through my hair.

I grabbed my bag to retrieve a comb. I pinched my cheeks to give them some color, and applied fresh lipstick. Assessment: not great, but better than before. Thank God for lipstick! I went back to my desk to enter cyberspace.

It was great timing when he showed up a couple of hours later. I had accomplished enough for the Lab this day. I saw his reflection in my monitor, and of course I smelled the forest river breeze.

"Hi!" I swiveled in my chair to face him and turned my palm out to motion to the guest chair. "How are you?" I wondered if he realized the smile I had for him came from deep within my soul.

"Good," he said with one of those probing looks that seemed to get right past the eyes and into my head. "I'm good. The question is, how are you?" He sat down.

I knew I still looked poopier than the comb and some lipstick could fix. His concern validated it, but it also touched me. I felt very fortunate to have him as a friend.

"Oh, Stratton." My eyes brimmed with sudden easy tears, as if I needed to further ruin my appearance.

My hysteria was a true test of our friendship as well as an assessment of him as a man. He passed both tests equally, with excellence. He got up from the chair, opened his arms, and compassionately said, "Come here." I stood up and started to wipe my tears with my sleeve, and he said, "No need. Use my shoulder." He took me in his arms tenderly, yet supportingly firm, and he held me close to him in a way I don't remember ever have been held. I deeply inhaled the forest river breeze and discreetly wiped my nose on my sleeve as I put my arm around his back. I felt two hearts beating—not merely one. It was as if my life up until then had been a melody that moved with the disappointments, joys, and sorrows of my heart. It played thinly, with tinny plinks at my loneliest moments, and loudly and off-key when I was sad or low. It soared lightly in a joyful melody at times, but in his embrace the melody morphed into perfect tone and pitch, and then became a fully accompanied lovely concerto.

Lately, my life melody had played intensely in a minor key, and though none of the torment had subsided, there was purpose and passion building to a powerful crescendo, not unlike the familiar depths of Rachmaninoff's Piano Concerto No. 2. I was no longer alone. It was like that last turn of a Rubik's cube clicking into place. All the patterns matched; there was order from chaos.

I rested the side of my head against his in complete trust and surrendered to the comfort. Tears subsided. Calmness prevailed. I felt secure and safe. I had courage to face whatever was imminent for myself and those around me for whom my heart was aching. I found a new bravery, and I knew I would tell him everything—all that was going on around me and within me, including everything about my past. I finally stepped back and gazed into those kind blue eyes. I knew that the security and comfort that I had found in his embrace I would always also find in that handsome face.

"Do you have time to talk?" I asked him sheepishly.

"Yes. I can leave now if you want to go somewhere."

We did. I logged off. He helped me with my coat. I walked up to his desk with him so that he could log off, get his coat and car keys, then say good-bye to Princess David. He held my hand all the way upstairs and then again all the way down. Princess David noticed this and gave us an approving nod accompanied with a slight grin.

We stepped out under the leaden sky. The bitter wind bit and whipped the edges of our coats while visiting each cell phone locker. After we put each other's numbers in our phones, he walked me to his car, which was parked more closely to the cell phone lockers than mine. He opened the passenger side door for me and helped me into his Victory Red Camaro convertible. He stretched the seat belt and offered it to my hand, then walked around to the driver's side. I was acutely aware of every little movement he made. I felt like he had become the center of my world and I was a satellite comfortably revolving in the magnetism of his orbit. When he slid into his seat and closed the door, muffling the rushing water over the retaining wall, I said, "This car suits you."

He grinned his response; he appreciated my comment.

I said, "I think my next car will be American. My first car was a gift from my stepfather."

"Where is yours parked?"

"As far southeast as you can go. I always park there."

"Don't park there tomorrow, OK?"

"OK." I realized that yes; of course, in spite of the Lab's increased surveillance of the area in which I usually parked, I should break my usual habit, in case Christine's attacker would be so bold to try again.

The wind whipped my coat when he helped me out of his car, so we didn't try to speak above the roaring water close to my car, but we had compelling communication without words. Each look; each touch so fervid. We had decided while we were in the Camaro to go to the Peet's near the Lab. It would be quiet in the afternoon. He settled me into my driver's seat, once again protectively handing me my seat belt, before securely closing my door. He followed me. I smiled within, thinking that his car following behind mine rendered new meaning to the phrase "I have your back." I thought, *No longer alone; no longer a little crazy with my loneliness.*

When we parked in the lot of the strip mall that housed "the Lab's" Peet's store, Stratton gave me his hand as I emerged from my driver's seat. He waited patiently as I closed and clicked the remote to chirp my car locks. When I turned to face him, he took my chin in his right hand, looked into my eyes, and inquired, "When was the last time you ate?"

"This morning. I had a hearty breakfast," I said defensively.

"You know it's nearly five, right?" He put his arm in a curve inviting me to link mine through. He turned us away from Peet's door and directed me down to the anchor building of the little mall.

The sign across the front of the building read *Canal Street Grille.*
Then he asked, "What kinds of food do you like and not like?"

"I like everything."

"Good. I'm going to order everything. I think you need a
steak." He opened the door and motioned me through, following
up with his hand at the back of my waist to direct me.

He did order almost everything. The restaurant was virtually
empty, so when we settled into a lovely booth, we had complete
privacy. The tinted windows filtered the brilliance of the sunset.
Our booth's window was facing west. It was like a shadow of
the purpling sunset. We were not done with the rain. This was
only a break in the billowing dark clouds, not unlike that break
that allowed me early this morning to see the waxing moon. The
forecasters promised we were in for yet another storm.

Over a grilled artichoke appetizer, I told Stratton how Norma
had torn my brother and me away from our daddy and grandparents.
I rambled on at that point about my conflicted feelings toward my
mother. "I suppose I love her, but I'm not sure if she loves me."

"Of course she loves you," he said immediately. "No one ever
loves us like our mother."

"Yeah, but I think she's different from most mothers." I tried
to explain. "I think she cares about how Ray's and my failures and
accomplishments reflect on her. I don't think she actually cares
about us."

"Hmmm." He shook his head thoughtfully. "Those two
statements are not mutually exclusive, you know?

"I suppose that's true."

"I don't know. My mom has always been so good to me."
He smiled. "Even when I was a somewhat smart-mouthed,
lazy, video-game-enslaved teen. She always sees the best in me.
Believing that brought me out of the video-game dark ages." I
started to cry. "Oh I'm sorry. The last thing you need is for me to
brag about how wonderful my mom—"

"No! I think it's great that your mom is wonderful." I sniffed and pulled a Kleenex out of the purse in my bag and dabbed at my nose, then my eyes. "These tears"—I pointed to each eye abruptly—"are because I just mentioned my brother, Ray. He's in serious trouble."

"So, as if you don't have enough to worry about with your best friend in the hospital attacked by a dirtbag, and no support from a confusing mother—" he shook his head again "—you also have a brother in trouble?"

I laughed. I supposed I was a bit hysterical. "Oh, I've only just begun. I have yet to tell you the worst." I swiped a piece of artichoke leaf through the yummy sauce that resided in the middle of one of the halves and scraped the delicious combination through my front teeth. I set down the rest of the leaf and took a sip of water before continuing. "My brother is—was—in rehab up until a few hours ago. He left, and no one knows where he is. My mother and my stepfather just left for Connecticut because of a death in the family."

"So there *is* a whole lot more?" he asked compassionately.

"Oh yeah. Much more. I'm going to tell you what's going on now, but I'm also going to tell you a story from my past that I've never told anyone."

He hailed our waiter, Chas. Stratton ordered me a rib eye steak with a loaded baked potato and a side of grilled veggies. For himself, he chose halibut with creamed rock shrimp, spinach risotto, and also grilled veggies. We waited patiently as Chas filled our water glasses. I sat silently watching Stratton. He had so much self-esteem and confidence. I bet he was a perfect gentleman even as a small boy.

When Chas left, Stratton turned his attention intently to me and said, "OK. Go on."

I took a drink of water and continued. I related as much as I could remember about the horrible day Laura died. Then I told him about the funeral, about Daddy and Norma fighting, and Norma waking me the next day telling me to pack. "But I already told you that part." I lifted Laura's cross. "This was my sister's."

He nodded recognition. "You always wear it." Then he said intuitively, "So you think her death is your fault?"

"Of course I do." I was strangely composed. I think having talked about it with Ray had helped me process the guilt that had gnawed at my core throughout my childhood. "But I've started to forgive myself. The bigger problem is that I think everyone else thinks I pulled the trigger."

"No way!"

"Way. Norma said so on the way here to California, and of course I haven't seen Daddy or anyone else since the day after the funeral." I felt a flush of embarrassment rush hot through my face.

"Where did you live before? Do you know what happened to the girl that did pull the trigger?"

"Vanessa." I said sadly. "No. I have no idea what happened to her. I don't know her last name. And I don't know where I lived before. I was so little." I took a deep breath. I heard him inhale too. "And you know what? I'm such a coward. I saw a man the other day that I know was there after Laura died. He can probably help me find Daddy. I think that even though it's been the desire of my heart and within almost every prayer of my life, I'm afraid to actually find Daddy. I'm sure he thinks I shot Laura too."

Chas interrupted a bit obsequiously to set our plates in front of us. He no doubt heard me say, "thinks I shot Laura." He was unable to hide his curiosity. He probably wanted to sit down to hear the rest, but after staying as long as he possibly could to make sure we had everything we needed, he finally went away.

Stratton asked quietly, "You saw a man? Where?"

"At the Lab." I swallowed. "When I met Kirin Puri several months ago, she seemed so familiar. Her elegant, graceful mannerisms." I nodded. "It was her father whose mannerisms I remembered. He came to her desk Monday when I was there."

"And you recognized him, but you didn't say anything? Do you think he recognized you?"

"I don't think so. I've changed quite a bit since I was four."

He lifted his right eyebrow and gave me a slight grin. "I'm sure you have. You've changed quite a bit since you were fifteen too."

I mused at that. "That's right. I was fifteen when we met. Wow! We've known each other for six years! Though we didn't see each other all of last year." We took some time to take a few bites. I noticed how comfortable the silence was. It was completely dark outside now, leaving the window as a poor gray mirror. Our reflections and the reflection of the tiny candle at our table glimmered distorted and pale. Even his distorted image was handsome. My steak was outstanding. The outside was dark and crispy, and yet the inside was delightfully pink and juicy. We exchanged tastings. His halibut was as tender and as moist as sea bass, and the rock shrimp topping was delectable.

"You have time, you know. Kirin's father will probably be here for a while, and even if he doesn't stay long, I'm sure you can reach him after he leaves. Do your arm and shoulder still itch?" He said this in response to me putting my hand up to the back of my neck as I considered scratching it. I jerked my hand back with restraint.

"Yes!" I said a little too loudly. "I can't believe on top of everything else I have this terrible itching on my neck and arm!" I took a drink of water.

As I set the glass down, he reached across the table to lift my right hand, "Every time I've seen you, I've seen your cross on you, but I've not seen this before." He studied the ruby ring. "It's beautiful."

I squeezed his hand beneath mine and said, "My Lady gave it to me yesterday." I gulped. "Which brings me to the very worst part."

He brought his other hand across to cover mine and looked concerned. "Are you done eating for now? I am. How 'bout we have Chas box this up and ask him to leave us for a while? D'you mind if I join you on that side of the table?"

I smiled. "I'd be delighted. Please come join me, sir." I removed my hand from his and patted the seat beside me. Stratton signaled Chas, who was not far away. After Chas boxed our food for us, Stratton asked him not to disturb our table again until we hailed him for dessert.

"Dessert?" I said.

"Yes. Today you need dessert," he said cheerfully. They have awesome crème brûlée, or maybe you'd like cobbler? You don't need to decide right now.

We settled into our privacy with full water glasses before us, tissue at the ready, and Stratton comfortably beside me with one arm around my shoulders and his free hand holding mine. I took a deep breath and said to my water glass, "I never liked George that much, but I love his mother. She is sort of my grandmother. I guess not even sort of. I'm pretty sure George legally adopted me. That would be the only way my birth certificate would be the way it is."

"Your birth certificate has George as your father?"

"Yes. I took it with me to get my driver's license."

"Then she *is* your grandmother, not just sort of." He smiled with his eyes.

"Her name is actually the same as mine—Margaret Randallman—but I call her the name I gave her when I was five. She wanted us to both feel comfortable in what started out as an uncomfortable situation, which is *so* like her. I call her My Lady. As the years have gone by and I became an adult, I sometimes call her My Lady Margaret, or My Lady M."

"Sounds royal," he said thoughtfully.

I looked at him. "Oh she is." I stopped as I felt my throat closing and the pain of tears pushing against the back of my eyes. I fought back and began talking rapidly. "She took Ray and me to church with her and gave us a place at her dinner table at least once a week. She taught us manners and how to swim, and taught me how to play the piano and . . . oh so much more." I stopped and took a deep breath. "And she's dying. She just told me yesterday." I lost the fight with the tears and needed a tissue.

"Oh! I'm so sorry." He squeezed me gently with the arm surrounding my shoulders.

I took another breath and continued as quickly as I could. "George doesn't know yet that his mother is terminally ill. She was going to tell him, but then his Uncle William died so she told him she had an infection and couldn't go to the funeral in Connecticut. Norma and George flew there today. They're returning late Friday. My Lady and George's Uncle William don't, er didn't, like Norma." I looked down at the ruby ring on my right hand nestled in Stratton's right hand. "She's always worn this. She gave it to me yesterday." I looked back up into Stratton's eyes. He got it. I knew he knew that if I could, I would trade all the jewels in the world to keep My Lady alive.

He took me in his arms and held me as close as the awkward booth/table arrangement would allow. After a time of silence, he released me, sat back from me a bit, and took my hand again, this time with both of his. "You will always have her love, even when she's gone. And she will live on through you in the things she has taught you and in the knowledge and wisdom she has given you."

My heart was pounding so hard, I thought he would hear it. *How could I be so fortunate to find such a compassionate, wise man, who cares about me? And besides that, he smells so good!* "Stratton?"

"Yes?"

"Was this our date?"

He laughed. "This was practice. Our first date is still on Friday."

CHAPTER EIGHTEEN

Day Two

When it was my turn to visit Christine, I was surprised at how peaceful she appeared. I expected her to be hooked up to a lot of apparatuses, but other than a bandage around her head, an IV feeding into the back of her hand, and a clip on her finger, she was resting quietly. She looked beautiful without makeup. Her eyes fluttered, and then she saw me.

"Oh, hi!" Her voice was strong. It was comforting to me. "Come sit down next to me." The IV tube wiggled as she motioned to her guest chair at the side of her bed. "Hey, look!" She turned the back of her hands to face me. "They removed my black nail polish. They probably thought they could monitor the color in my fingernails." She turned her hands around to study her nails and wrinkled her nose. "Fat chance." She had worn the dark color for so long her nails were dark yellow. "So, will you still let me drive your Beemer someday?" She grinned.

"Of course." I sighed. "Gosh," I reached my hand across to take hers. "It's *so* good to see you awake." I felt the far-too-familiar tightening in my throat, but knew if the tears I fought back started to flow, they would be tears of joy and relief.

She said slowly, "How is everyone? What day is it? Have you had your date with Stratton yet?" *All so good,* I thought. *Her speech is slower, but her mind and her memory are good.*

"It's Thursday and our date is tomorrow, but he took me out to dinner after work last night." I lifted both eyebrows and smiled.

"Hmmm. Sounds serious." She winced.

"Are you OK?"

"Oh, my head hurts—sometimes more than others."

"I need to let you rest, but when I come back, I want to know what you think of Jake."

"Jake? How do you know Jake?"

I smiled. "He showed up here the night you bonked your head and every time I've been here since—except this morning, he was outside the ICU."

"Really?" She blushed and looked past my shoulder. Jake was standing at the door with a bouquet of lilacs and white chrysanthemums arranged beautifully in a vase. "Hey, Jake." She batted her eyelashes twice. "Meg just told me you've been here waiting for me to wake up."

"Hi, Teenie. Er, hi, Meg. Maybe I should come back at a different ti—"

I interrupted him. "No. Hi, Jake. Please stay. I have to go to work anyway." I got up from the chair and took the vase from his hands. I put it on the shelf above the sink so Christine—or "Teenie"—could see the flowers from her bed. He sat down in the chair. I saw him look at her hand. I sensed that he wanted to reach for it as I had.

"So, can you text with all that stuff connected to your hands?" I asked teasingly.

"Yeah," she said enthusiastically. "My mom charged my phone." She pointed to her side table, which wiggled the tubes again. "Text me when you get your phone out of its locker. If I don't have company or people poking and prodding me, maybe we can chat on your Bluetooth on your way home. Just like old times."

"OK." I smiled contentedly and gave her an affectionate look. "I'm so relieved that there are going to be new times."

"Yeah. Me too." She nodded. "And I still want to drive your car."

I laughed. "Easy request." I turned to go and almost collided with Detective Gorsky in the doorway. "Oh, hi! I was just leaving." I was surprised that in spite of feeling his rock-hard muscles in the close encounter and the fact that he smelled great and looked at least twice as gorgeous as he did the other day, I felt no attraction. There was a Stratton melody in my heart that was apparently immobilizing all other desire.

Detective Gorsky gave me a knowing nod. I smiled and nodded back to him, then turned again to the small room. "Christine, this is your friend, Detective Gorsky. He'll have to give you another card. I had one of the paramedics give me the one you were, er, *carrying*, so I could call him while you were here Monday night."

Christine's eyes got wide, and she looked down at her left breast. "I hadn't thought about that yet. I still haven't figured out where my br—" She looked at Jake. "My clothes are." She dimpled. "I'm sure I'm a mess."

"You look beautiful," Jake said.

"Well, bye to all of you," I walked around to the other side of the bed and lightly kissed Christine's bandaged head. "Bye, Teenie." I gave a thumbs-up to Jake as I said it, then I crossed the room and turned to give them all a little wave before I went out the door.

My mind started racing. I thought about how she looked, how great it was to see her awake, and how bold Jake was to tell her she looked beautiful. I wondered if she remembered anything that would help Detective Gorsky. I thought about how the few intimate hours with Stratton had changed me and I liked it. As much fun as flirting with Detective Gorsky had been, feeling comfortable and complete was much more satisfying and delightful.

I stepped out of the elevator and felt my handbag vibrating. It was Janet, on desk duty at the center. They had Ray back in his room.

The kind person who found him sleeping under a park bench could have ignored him and left him there, but after I heard the full story, I was certain that God had sent an angel to answer my prayers. The young man had been jogging through the park, but he unselfishly interrupted his workout. Ray had the sense to take his good coat, which probably got him through the night and caught the attention of the jogger. He sat Ray up and insisted that there must be someone he could call on Ray's behalf. Ray rallied in consciousness enough to give the guy his sponsor's number. The man stayed with Ray until people from the center came. No one knew the man's name, so there was no way to thank him. I whispered my gratitude to God and asked Him to thank the man He sent.

"I'll be right there," I said to Janet. I was shaking involuntarily as I got close to my car in the hospital parking lot.

"Meg?"

"Julie!"

"Oh, Meg! Are you OK? Did you see Christine? Is she OK?" She put her arms around me, probably hoping to stop me from shaking.

"Oh, Julie." I hugged her back. "Yes, I saw Christine. She's good. She looks really good. Really." I was beginning to calm down. I pulled back a little. "Jake is with her." I checked her face to see if she believed me. My hysteria had no doubt upset her. "And the Walnut Creek detective that she called . . ." I realized that Julie may not have known how closely Brenda's murder had touched Christine.

Julie stepped back a little too, but left her hand on my arm. "I know about Christine's call to the detective. We talk about everything."

"Of course you do. I should have known that. You have such an enviable relationship." I gave her another hug, partially because I wanted to reassure her that I had stopped shaking, but mostly because I wanted another dose of sisterly comfort.

Again Julie stepped back. "Something's upset you, Meg." She patted my arm this time. "Do you want to talk about it?"

"You sweet girl. Christine is so blessed to have you as a sister." I took a deep breath. "I don't want to talk about it because I have to go, but I don't mind telling you what upset me. My brother is a recovering addict. At least he was recovering until yesterday when he left the facility that was helping him get control of his life. He's been found, and for now he's safe." I pulled my car keys out of my pocket. "I need to go see him right now."

"Oh!" Amazingly her monosyllable expressed immeasurable compassion.

"I can't wait to see how he's doing."

"Thank you. Now I need to go see my sibling too." We both waved bye.

On the way from John Muir to the center, I opened the compartment that would permit me to think about Ray and realized that I should have heard from Norma by now. On my way through the John Muir parking lot, I started to send a text to Stratton, and though I knew he wouldn't get it until after work, sent it anyway. I knew he would rejoice with me because Ray was safe.

I called Karolina and said I would probably not make it in at all today. She said she would get someone to monitor the Security mailbox and not to worry. I teared up when she said, "Take as long as you need." How could I be so blessed to be surrounded by such nice people? I was truly meant to take that job at the Lab.

Ray looked awful. His cheeks were sunken. His watery eyes were bloodshot and rimmed with red. I wondered how he had so much water in his eyes because he looked dehydrated. He was sitting on the top of the covers of his bed. His clothes were filthy, and he was hooked up to an IV. He had a small blanket over his lap.

"Hey, Deedee." His embarrassment came through. "They won't let me shower until they're happy that I have had plenty of fluids." He reached to his side table and obediently took a pull on his water glass. "Double doses. I really want a shower."

"Oh, Ray!" I came close enough to hug him, carefully steering clear of the IV tube. I said softly as I hugged, "I've been so worried." I sat down in the guest chair. We were both silent for a while.

"They were right," Ray said with conviction and a nod.

"Who was right?"

"The center." He took a deep breath and studied the bandage holding the needle in his hand. "I need to entirely separate from some of my friends. Veronica came to see me a couple of days ago."

"Veronica? Is she the one who couldn't wake you up when you had to go to the hospital the first time?

"Yeah." He looked up from studying the needle. His eyes met mine. "I thought I loved her, but I don't think what's been going on with us is love. It's too toxic."

I nodded and said in a tone that I hoped didn't sound like I was judging him, "So, now are you ready to start over?"

"Yes. This time I'm going to stay with the program and stay in touch with my sponsor. I've got to do this, Deedee." He looked straight ahead and said to the painting on the wall in front of him, "I don't want to be a worry for you anymore. I want you to be as proud of me as I am of you."

I got up and hugged him again and held him for a while. "You can do it. I know you can. I suppose it's good that you want to do it because you have me cheering for you, but ultimately, you have to do it for yourself." I sat back down, and we resumed another session of silence.

"Have you heard from Mom?"

There was no use sugarcoating it. "No. She should have gotten the message I left her on her cell by now." I felt so horrible for him. "I told her you had left the center." He must know that she apparently didn't care enough to return my call. I thought about all the other things I had withheld from him, but decided this was still not the time to tell him about Christine or My Lady Margaret.

He studied my face. "It's OK, Deedee. It's not your fault she's the way she is. I think deep down inside she does the things she does as a defense. She must know that she offends people with her bullying tirades, but she can't help herself. I bet she's trying to give people a reason to dislike her, thinking that they already do."

"Well, I could never understand what caused her to be the way she is, so I won't disagree with you, but I think she is so full of herself no one else really matters." I reached for his hand. "I often wonder how she was treated as a child. My Lady and I talked about her parents once. I realized that I knew nothing about Norma's family. Nothing! She could have been spoiled by parents who created a narcissistic, prima donna brat, or maybe she was abused or something and she learned to be mean to everyone to manipulate her way through life. I dunno. I just know that she's never been emotionally available to us, and I doubt that she is to poor George." I felt my handbag vibrate next to me. I pulled out my phone and looked at the screen. "Speak of the devil."

Ray's lifted both eyebrows. "Mom?"

I nodded. "Hi, Norma. I'm sitting here with Ray in his room. He's safe." I grinned at Ray, "He's not very clean, but he's safe." There was silence on the line very different from the comfortable silence Ray and I had just shared and light-years away from the contented silence during dinner with Stratton. "Hullo? Norma? Are you there?"

"Yes, Margaret." More disturbing silence. "Your *mother* is here on the line. So your runaway brother has returned to cost George more unnecessary money?" Her voice was cold and mean.

I surmised that this was more about the reading of the will than it was about Ray's relapse. "Yes. He's contrite and ready to start over. I believe he's in the right place physically and emotionally." I didn't think Ray needed to know how unsympathetic and unkind she was. "I know you were worried, but he's going to be better than OK. I believe in him. He's going to be victorious." I winked at my little brother.

"Well." More icy silence. "We'll see, won't we? His track record sucks. He doesn't care about anyone else but himself." For sure she was blind to the irony of her words. "He's a complete embarrassment to me. I'm sure the people we are sending all that money to are wondering why we would bother. Quite frankly, it's not my idea to continue Ray's treatment. It's George's, but he never listens to me."

Again, it was unbelievable how she saw herself and others around her. I tempered my response to protect Ray. "Yes. We'll see how well he does with our support. How is Connecticut?" I asked lamely.

More aggressive silence. "Margaret, you'll be getting a call from Uncle William's lawyer. I gave him this number."

"OK," I said evenly.

"George and I will be on an early plane to San Francisco tomorrow. We left my Mercedes there. We should be home at a reasonable time since we gain three hours back."

"Well, depending on what time you arrive, I may be out. I have a date."

"A date! With who?"

I didn't even consider correcting her grammar. I sensed her seething at the other end of the line. I suspected that she knew she had lost control of me, and she didn't like it. She was probably calculating how to control the fortune Uncle William had left me, and the news that I was adding an important dimension to my independence by dating someone she didn't choose for me was disrupting those calculations. "A guy I know from work. His name is Stratton. We were at Stanford together too."

"Well. I s'pose you are old 'nough to go on a date without checking with me and George."

"Thank you. I think I may have been a long time ago, but I'm twenty-one now, remember?"

"Y-yes." I realized now that during our conversation her speech had slowed a bit and was beginning to slur. I looked at my watch. It was probably happy hour for her no matter what time it really was in Connecticut, but it was after three Pacific, so indeed happy hour had begun in earnest there. "Well. I need to go. George and I are about to go in for an early dinner. We need to get up very early. Too early. It's nice to fly fursst class though. They take such good care of me."

I didn't say what I was thinking. *Just you? Do they take care of George too?* But I didn't. I just said cheerfully, "OK. Safe trip. Maybe I'll see you tomorrow." I had no idea how prophetic the "maybe" was.

CHAPTER NINETEEN

Day Three

"Have you heard from your mother or George?" My Lady and I were settled with tea exactly seated as we often had in our past. I was at the end of her couch, and her wheelchair was beside me. Except for being so thin, her disease was not blatantly evident. Her color was improved. Coughing and gurgling sounds had subsided. Her face, though, looked like it was being pulled down from inside her skin, and there was pain in her eyes.

"Y-yes." I didn't want to upset her, but I continued. "She called when I was at the center with Ray."

She lifted her right eyebrow. "And?" she questioned, knowingly.

"And Ray had a relapse." She patted my hand comfortably. "And I think Norma is angry about the reading of Uncle William's will." She patted again.

There it was. Just a look, but it was filled with the capacity to comfort me with her limitless wisdom, understanding, and compassion. I choked back tears and tried to force the thought of how much I would miss her from my mind so she would not read it in my eyes. "Both predictable," she said simply. "Not surprising in either case, but nonetheless disturbing about both."

"Do you think Ray will keep relapsing?" I said wearily.

"No one can know for sure." She took a sip from her flowery, fragile teacup. "It's up to him to use the tools they are providing." We both turned our attention to the storm outside her living room French doors. The rain plummeted noisily, straight down and with full force demanding our attention. Her patio, unable to drain quickly enough, filled instantly and evolved into a small pond. Some of the winter finches took refuge under the patio overhang, clinging onto whatever they could. Some settled on saturated branch tips that were lengthened by the weight of the water in the bushes and therefore extended into the shelter. Other resourceful birds clung directly to sides of the stucco walls.

She turned her attention back to me. "You cannot fix this for him. You know that, right?"

"Yes," I said sadly, but then added confidently, "The center has given me a few tools too." I smiled at her. "My Lady, you're amazing. You know that, right?" I echoed her question, but continued without requiring her to answer. "You are always so wise, so positive, so gracious, and so kind." I rested my hand on the top of her arm. "You look like you feel better today."

"Yes. I do. The doctors have successfully tamed many of my symptoms. They reached a balance for now that keeps me alert but comfortable." She studied the floral pattern in her carpet, then looked out to see the deluge subsiding. The little birds were not quite ready to leave their haven. She said to the French doors, "I'll have some good days and bad days before the end."

"Call Christine," I commanded into my Bluetooth. "Hey, Teenie. How are you feeling today?"

"Hey, yourself," she said strongly. "Good. Really good." She chuckled. "Teenie. He always called me that when we were kids. Are you on your way to see me?"

"No. Sorry. I've been such a slacker at work lately. I need to get to the Lab. Truthfully, I lingered too long with My Lady. She was doing amazingly well." I gulped away the memory in that compartment for the moment and changed the subject. "Sooo . . . Jake. He seems like a sincerely great guy."

"Yeah." She chuckled again. "Just cuz I dress like a vampire doesn't mean I prefer them." She paused. "Meg?"

"Yeah?" I echoed.

"As I see myself without all the black for a couple of days, I kinda like it. My hair has grown light-brown roots. I'm thinking about cutting it really, really short and letting it turn lighter."

"I think you will look beautiful no matter what you decide, and apparently Jake does too." I prodded. "Hey, Teenie." I pulled my car up to the Lab turnstile. "I'm almost ready to wave to handsome Jorge."

"Oh! Tell him hi from me too!"

In spite of the excellent noise-canceling technology of my Bluetooth, I was sure she heard the storm when I pushed the button to lower the car window and yelled above the uproar, "Hi, Jorge!" He waved as I pointed to the Bluetooth extension of my left ear. "Christine says hi too."

He showed me his beautiful white teeth, gave me a thumbs-up, and a "queen's wave" that mimicked the one Christine and I normally used to hail him. Then he rotated this arm and hand to pantomime that I should roll up my window as he shouted over the storm, "Hi back, and tell her to get well and come back soon."

I welcomed the quietness as the window reached the top and slid into its weatherproof slot. I relayed handsome Jorge's message.

"Yeah. I might get outta here very soon. Sooo, date with Stratton tonight, yeah? What are you going to wear?"

Some combination of excitement and apprehension struck me mid-abdomen and sent signals out from there to the rest of my body. "I have some idea, but I haven't quite made up my mind."

I turned the car automatically toward my fave parking place, but hesitated remembering my promise to Stratton. I searched, but at that time of the day, most of the places closer to the building were taken. "I have three choices sitting out on my bed. I had to close my door so Midnight couldn't eliminate any of them."

Christine giggled. "Any of them show off those fabulous legs?"

I felt my neck and cheeks blush though no one could see me. "One does." I finally found a vacant spot under a liquidambar closer to the covered breezeway, but still on the wall. I turned off the engine. "It's really stormy. I better let you go, cuz I won't be able to hear you after I open my car door."

"OK, bye. Call me again when you're on your way home. If I have people poking me or if we miss each other, don't forget I vote for showing off your gorgeous legs."

"OK, bye." I pushed the button on my Bluetooth, looked down at my handbag and umbrella on the passenger seat, then surveyed the sheeting rain on my windshield. I tried to judge whether it would be worth it or not to fight the umbrella. I decided it was. I draped the long strap of my bag over my left shoulder and placed the bag securely on my right hip. I picked up the umbrella and opened it slightly as I pushed open my door. A gust of wind pulled the door from my grip, so I closed the door and the umbrella and decided to run for it.

One of the remaining leaves on the liquidambar trees whipped across and stuck like a slug to my left cheek, catching in the edge of my Bluetooth. *Oh bother.* I just left the leaf for the rain to wash away as I ran for the cell phone lockers clutching my bag, umbrella, and coat close to my body. As usual nothing, not even this boisterous storm, surpassed the roar of the noisy channel of water beyond the wall.

I stowed my phone and Bluetooth, connecting them to the dual port charger within my locker. As I stepped into the warmth beyond the vapor lock, I smelled the Peet's Coffee cart and took a few steps in that direction before spotting Chip. I wasn't in the mood for his creepiness any day, but especially not today.

I flashed my lanyard to the guard at the desk before heading up the escalator to territory forbidden to Chip's limited-access badge. I spread my soaked trench coat out over Christine's chair and part of her desk in her empty cube. As soon as I logged in, my interoffice instant-messaging program chirped at me. The dialog box was entitled, Stratton Davis. I smiled.

SD: Hi, beautiful! How's everyone?

MR: My Lady, Christine, and Ray are all better today. Thanks for asking.

SD: Have time for a cuppa coffee in a little while?

MR: Maybe. Let me see what's up on our little corner of cyberspace. Can you ask again in about two hours?

SD: Sure

It was not meant to be. I was so deeply engaged with my keyboard and monitor that I jumped when my phone rang. "Good afternoon, this is Meg Randallman."

"Meg, my dear." My Lady's voice was even, but laced with apprehension.

"My Lady?" I asked, dumbfounded. It was the first time she had ever called me at the Lab.

"Yes, dear, it's me. I'm afraid I have bad news." My mind raced to Ray, but realized instantly that it didn't make sense. The center would have called me, not her. "There's been an accident. George and Norma."

"A plane crash?" I heard hysteria rising in my voice. I glanced at the clock and tried to make my brain switch to information I had on file there about travel arrangements.

"No, my dear. I just got a call from the California Highway Patrol. They were in Norma's car on 580."

"Fursst class," I quoted stupidly.

"Pardon me?"

"Sorry. It came out involuntarily. Norma had started drinking when we talked last evening. She called it 'fursst class.' They serve free cocktails in first class."

"Oh yes. I see. Probably. I don't know who was driving or if there were other vehicles involved. They have been taken to Pleasant Valley Medical. It's not renowned for trauma, but it was the closest emergency facility that had blood in stock. Apparently, they both needed it immediately. George has been stabilized, but Norma is in critical condition."

"Oh no!" *Please God no.* I felt the familiar rush to my bowels that seemed to be my reaction to shocking news. "I'll leave right now."

"Of course, my dear." Her voice cracked, and then I heard a deep gurgling breath. "Please call me as soon as you can."

As I was waiting for all systems to shut down and log me off, I looked at the glut of unopened paper mail on my desk that had piled up in my absence. I pulled out my laptop case and started stuffing it in. It was Friday, I thought. Maybe I'll have time this weekend to at least open it, purge the unnecessary, and prioritize the rest.

As I stepped out of the vapor lock, the late afternoon sky was so laden with dark clouds, it was darker than dusk. The wind whipped my coat as I took my phone out of the locker. I looked down at my handbag draped across my shoulder, covered by my laptop case. The flap that closed the handbag was facing in, not out. It was overwhelming to think about rearranging the load and unsnapping my handbag to put my phone away where it belonged. I was not willing to part with my gloves, even temporarily, and though I knew it would be uncomfortable with the Lifeproof cover on it, I reached through my coat and V-neck sweater to deposit my phone and Bluetooth earpiece into the convenient pocket of my bra that also conveniently pocketed my left booby.

I decided to try the umbrella on the downwind return trip to my car. It took a great deal of effort. I held the handle as high up toward the umbrella as possible, pulling it downward to touch my head and surround me. I was virtually blind to anything outside my miniature shelter.

The rushing water and the storm masked the sound of my attacker's footsteps. Just as I let go of the umbrella with one hand to retrieve my keys and car remote from my coat pocket, several things happened almost simultaneously. The umbrella lifted in a gust of wind. I saw a hooded man with a ridiculous, almost clear, shiny plastic mask. I screamed and pulled my laptop case from over my head and threw it with all the force I could at my attacker. The opposing force thrust me backward to land with each foot on a nasty little ball, and another gust of wind tossed me over the wall into the raging water of the ditch.

I have no idea what happened to my umbrella or my shoes. My lungs and heart felt a tremendous shock as I plunged deeply into the freezing torrent. The force submerged me completely, but I bobbed up briefly and caught a burning breath into my icy lungs. It crossed though my mind that those shoes I lost were expensive Italian leather, but as I kicked my feet, attempting to right myself in the water, I was grateful that I had worn flats today instead of boots.

The corrugated pipe gaped toward me. I kicked furiously and thrust both arms to grab the side of the huge pipe. I was successful, but I paid a price for my efforts. As long as I held on where I was, I would not be able to take another breath. I was underwater.

I walked my hands up the side of the pipe, and at what seemed like the last possible moment, I gasped for a lifesaving breath. A medium-sized tree branch that had met with the same fate as I hurtled past my face and grazed my thigh. The nub of a smaller limb sticking out of that branch felt ever so much like a knife as it pierced through my slacks and sliced several inches of my flesh.

I looked upstream to see the masked face peering over the wall. Something about the arrogant movement of his head was familiar. The head and hands on the wall jerked back from view.

My hands were slipping from the inside of my gloves. Through my mind's eye I could see My Lady's ruby ring on my right hand. I let go with that hand and rubbed the glove off carefully against the edge of the pipe, gingerly starting at the fingertips. As the glove fell away and slapped my face on the way downstream, I grasped the edge of the pipe again securely with my bare hand. I manipulated my left hand free of its glove.

Another branch streaked past, smacking my back. I had turned into its path while I was twisting off my gloves. I opened my mouth involuntarily to say "ouch!" and got a mouthful of oily leaves. I spit and spit and spit to get as much out as possible. I used my glove-free left hand to turn the ring on my aching right hand so that the diamonds and ruby were on the inside. I took a deep breath, then let go, grasping the precious jewels in a fist. I was immediately plunged into the blackness of the tunnel and once again thrust deeply into the debris-loaded water.

The strap of my handbag wrapped around and pulled tenaciously around my neck. Keeping my right hand fisted, I used both hands to free myself from the strangling handbag, and then started a concerted effort to release my trench coat as it caught on something in the deep and held me stationary. Branches, leaves, and unidentifiable debris pelted me continually as I struggled to free myself from my trap. I thought my lungs would burst.

Before that moment, it had not occurred to me, but now I thought for sure I was going to die. My trench coat finally let me go, jerking my left shoulder violently. I was free. I bobbed to the surface and caught another life-giving breath. The darkness fell away and the torrent gushed me out of the pipe.

My bottom bounced hard on the bottom of the ditch as it widened. The water was still moving rapidly, but it was shallower, and it allowed me to manipulate to a face-up position and balance myself to continue to glide rapidly, gratefully breathing the wet wind. I determinately kept my right hand frozen into a fist.

The banks rose higher. First the left bank reverted from concrete to rich foliage on a green, mini hillside. Then the right burst forth, flourishing with plants and bushes thriving in the abundance of drink. The ditch widened yet again. My bottom bounced the river floor again, this time scraping my back against rock. The movement slowed. I was floating almost peacefully, and I began to hope that I might survive after all.

The sky above me filled with naked branches, and then with willows that trailed their hair along the left bank. It had stopped raining, but a few heavy drops from the trees splatted heavily on my face. A glimpse of daylight sought me though the treetops. I suppose I knew I was cold, but I was numb.

Another curve in the ditch combined with yet another widening. The next curve deposited my anesthetized body on the outer right bank across from an enormous willow. Most of my body was ensnared beneath the water, but my arms, chest, and face felt the chill of the biting wind. A clump of leaves entwined within tiny branches rounded the bend, scraping my cheek. A cluster of spiky branches were holding my ripped clothing and biting my skin. I could barely feel them in spite of the fact that they were probably poking tiny holes in me.

Oh well, I chuckled, *for the first time in days, at least I don't feel my spider bites and am not fighting back tears.* Then, of course, the latter was not true. I was weary, and once again I realized that I had deceived myself. I was probably going to die. Nothing above the high banks indicated I was close to anyone that could find me or help me. The winter day was losing its dim daylight. The darkness was closing in on me in my fresh trap of branches. I cried as I thought of My Lady, Christine, and Stratton. Then Ben, Karen, Einstein, and Midnight, prompted more tears. I thought about the lifetime of senseless blame and fury I had directed at Norma. I prayed I would make it to the hospital to tell her that I loved her and that I forgave her. *Please God. She has to know I forgive her; I can't stay here and die.* What a waste of energy to blame myself and lash out in my rebellion toward my mother for taking us away from Daddy. *And Daddy. I'm going to die and never find Daddy.*

I felt a strange calm as the tears subsided. I was numb. I was alone in the middle of nowhere, lying there thinking what a shame it was that I wouldn't be able to tell anyone that I knew who my attacker was. No ridiculous mask could disguise Chip's arrogant movements.

Another branch rammed my stomach. The flow was slower than in the ditch above, but still vigorous.

I lay there for some time trying to think, but I was so spent, I just concentrated on breathing. I was so cold. The water continued to flow past with stuff that kept slapping me or poking me. I didn't care. I began to fall asleep, so I decided to say my usual bedtime prayers. They were not coherent. I was not coherent. I dozed off saying to Jesus that I thought I would see Him in person very soon.

My left breast vibrated. I tried to undo my fist. At first I thought it was hopelessly frozen. I put it into my sweater anyway, and two fingers obeyed the signal from my brain. I scooted out my phone, and the Bluetooth flipped into the passing stream. The phone started to float away also, but I was able to grab it with my left hand just as the phone stopped vibrating. Missed call. Stratton.

I took a sighing breath. As I lifted one of my working fingers to touch the screen to call him back, the phone vibrated again, so I touched it to answer. He had not given up. *Dear God. He had not given up.*

My voice croaked something barely audible and nothing like I intended. "Hi."

"Meg! Where are you?" I had never heard his voice so urgent and tense. "Security saw and caught that sleazeball Chip. He's not talking for a change, but he was near your car, which is still in the parking lot. Where are you?"

"I'm in the middle of nowhere, somewhere way downstream from the Lab. I fell over the wall into the ditch."

"Oh, my poor dear sweetheart! I need to find you!" In the momentary silence, I thought he had gone, and with the broken phone connection lost all hope of rescue. I was so drowsy. I was surprised to hear his voice again.

"I know! Do you have the Find My Phone app on your phone?"

I croaked, "Yes."

"What's your Apple ID?"

"TVaddict at AT and T dot net."

"What's your password?"

"Movie–123. Uppercase M."

"Hang on, sweetheart. I'll be there with an emergency crew as soon as I can. How much juice does your phone have?"

I looked at my screen. "Ninety-five percent. I plugged it in at my locker."

"OK. Leave it powered on, but I won't call you back until we are very close. Are you hurt?"

"A little sliced. I'm still mostly in the water, but on a bank." A cluster of leaves caught in my armpit while I was holding my phone.

"If you can get out of the water that would be good, but whatever happens, don't lose your phone! And, Meg."

I was feeling very sleepy, and I'm sure it came through in my "huh?"

"I'm praying for you."

"Thank you." I felt my throat choke on what would be tears, but none came.

It took exactly thirty-seven minutes for my rescuers to reach me. I tucked the phone safely into its favorite pocket while I clumsily struggled up the bank out of the water, leveraging the branches of the bramble bush that had trapped me. Once more at rest, I pulled out my phone. I had nothing else to do except watch the clock. I felt so sleepy, and strangely, I was trying to remember how I got here.

However, even in my growing confusion I was able to recognize that the phone was vibrating when Stratton called me again, and I could hear the approaching helicopter. "They're on their way, sweetheart."

"I know. I can hear them. Stratton?"

"Hmmm?"

"I-I like it when you call me th-that." I had begun to shiver uncontrollably. "I feel so sleepy."

"Well then, sweetheart it is. See you soon, sweetheart. I think half the Lab is waiting for you here at the Pleasant Valley Medical Center. They said they would bring you directly here since it's so close. They said I could wait on the roof for you. Please turn your phone flashlight on now and signal so they can find you fast."

"Stratton. Can you talk me through the buttons I need to push?" I heard the quietness of my voice and wondered if he would be able to hear me. "I seem to be confused. I don't know what buttons to push."

Very steadily he said, "Just turn your phone toward the lights above and touch the screen every few seconds. That will be enough light for them to find you."

"OK." I barely heard Stratton still talking to me. The helicopter was landing in the field above my perch on the bank. Two people were there shortly. I was so lethargic, I didn't even object when they stripped me of my wet clothing and took my phone. After wrapping me in warm blankets, including over my head, I felt them strap me to a board. The thunderous noise didn't hinder me from coasting off to sleep.

I was air-lifted to the roof of the building that I had intended to hurriedly drive to when I left the Lab less than an hour before. As the paramedics wheeled me through the elevator doors on the roof, I woke from my stupor when I heard Stratton's voice say, "Hi, sweetheart. This is Director Taylor, your boss's boss's boss. They said he could come with me up here to take the elevator down with you."

I opened my eyes toward the direction in which I heard Stratton, but mustered the energy to turn my head so I could politely acknowledge the man Stratton introduced as my boss's boss's boss. The elevator came to a stop as he came into focus.

"Daddy?"

CHAPTER TWENTY

Recuperation

I must have fallen asleep again for quite a while. I woke in a single room with a nurse hovering over me and the inevitable plastic tube hanging from a plastic bag connected to my hand with a taped needle. I looked down at the hand to see another apparatus clipped to a finger. It had a tiny red light on it. My Lady's ring was gone. I willed myself to move my other hand, and it complied. I reached up to confirm that Laura's cross was still around my neck.

"Well, hello there, sleepyhead." The nurse smiled at me. "As long as you're awake, let me check you over a bit."

She put her stethoscope into her ears and touched the other end to the top of my left boob. I realized she was a doctor, not a nurse. Her name tag read "Dr. Nancy Varion." I gave her a questioning look.

"Yes." She nodded. "Your heart sounds good. Deep breath, please. Again. We were concerned about your heart and lungs for a while, but you're a strong and healthy woman. You weathered hypothermia better than others might have." She ran a light in front of my eyes. "Do you think you can roll over a little that way so I can check the stitches on your thigh?" I remembered the branch that tore me.

"Is it still Friday?"

"Nope. It's Saturday. You had a good night's sleep. What's that look for? Don't you like to sleep?"

"No, I mean, yes." It felt like blood beneath my eyes was sinking in disappointment. "It's not that. I was supposed to have a date last night."

"Oh!" She grinned at me. "You had him by your side all Friday night. Not as enjoyable as a date, but you certainly have a loyal friend." I flinched as she peeled back the bandage.

"Sorry," she said. She applied a soothing ointment and then a new bandage to my thigh. "This looks good too. You bled quite a bit. The good news is it cleaned the wound a little before you got here. The bad news is we had to give you a pint of blood."

With a loud snap, she pulled off the rubber glove that she had put on to apply my ointment. "That's why your loyal friend is not here. He wanted to give us back a pint out of gratitude." She covered me back up and twitched the covers into place. "He said he wanted to take a shower before he came back. What?"

"He always smells so good."

"You *are* a lucky girl." We both chuckled.

"I'll be back this evening. We will probably be discharging you tomorrow morning. Right now, I want you to drink as much fluid as is comfortable, stay warm, and get as much sleep as possible, though I realize that a hospital is the least likely place to get uninterrupted sleep." She nodded her head wisely. "I'll send the comfort team in to take care of everything."

"Wait, please." She turned from the door. "First. Thank you, Doctor—"

"Dr. Nancy." She smiled.

"Thank you, Dr. Nancy, for all you are doing for me. Second, I was wondering if you could get some news for me and if I could have my phone." I looked down at my right hand. "And hopefully I was still wearing a ring? Ironically, I was on my way to this hospital last night, but I intended to drive, not come by water and air."

"Your friend has your phone and your beautiful ring. Actually, you slipped the ring off and gave it to him. You also signed a HIPAA-compliant release form that allows us to tell him about your condition. He asked me to remind you of all this, if I was here when you woke up. We thought it was likely that you were making good choices, but that you were not going to remember them."

She twitched the covers unnecessarily, then smoothed them neatly down the edge of the bed. "Before he left, he asked me to tell you that he used the phone to call someone he said was listed as 'My Lady.'" She smiled again. "And then some others." The smile disappeared. She said tenderly. "I know what news you want."

I felt dread during her thoughtful pause. "Your parents are still here. Your father is beginning to rally. Your mother is still in critical condition. In a little while, you can go see them. I've arranged for wheels." She smiled kindly and motioned to the IV bag and tube. "You'll be detached from all those connections soon."

The nurses and other comfort-care people brought me a warmed blanket, then hot broth and tea, and then some smooth berry yogurt. Incurably vain, and knowing that Stratton would be back soon, I requested that someone hand me the hospital phone. I called Ben, and after asking about Midnight and Einstein, I gave him directions on how to find my hairbrush and some emergency cosmetics.

He said that Stratton called him last night. My Lady told Stratton that Ben would want news of me right away and that my "babies" would need his attention. I wondered where my handbag ended up. It was more valuable than anything that was in it, except perhaps my Kate Spade wallet. I made a note to call American Express to cancel my credit card, and then my mind rabbit-trailed down a path of consternation. I wondered how much trouble it might be to get a new driver's license. I remembered exactly where my pricey trench coat was, and resigned myself to its loss, as well as the handbag and wallet.

I held off from the offer of hospital coffee hoping for a great cup rather than a mediocre one, and it was worth the wait. Stratton showed up with a large Peet's cup. He beat Ben in arrival, but in spite of my appearance, I was delighted to see him and the large cuppa.

"So, Sleeping Beauty. How are you feeling today?"

I could feel the blood rise into my face. "I'm really good. I don't know why they need to keep me until tomorrow. I think I could go home now." He came around to the window side of my bed and sat down facing the door to the hospital hallway.

"They said you're doing well, but they want to keep an eye on your vital signs a little longer, and they don't want to send you home with the onset of an infection."

"They're going to let me get up to go see my parents, though, as soon as they take out the tubes." The IV bag wiggled when I raised my arm and stirred the line.

"Speaking of parents. Do you remember calling Director Taylor 'Daddy' in the elevator?"

"Oh! I thought that was a dream!" I stared at him stupidly. "So it really is Daddy? Are you sure? I could certainly be considered delusional."

"No dream. No delusion. He recognized you too. He and I spent a lot of time in the waiting room last night."

"But his name was, Francis, er is, not Franklin." A flood of memories clashed with each other in my brain. Most of what I remembered was, of course, imagination. "Now that I'm about to meet him again after seventeen years, it feels awkward. I'm excited to see him, but I'm apprehensive—so many years of separation and change. I've wondered how my grandparents are, but I'm not sure I want to know." I gulped. "And there's Laura's death."

I took a deep breath and involuntarily covered my face with both hands. After massaging my hairline three times, I brought them down again and studied the jiggling IV tube. I said to the IV bag, "I am sure it must be awkward for him too."

His eyes followed mine to the IV bag and said, "Actually, yes. He said the same thing. He is excited, but a little afraid of how you'll receive him. I got the impression that he thought your mother may have tainted his memory."

We turned back to looking into each other's eyes. I scoffed. "No. Not tainted, but certainly not nourished. She has never spoken of him at all. It's as if he never existed." I took a deep breath. "I'm so glad I told you our story the other evening." I blushed remembering the intimacy. "Without knowing it, I set you up to be a liaison."

I took a sip of the delicious coffee. I was about to launch into a battery of questions about the conversation between Daddy and Stratton in the waiting room, but both Ben and Detective Gorsky stood politely outside my door negotiating who should enter first. Ben came in first and stood at the opposite side of my bed from Stratton. He nodded across me to Stratton, who nodded back. Detective Gorsky stood at the end of the bed, facing me. Ben looked nervous and uncomfortable.

I started to introduce everyone, but suddenly Ben set my cosmetic bag and a Nordstrom bag at the end of the bed, and then bent down to hug me. I felt him shaking. It profoundly touched me. I also started to cry.

When he stood back, he pulled a few tissues from the box on my side table, wiped his nose, and said, "My precious Meg." After more tears and somewhat furious wiping with the tissues, he said, "It's so good to see you. You look good—really, really good. You don't need that bag so much." We both laughed. I grabbed my portion of tissues.

I waved my hand back and forth introducing each of the men. "This is Ben, this is Stratton, and this is Detective Gorsky." Detective Gorsky reached his hand to Ben first, and then to Stratton.

Stratton reached across the bed to shake Ben's hand and said, "You drove Meg to Stanford." Ben nodded yes and smiled proudly. Then they each muttered their own versions of "how do you do" and "nice to meet you" greetings.

Ben said earnestly, "Mrs. Randallman sends her love, but she's too weak to come today." He swabbed across his face one last time with a tissue. "She sent you a gift though. She said you needed this, right now, today." He handed me the handles of the Nordstrom bag.

"Oh, that's OK. I'm fine. I'll call her in a little while—Oh! This is beautiful!" I unfolded a gorgeous royal-blue silk robe. I laughed and looked down at the ugly hospital gown. "She's right. I definitely need this right now, today. Please tell her I'm fine, and I'll be home to see her tomorrow. I think I'll be able to go down to see George in a little while. I'll call her after I see him."

"Yeah. I'm going to stop down there myself right now." He seemed to have recovered from our emotional greeting.

I clutched the silky blue fabric to the front of my blankets that were not exactly covering my less-than-sexy gown. "Thank you, Ben for bringing me this." I stroked the lovely silk. "Please give my love to Einstein and Midnight, and tell them I'll be home tomorrow." I laughed. "If Einstein seems too neurotic, maybe you can help him Skype with me later." I picked up my phone that Stratton had placed on the tray.

Ben shook his head knowingly and grinned. "Sure. I'll tell them you'll be home tomorrow." He chuckled and looked across at Stratton. "Sometimes I wonder if they actually do understand everything she says to them." Stratton smiled and nodded.

"Of course they do," I said cheerfully. "They are both very smart."

"Well, I won't argue with you, little lady. If anyone could raise a genius parakeet or genius black Labrador, it would be genius you. I'll be going now." He pointed to the cosmetic bag at the end of the bed. "You just call or text if you need anything else. I'll let you know if your parakeet is so ditsy that he needs to Skype."

He reached his hand again across the bed to Stratton, smiled broadly, and added an affirmative nod. "Nice to meet you after all these years of hearing about you."

Stratton took his hand. His eyebrows lifted curiously. He turned his head toward me as one corner of his mouth smiled. Ben shook Detective Gorsky's hand on his way to the door, and then gave me a baby wave good-bye. I was draining my Peet's cup, but as I placed it on the side table, I returned a baby wave with my other hand. As I set that hand back down on the bed, Stratton wrapped his large, warm hand around it. I turned my palm up to clasp his in a visible, accepting response. The invisible response was like pyrotechnics exploding inside my heart and tummy.

I smiled at Stratton, but then turned my head to give Detective Gorsky my attention. "Would you like to sit down? There's another chair against that wall." In long strides, he reached for the chair and effortlessly slid it to my bedside. I began questioning him at just-finished-a-large-coffee speed. "So is Chip Swain under arrest? Do you think he's the one that attacked Christine? Do you think he murdered Brenda? I would suppose that he's not alone in this, right? He's not smart enough. Did you see that ridiculous mask?" I took a breath. "I knew it was him. He has such unmistakable, arrogant gestures and movements."

He laughed. "So soon? My interview has begun?"

"Sorry." I looked at Stratton. "It's Stratton's fault. He brought me a large coffee." I nodded toward the empty cup.

"I can actually answer most of your interview questions because we've made three arrests and those are therefore public record. We arrested Swain right after you decided to take a swim rather than hang out with him." He smiled. "And he doesn't appear to be a mastermind."

I grinned. "I find that easy to believe."

He grinned back. "He's not the sharpest knife in the drawer."

"Yeah. I supposed the real 'stupid criminals' were the ones that entrusted him to carry out their dastardly plans."

"A poor choice, indeed. Swain insisted that he didn't murder Brenda. He confessed to attacking Christine, but he insists that he only meant to grab the laptop, not hurt her. He says that he didn't intend to hurt you either, but he is responsible for her injuries and yours, regardless of his intent."

"Do you believe him? I mean, do you believe he didn't kill Brenda?"

"Actually, yes. We told him he would need to give us names or he'd be taking full responsibility for murder as well. So he did. Those are the other two men in custody." I looked up to the right, and he twisted his mouth slightly. "I can tell you this: now that we have these men in custody and evidence gathered from subsequent search warrants, we have a nice sum of convicting evidence, other than just Swain rolling on them. They also rolled on each other and both rolled on Swain.

"The summary is this. Of the two other men, one is the *mastermind* as you called him. He's the moneyman. He hired Swain and the other man. The second suspect is more of a *minion*. He found Swain by following him from the Lab to his place of business, Ready Business Machines. They targeted him because his company vehicle identified him as someone who had not been through the comprehensive Lab background checks and was less likely to be loyal to the Lab. They were right. Swain was willing, for a price, to find out who managed Lab cyber security passwords and turn their names over to moneyman. That's how they got Brenda's and Christine's names."

I gasped. My hand flew involuntarily to my chest. "Christine was in great danger!"

"Yes," Detective Gorsky continued. "Until you came to work here." He nodded. "Then she was no longer the target."

"Then Chip pointed them to me?"

"Not exactly. Swain took it upon himself to get your laptop hoping to get a big payoff. As we guessed, he mistook Christine for you.

"After Brenda was murdered, moneyman *says* he stopped the espionage attempt when he found her laptop useless. He also says he hadn't planned for the minion to murder Brenda."

"Somebody needs to take responsibility for Brenda's murder." Stratton said angrily.

"All three of them will." Detective Gorsky nodded in agreement. "Neither Swain nor the minion were ready for paydays to stop. Swain overheard two employees at the coffee cart talking about a new technology that put the password security device as software on the laptop. He told the minion, who decided to follow Christine for a while hoping to see her carry her "new technology" laptop into her home. He thought he saw it with her one evening, but there were too many people around so he decided to follow her to work the next day, hoping she would make a stop on her way to work. She didn't. And then you started following her so he abandoned that plan."

"Oh good! I did something right!" I thought *That is a small consolation.*

"Yes. It was very brave of you and it protected Christine. However, from the confessions, it sounds like something else happened about the same time."

"What?" Stratton asked.

"The minion told Swain what he was doing and that you were making it difficult. Swain told him to back off. He said he knew who had the passwords now and he would use his advantage of having a badge at the Lab to get the right laptop."

"Mine." I brought my right hand to my face, covering my eyes and forehead. "Christine would not have been hurt if it were not for me." I looked at Stratton, feeling again the skin sinking beneath my eyes. "Once again, someone took my place."

Detective Gorsky tilted his head and gave me a querying look, but he didn't ask me what I meant.

Stratton retrieved my hand as I returned it to the bedside. "This is not your fault. Try to let the burden fall where it belongs—on these greedy, ruthless men."

Detective Gorsky said, "Did I sufficiently answer my interview questions?"

I grinned. "Yes. You are very kind, thank you. You can understand why I'm so concerned and curious."

"Yes, of course I do. And your enthusiasm is an indication that you're doing well." He looked down at our clasped hands. "Very well indeed." He nodded knowingly. He reached into the breast pocket of his jacket and pulled out a pen and notebook. "There won't be a trial for a very long time, if at all." He looked down at the notebook and wrote as he spoke. "You said you knew it was Chip Swain who threw you over the wall because, even though he was wearing a mask, you recognized the way he moved?"

"Well, to be fair. He didn't throw me over the wall, but he startled me to the edge, where I threw my briefcase at him, and the opposing force momentum plus the wind, my umbrella, and the nasty little balls sent me over."

Stratton and Detective Gorsky asked simultaneously, "Nasty little balls?"

Over Detective Gorsky's shoulder, I saw Daddy at the door.

CHAPTER TWENTY-ONE

Daddy

Stratton and Detective Gorsky followed my stunned look toward the door and rose simultaneously to take their leave. Congregating awkwardly together, Stratton introduced Daddy to Detective Gorsky, and then they both quietly disappeared, leaving Daddy and me alone for the first time since he gave me a Bible and walked out of my bedroom door seventeen years before.

He stood there for a moment in uncomfortable silence. He looked down at Laura's cross around my neck, and then connected again with my eyes. I knew that he was fighting the same overwhelming, confusing emotion that I was. So many years. We were strangers and yet not.

I said, "Hi, Daddy," and surrendered to the tears that were choking my throat. "Would you like to sit down?" Shaking the IV tube, I motioned to the chair that Detective Gorsky just vacated.

He moved to the chair, never taking his eyes off my face. His eyes were gleaming with extra moisture. I took a tissue to blot away my tears and my nose. He said, "Maggie. It's so good to see your beautiful face."

I blotted again and said shakily, "Thank you. It's good to see you too." I laughed at the understatement.

"I would have known you anywhere. Ajeet told me he thought it was you that he'd met at Kirin's desk."

"So he did recognize me." I studied his face to see if I could tell if he blamed me for Laura's death or for yielding to complacency when I was old enough to search for him. All I saw was love.

"Yes. But your name is Meg Randallman, so at first he wasn't sure. Kirin told him you weren't married so he wondered, but then he was convinced he was right. Since Meg is another name for Margaret, and"—he pointed at the front of my stylish gown—"he helped me pick out that cross for Laura. Plus, you gave yourself away. He was sure that you recognized him as well." He was looking at me with wonder. "He's a great friend. I don't know where any of us would be now had it not been for his patience, kindness, and commitment to us. He is so wise. He suffered a great loss of his own many years ago and pioneered a path of forgiveness that he shares with those of us who need to forgive and be forgiven. He brought us through the loss of Laura, and then you and Ray."

"Us." I gulped. "Are Grama and Grampa still alive?"

"Yes. Thanks to the healing power of forgiveness."

He reminded me of Ray as he pushed back the thick, wavy hair on the top of his head with his right hand. Silver strands prevailed at the sides of his face and were dispersed throughout the rest of predominantly dark hair. "Dad had the hardest time of all getting over Laura's accident. I called them to tell them I found you. I bought them airline tickets. They should be here sometime soon."

The awkwardness—a fabricated barrier constructed of doubt and reservation during seventeen years of separation—that had reigned in the room from the moment Daddy stepped into it, suddenly collapsed. "Oh Daddy! I've missed you all so much." I cried freely and opened my arms.

Daddy leaned in to hug me. Our chests shook. We cried opening in an embrace that would have to compensate for years' and years' worth of hugs we should have known. "I've missed you too, Maggie."

After a while, he sat back into his chair, took several tissues, and then handed me the box. We smiled at each other as we both went through the process of gaining emotional control. We took several shuddering, deep breaths.

For the first time I envisioned how Grampa Red must have felt. Even though they thought I shot Laura, it was his gun, loaded, in his shed. "Did they arrest Grampa Red?"

"Yes, for child endangerment and some other firearms charge, but they didn't keep him in custody very long. There was a hearing. You see, the tail of his shirt had gotten caught in the lock as he was leaving the shed. He remembered it catching, but he pushed on the door after he locked it and it didn't give. A detective found the piece of material that matched Dad's shirt. They knew he had not been careless or negligent. I believe the judge was compassionate because he could see that we had all suffered enough." His gaze on me relaxed as we talked. He looked down at his hands. "I think he would have preferred to be prosecuted and severely punished. He blamed himself and wanted everyone else to also."

"I didn't shoot Laura."

His eyes shot to mine in alarm. "Of course you didn't! What made you say that?"

"Norma said she had to take us away because I killed my sister, so I figured you all thought the same."

"Oh, honey! All these years?"

I nodded, choking back more impending tears. My heart hurt.

He said, "Vanessa told the police everything that happened. She was surprised when the door of the shed gave way to her leaning weight. She was shocked that the gun was loaded." He tilted his head to the side and squinted his eyes slightly. "Your mother knew that Vanessa had come forward immediately . . .

hmmm," he sighed. "Vanessa's testimony was invaluably relevant to the ruling in your grampa's hearing."

"What happened to her?"

"Actually, our horror turned out for her good. The accident caught the attention of Child Protective Services. She was put into foster care. Turns out that the people who took her in knew Ajeet, so he was able to keep tabs on her. In fact, he was able to talk to her and help her forgive herself, just as he helped your grampa."

"Wow! What an amazing man." I felt a tremendous burden lifting from my heart.

"Yes. I am most fortunate to have him as a friend. He was the reason I was in college when you left. He talked me into going back. I had dropped out when I married your mother so I could work more hours at my well-paying grocery store job. Ajeet convinced me that with a degree or two, I had a bright future at the Lab. I asked your mother if she could work for a while so I could improve our future. I quit the grocery store and took a part-time job at a Texaco. I've often wondered if that was too much to ask of her." He took a deep breath that seemed to shudder in his chest. "I blamed myself for driving her away." His eyes brimmed again with tears. "And she took you and Ray."

"Oh Daddy, I'm so sorry. It wasn't your fault. I think she had bigger plans than you and *nothing* you could have done would have given her contentment. At first, after she kidnapped us from you and married George, she seemed content with affluence, but it didn't last." I felt no need to tell him how I knew. My enemy, complacency, growled at me and mocked me for not searching for Daddy to comfort him. I saw now that for my part, our separation had been all about *me* and *my* loss. If I hadn't been so selfish, I would have driven myself to find him for *his* sake.

"I guess that could be true, but I have always felt it was my fault. It was hard, but I had to keep going." He nodded once in a determined way. "Stratton told me last night that your mother remarried." He looked defeated. "Ajeet helped me move on from my self-condemnation. Then he helped me embark on my career at the New Mexico Lab. After I got my doctorate, he introduced me to the hiring manager. By then, that manager had been well-primed and was waiting for me to join his team." He grinned.

"New Mexico? Is that where we're from? Is that why he wore white?"

He chuckled. "Yes. I had forgotten. He always wore white in those days. He used to tell us Americans that we were crazy to wear any other color in the heat of New Mexico summers. He lessened his resolve some over the years." Another incredulous look, "Of course. You would not have known where you were from. That would be why we never heard from you! I was so afraid you were"—he paused to take a breath—"dead. Yes. We lived in Las Lunas when your, er, when you left. It's a suburb of Albuquerque."

"I remembered Nueva Lane, but that was all. At first, when I was little, I was determined to run away and find you, but I never did. I didn't know where to run to. Then when I saw Ajeet the other day, I was a coward. I wanted answers to all the questions that I've had inside all my life, but I was afraid that you all believed I killed Laura."

We sat quietly for a moment. Our conversation was processing rapidly in my well-caffeinated brain. Then I said teasingly, "So, your name is Francis?"

He grinned. "Oh. It's way worse than that! It's Francis Albert."

"Like Francis Albert Sinatra?"

He chuckled. "Yes. Your grama and her mother before her—your great-grama, Louise—loved Frank Sinatra. So, tada!" He displayed jazz hands. "I can't sing worth a darn, but I've spent a lot of years on the piano and the guitar. I often play them at church services or gatherings."

"Gosh! I thought your name was Franklin."

"Franklin?"

"Uncle Tom used to call you Franklin."

He laughed overtly. It took a moment to compose himself before he could tell me why. "When Tom and I were kids, we would collect recyclables to get cash to go to the movies or the comic book store. Whenever we got a ride to the recycling center, I would say, 'Do you think we'll get a hundred dollars?' Tom would say, 'At least a hundred dollars.' Then after we would cash in for—I'm sure I don't have to tell you—way, way less than a hundred dollars, I would say, 'I wish I had a hundred dollars.' Tom would say, 'Yeah, right! Not today. No Benjamin Franklins for Franklin.' He thought our comedy routine was worthy of changing my name from Frank to Franklin."

We both laughed as I processed my thoughts and wondered if it would have made any difference if I had known his real name. Then I asked warily, "Did you remarry?"

"No. I didn't know your mother had divorced me."

"Actually, I think she skipped that part when she married George and changed our names." I wrinkled my nose. "I often wondered how she pulled it off."

"I tried searching for you by your social security numbers. When nothing turned up, that's when I wondered if you had all . . ." He took a deep breath, "died."

"She changed our social security numbers, and then George adopted Ray and me."

"I didn't know you could do that."

"I know, right? My adopted grandmother hired a private investigator. It looks like Norma, Ray, and I all suddenly appeared in history in 1998. The PI may have been more successful locating you if I had given your name as Francis, not Franklin." We both chuckled again. "But you know what? When I went to get my driver's license, the name on my birth certificate was Margaret Randallman, and George is down as my father. My birthplace was changed to Pleasant Valley, California. The only thing that was correct was my birthday, I think! Is it May eighth?"

"Yes. That's your birthday." He studied the blue sash of my robe that had draped itself as a beautiful ribbon across the bed, and then he looked up. "It's not easy to forge official documents." I could see sadness in his eyes and was sorry I told him.

"Well, you know how persuasive she can be. She probably worked a poor clerk somewhere and wore him down until he was liquefied by her long-lashed green eyes and became putty in her beautiful hands."

"You call her Norma?

"Yes. Ever since the day she took us away from you."

He lifted his right eyebrow. "You sound bitter."

"I have been most of my life, but when I thought I was dying in that freezing water, alone, away from anyone who could help me, I realized how much of my life I have wasted defying her and trying to hate her."

His eyes filled with tears again. "Yes. Spitefulness is a cruel master."

We were silent for a while. I reached out to take his hand. He squeezed mine, then I said, "Do you know where Norma's parents are?"

"Not really. I met her when she was living with her mother's mother. She was working in a diner in Corrales close to the grocery store where I worked. She was only seventeen, but almost eighteen. Her mother left her father—"

I scoffed an interruption. "So it's inherited?"

He chuckled. "Yes, I guess, but it doesn't need to pass to you." He brushed back his waves with his hand again. "After her mother left, she said her father made some inappropriate comments that caused your mother to think that inappropriate behavior might follow. She snuck out her bedroom window with a backpack stuffed with everything she could carry and hitched a ride from

Santa Fe to Corrales with a cousin who was a truck driver. All of this, of course, is the way I'd heard it from your mother. I learned later that she had a tendency to tell stories the way she wants people to hear them, and then she begins to actually believe them. Her story may have been a lot more depraved and terrifying. She said her father was a heavy drinker—"

"Alas. Another family tradition."

"Oh?"

"Yes. Both she and Ray."

He looked distressed. "Ray?"

"Yes. He's doing pretty well, and his addiction is to drugs more than alcohol, but I think he is going to be OK. We can go visit him together as soon as I get out of here. Oh Gosh! I need to call him!"

"Actually, Stratton called him last night. Now I understand why Ray didn't come here immediately, and why Stratton was somewhat evasive of my questions about Ray. He said you knew more about Ray's whereabouts and that I should talk to you."

I sat quietly again, my mind still racing. "So I have a great-grandmother in Corrales, New Mexico?"

I could hear his breath go in. "No. I'm sorry. She died during the time I was, er, courting your mother. I suppose as I look back now, she was courting me."

I smiled. "Or seducing you?"

He laughed. "I suppose that was it. She had turned eighteen and was on her own. Her grandmother lived in an apartment. There was nothing there to help her start out on her own. I probably looked like a life raft to her sinking ship."

"Oh, Daddy. It had to be more than that. You're so handsome and kind. I'm sure she fell in love with you."

His countenance fell, and he said sadly, "I'm not sure if we'll ever know. I hear she's not doing very well."

I asked in disbelief, "Did you stay faithful to her because you still love her?"

"I stayed faithful to her because I took a vow," he said sheepishly. "Whether I still love her or not, I don't think I have an answer. I do know that I forgave her a long time ago—"

I interrupted again, "Lemme guess—because Ajeet helped you, right?" I chuckled.

He chuckled too. "Yes, that is in fact true. He stuck around as much as he could during those dark days and reminded us over and over that forgiveness is a choice."

"So maybe I should ask him to help me." I paused to swallow and take a breath. "I didn't shoot Laura, but it was my fault she died." Another breath. "Vanessa was aiming at me. Laura stepped in front of me."

He studied my face carefully, then asked very gently, "So she died in your place?"

"Yes. I suppose that's why I feel responsible and so guilty. She took my place to save me."

"She wasn't the first."

As I was trying to assimilate the overwhelming truth of Daddy's statement, a care-team nurse entered my room rolling a cart. "Hello. May I interrupt you for a few minutes?"

"Of course," said Daddy considerately. "I'll wait outside, shall I?" As he rose from his chair, he bent over to kiss me on the forehead just as he had the night he gave me my Bible. "I love you pumpkin." Tears again for both of us.

"I love you too."

CHAPTER TWENTY-TWO

Reunions

Stacy, a strongly built woman with short curly brown hair and sharp amber eyes, took my temperature, counted my heartbeats, and freed me from the wretched tubes. She asked me to turn sideways to sit on the bed with my legs dangling for a moment and take a nice deep breath. She said, "Ready?"

"Sure. Let's do this. Could you bring that cosmetic bag?"

"I'll get it in a minute. I'm going to walk with you to the bathroom."

As soon I stood, I felt my legs go wobbly, and my head began to spin. I grabbed onto her waiting arm. "Whew! Stacy. I'm glad you're here!" She stepped closer, took my hand from her right arm, and put it on her left. She put her right arm around my back. "There you go. That's good. You'll get stronger soon."

I refreshed myself in every way I could in that tiny room. Stacy gave me a new charming hospital gown that was just as lovely as the first, but clean and fresh. She also brought my cosmetic bag. After cleansing as well as possible without a much-longed-for shower, I applied a little makeup, finishing with dark-red lipstick *There*, I thought, *what a difference lipstick makes.*

I looked better, but I leaned heavily on the sink and took a deep breath. I felt weak, tired, and a bit dizzy. Stacy allowed me privacy, but waited outside the bathroom door. With one arm still pressing forcefully on the bathroom sink, I used the other to turn the doorknob and push the door open. "Boy. I think I need to get back to bed!"

She was waiting, holding the blue silk robe ready for my entry. She helped me with it as I clung to the support of the bathroom sink with one hand and then the other. Outside the bathroom, Stacy had a wheelchair locked and ready. "Sit here for a moment," she said.

She handed me a glass of ice water with a straw, and faster than I could tell it, she changed the sheets on my bed. She dropped the sullied sheets into a cloth hamper near the door, and then opened the door. An older couple stood in the doorway with a bouquet of flowers. Behind them was a very anxious-looking Candy Striper, hospital volunteer.

I felt my face lift into a smile. My heart was so filled with love that I forgot all about the dizziness. "Grama! Grampa!"

They really didn't look that much different to me than they had seventeen years before. They were both a little thinner, and Grampa Red was not so red anymore, but either Grama had good genes or a skilled hairdresser. I felt the tiny frail hands of my grandmother wrap around one of mine, and then they were both hugging me and dripping tears. We all mumbled expressions of love and missed-you language.

Before we could actually settle into a conversation, the nervous Candy Striper interrupted our reunion. "I'm so sorry. I really am, but I was told to come get you. I'm to take you to your mother's room immediately."

I connected with the fear and urgency in her eyes and knew the reason for the summons. I exchanged glances with each of my grandparents. "Did you know Norma had been in an accident?" My heart ached. I needed more time with Norma. I wanted to apologize for being defiant. I did not want her to die, not now.

"Yes." My grandfather's comforting voice sounded exactly the same. "Frank told us before we left home. You go along now. We'll wait here for you." He kissed me on the forehead as Daddy had a short while before. I was certainly stocking up on love and kisses today.

Stacy stepped out of the way so Cindy the Candy Striper could wheel me away. Daddy and Stratton were outside in the hall. "Daddy. You better come with me." He gave me a knowing look, patted my shoulder, then fell into stride alongside my chair.

Stratton sketched a wave and said comfortably, "I'll wait here with your grandparents."

George was seated beside her bed. He was bruised severely on the bridge of his nose. His eyes were blackened. His right hand was in a sling. His left hand was holding Norma's. He rose when he saw us, but I said, "Please, George, don't get up."

I looked at her then. She was gray. She looked asleep. "Is she—?"

"She's still alive, but the doctors say it's not for—" He broke off the word and looked down at her. "There's been a lot of internal bleeding." I could hear his breath go in. "Not sure if she'll regain consciousness."

My heart hurt as I listened to him. It seemed to me that she would not wake up. I remembered my thoughts as I lay tangled on the bank in the water and prayed she would not only wake up but be coherent enough to know that, in spite of the way we had treated each other, I loved her, and if she needed it, to know that I forgave her.

Memories clashed with each other and fought with guilt. I had defended myself against my mother's self-centeredness and rejection with denial. I contrived apathy and sometimes even imagined that I hated her, but as I sat there remembering more than I wished to, I knew that I didn't hate her. I also clung to a shred of chance that all along she really had loved me.

I came to my senses and remembered my manners. "George, this is my father, Frank Taylor. Daddy, this is my stepfather, George Randallman."

Daddy echoed my sentiment when George started to rise. "Please. Stay seated. Perhaps we can shake hands later."

George turned his eyes from Daddy and sat back down abruptly. I wondered if he ever thought about the man who lost his wife and children the day George facilitated Norma's crime. His sudden movement shook the bed, then he reached again for Norma's hand.

Norma's long lashes fluttered. She opened her sunken green eyes to follow the sound of his voice, then fixed them on Daddy's face. "Why? Is it ever Frank?"

"Yes, Norma. It's me." Total awkwardness filled the room. It was hard to read George's puffy bruised expression. Norma face was too docile to read too, but it was obvious to me that Daddy was undoubtedly still in love with his wife, who had deserted him and ripped his children from their home.

"Where are we? Did we land in New Mexico?"

"No. Norma. You're in Pleasant Valley. You and your husband, George"—he nodded to the other side of the bed—"landed in San Francisco yesterday. There was an accident."

Norma turned her face toward George and mumbled so softly, it was difficult to hear her. "Oh my. George, honey, are you hurt very badly? I'm so sorry. That big truck. I remember now. That big truck pulled into our lane. I wanted to take the off-ramp. I couldn't stop in time."

Her eyes then moved back to me. "Margaret—" Her voice was getting weaker and seemed farther away. "You're in a wheelchair." She stared at me. Her eyes seemed vacant. I thought she was gone, but she had two more words to speak before she left us. "Ray." She turned her glassy gaze back to Daddy and said, barely above a whisper, "Frank."

My throat closed up, and tears rolled down my face. I pulled the wheels of my chair to draw close to her, put my hand on her forehead, and gently dragged my fingers down to close her eyes as I had seen people do in movies. I looked across the bed at George. He looked like he had been suddenly turned to stone, instantly gaunt. I looked up to Daddy to see tears that he did not apologize for.

CHAPTER TWENTY THREE

Reception

The last time Hillhollow hosted so many people was when George and Norma got married. Some of those same people, who still worked with George, came to the reception that we held in lieu of a memorial service for Norma. I asked George if I could invite my grandparents to stay with us instead of checking them into a hotel. He insisted that I invite Daddy too. It was too cold to spread the party out onto the veranda, so the hollow rooms of Hillhollow were filled with warmth and well wishes that I had never known.

Ray was released to join us. I remembered my "reality therapy" training from the center, so as soon as I recovered from my tears at our mother's deathbed, I immediately called him to tell him the whole truth—all that had happened. Norma's passing did not seem to upset him too much. His reaction to seeing Daddy, Grama, and Grampa, was pure enthusiasm and excitement. When Ray arrived at the reception, he seemed a little worried about George and me. He kept asking us how we were feeling. I was praying that none of it would disrupt his fragile life balance.

As Ray and I moved around the huge Hillhollow downstairs rooms, we talked about how lonely Norma must have been. Not one of the people who came could be called her friend. They came expressing their condolences to George, Ray, and me. Matt's father came, but Matt did not. I could tell Ray totally approved of, and liked, both Stratton and Christine. I knew Ray was resisting the temptation to tease me about Stratton but that his restraint would only hold for today.

I loved watching Daddy and Ray together. They had no problem connecting. It was amazing to me that Ray's mannerisms—even his walk—was so like the father he had spent so little time with. Their simple affection for each other brought joy to my heart. I suspected that Daddy would be arranging a transfer from the New Mexico Lab to California.

My Lady was not strong enough to come to the reception, but in the few days between Norma's passing and the gathering, she rallied to receive visits from my grandparents and Daddy. George and I knew that would not be long before we would be holding another reception.

After everyone except Stratton was gone, including Ray, who returned to the center, George withdrew to his room. Daddy settled in an easy chair in front of the fireplace with a book, but fell asleep almost immediately, leaning back snoring softly. My grandparents retired for the night into the lovely suite of rooms made ready for them. I had kissed them both and reminded them that I wanted them to stay as long as they could.

Stratton said, "Well, it's time for me to go unless you need help cleaning any of this up." He motioned to the remnants of the reception around the rooms, but mostly piled on the island in the kitchen.

"Not necessary, a whole crew will be here in the morning."

He took me into his arms, held me closely, and said to my hair, "So would you like to have dinner with me tomorrow evening?

CHAPTER TWENTY FOUR

The Date

"This place is lovely!" We were seated across from each other over a red-and-white checkered tablecloth. I was on a leather cushioned bench. Stratton's chair was opposite me. The adjacent tables that shared the wall-length bench were empty.

"You are lovely." He said simply.

I smiled at him and felt the heat of my blushing cheeks. I felt so comfortable sitting across from him. "You know what, Strat? I feel like we know each other so well in all the important ways, but I know hardly anything about your family."

He lifted his eyebrows, and nodded. "Fair enough. Unlike yours, my story is simple to tell. Rather boring actually. Stable home in Silicon Valley. Loving, supportive parents. Happy people in happyland." He chuckled and did a brief jazz hands accompaniment to the word he made up. "I already told you that my mom is awesome. So is my dad. He was one of the first employees at Google." My eyes widened. "Yup, stock options. My family is filthy rich."

"Do you have any siblings?" A waitress, with huge blue eyes and golden hair stretched back into a bun on top of her head, interrupted us. Stratton ordered spaghetti and meatballs. I decided on eggplant parmesan.

"Yes. A younger sister, named Sandy. She's your age—twenty-one."

I had a hopeful thought flutter within. *Another sister?*

"You'll love her. She's really smart. She's a character with a subdued sense of humor that sneaks up on you. And"—he lifted his right eyebrow and nodded knowingly—"she loves movies."

"A brainiac like her brother." I grinned.

"Unlike you, though, she's just now getting her undergraduate degree at Stanford because she took a little longer to go through high school than you did."

"She probably had other interests in high school, like classrooms, friends, proms, and such." I was so content at the moment that I could reminisce about my lonely years without any painful sting. "I didn't have anything else to do except blitz through my studies."

"So." He took my left hand in his right across the table. "How are you doing? Really. How are you doing with the loss of your mother?"

"I'm doing OK. I am feeling a bit disappointed that I didn't get a chance to—to tell her I loved her and how sorry I am—er, was—that I treated her so defiantly." I steadied myself and swallowed the pain in my throat that was pushing for tears. "I had a huge change of heart toward her while I was languishing on that bank in that freezing water—um, did I remember to thank you for saving my life?"

He smiled. "Yes. Several times while you were giving the hospital permission to give me your health updates and while you were handing me your ruby ring."

I held out my hand and studied My Lady's beautiful gift. I realized again how closely I was living on the edge of emotion. I took a deep breath before continuing, "Oh, good. Well anyway, back to your question, I have regrets. While I was lying there tangled in brambles, thinking that for sure I was going to die, I wanted to reconcile. I felt like there was so much bitterness between us. Then, when Daddy told me how horrible her life was when he met her, I felt even more contrite and more forgiving." I inhaled, and then said to My Lady's ring, "It didn't happen. She only woke up for a few minutes. There was no time to tell her. All she said to me was, 'Margaret, you are in a wheelchair,' but her eyes were so glazed I don't know if she could even see my face."

"You didn't have a chance to tell her, but the important part is complete."

"Important part?" I asked.

"The change you made within your heart and mind is way more important than telling her. Have you ever heard the saying, 'To forgive is to set a prisoner free, then to find the prisoner is me'?"

I shook my head and pondered the saying.

"Through all the confusion and conflicts of your relationship, I think she knew that you loved her. Just like you had the natural tendency in you to love your mother, she had the natural tendency to love her children. Did you ever tell each other that you loved each other?"

"Yes. I suppose we did. I can remember a couple of times."

"I think love was always there, but it was masked by insecurity in both of you."

"Well, thank you." I squeezed his hand that was still holding mine and looked up from studying the ruby. "I guess we will never know." We had some of our comfortable silence, and then our delicious food arrived and we ate silently for a several minutes.

"Stratton. Something I didn't tell you when I blathered out my whole life story to you at our practice date is that the night before my mother deserted Daddy and kidnapped Ray and me, I looked out the window of my bedroom and wished upon a star. I wished I could start my life over. I remember that there was a half a moon in the sky. I was too little to know whether it was waxing or waning, but after what followed, I'd bet on the latter. Anyway,

I know that it wasn't some kind of magic or Jiminy Cricket that granted my wish to start over. It was God that heard me. Do you think He would have answered so cruelly by ripping me away from my New Mexico home?"

"I think it's more likely that He heard your heartbreaking prayer, knew that there was a second strike of tragedy coming, and caused it all to work together for your good. He directed your journey so that you would find your lady Margaret, Christine"— he lifted a meatball on his fork as a salute—"and me." He grinned before taking a bite.

"You're right. I'm sure you're right. That makes so much more sense than the confusion that has befuddled me and the subsequent unjustified anger that I've harbored toward God." I sighed. "What a waste of energy! I should have realized that all along, He had a plan for my future. He was protecting me and nurturing me even though I didn't deserve it." I set down my fork and took a drink of water. "It could hardly be a coincidence that I found a career in the same company where you and Daddy worked. He took my pain and turned it to joy."

Always a gentleman, Stratton helped me with my coat. As we stepped into the cool, wholesome air I breathed it in deeply. This set of storms had passed. The rain-washed pavement of the restaurant parking lot and the shrubbery surrounding it glistened in the moonlight. We walked arm and arm to the passenger side of his car.

I took another deep breath, savoring again the clean fragrance after the rain mingled with Stratton standing intimately close to me. Forest river breeze.

In the radiant light of the full moon, he lifted my chin with his hand and said, "You wore flats. You don't need to, you know."

"So you don't mind that I'm taller that you?"

"Nope. I think it's hot. I love it when you wear high heels."
He smiled mischievously and said, "Besides, someone has to be tall enough to reach the top shelves in the kitchen." Then he kissed me.

CPSIA information can be obtained at www.ICGtesting.com
Printed in the USA
LVOW12*1406121213

364883LV00014BA/862/P